GAME OF SCONES

Knocking again, this time even louder, I glanced around. Big windows faced the veranda. It felt a little improper but I peered inside.

"Mrs. Farmer?" I tapped on the glass and waited. Nothing. No Elsie. Now what?

I had been specific about when I'd be there, but maybe she was in the back. I went down the porch steps and walked around the side of the house. There was a detached garage in the backyard and the garage door stood open. Elsie's car, a white Cadillac, was parked inside. So she *was* home.

"Hello," I called. "Is anyone back here?" As beautiful as the flowers had been out front, the backyard garden was even prettier. One section surrounded by a miniature picket fence seemed to be devoted to different colored roses. Roses are my favorite.

I caught a movement out of the corner of my eye and turned just in time to see a figure slip between the tall bushes at the back. "Hello," I tried again, but whoever it had been was gone. Stepping into the backyard I noticed a brightly colored pile of clothing on the ground. Maybe Elsie had been hanging out laundry and that's why she hadn't heard my knock. You'd be surprised how many people in St. Ignatius still hung their laundry out on a clothesline. My house (Greer's house) had one and I loved it. There was nothing like the smell of fresh line-dried sheets.

I wandered further into the garden. Once I was close enough to the pile of clothing, I realized my terrible mistake. A scream rose in my throat but no sound came out.

What I'd mistaken for a pile of clothing was Elsie, her body prone, her glasses askew, her eyes open but sightless, a scone clutched in her outstretched hand...

Game of Scones

Mary Lee Ashford

LYRICAL UNDERGROUND
Kensington Publishing Corp.
www.kensingtonbooks.com

LYRICAL UNDERGROUND BOOKS are published by

Kensington Publishing Corp.
119 West 40th Street
New York, NY 10018

All Kensington titles, imprints, and distributed lines are available at special quantity discounts for bulk purchases for sales promotion, premiums, fund-raising, educational, or institutional use.

Special book excerpts or customized printings can also be created to fit specific needs. For details, write or phone the office of the Kensington Sales Manager: Kensington Publishing Corp., 119 West 40th Street, New York, NY 10018. Attn. Sales Department. Phone: 1-800-221-2647.

Lyrical Underground and Lyrical Underground logo Reg. US Pat. & TM Off.

First Electronic Edition: December 2018
eISBN-13: 978-1-5161-0504-5
eISBN-10: 1-5161-0504-4

First Print Edition: December 2018
ISBN-13: 978-1-5161-0505-2
ISBN-10: 1-5161-0505-2

Printed in the United States of America

Chapter One

"If you can't stand the heat, get out of the kitchen," my Aunt Cricket is fond of saying. And though that *is* great advice, everybody can't actually leave, can they? I mean, someone has to stay in the kitchen and take the heat or nobody eats.

Today that person was me, Rosetta Sugarbaker Calloway, aka Sugar to my friends.

Up until six months ago, I had been a highfalutin senior food editor for a major magazine headquartered right here in the midwest. Corner office, nice salary, corporate trips. Now, thanks to a downturn in advertising revenues which resulted in downsizing at Mammoth Publishing, I had a new calling.

Cookbooks.

In partnership with Dixie Spicer, a woman who is, without a doubt, the best cook in Jameson County if not the whole world, I'm the Sugar half of Sugar and Spice Publishing. The Spice part comes in, not just because it has a nice ring to it, but because Spice is Dixie's nickname. A moniker she claims came about because of her last name, Spicer, and her hair color, which is a rich cinnamon. To tell you the God's honest truth, the nickname probably had a lot to do with her personality, but more about that later. In any case, Dixie and I publish cookbooks.

Now, probably not the kind you're thinking. Not the big fancy celebrity or TV show-driven ones on the shelves at the big box bookstores. These are community cookbooks. They're the kind your church or your kid's soccer team puts together, usually using the sale of the books as a fundraiser.

Most days I thought my exit from the corporate grind and the new venture it had brought about was brilliant, but today my role had turned into more damage control than publishing professional. The *St. Ignatius Founders' Day Commemorative Cookbook*, our inaugural project, was due to the printer in six weeks and I'd thought a brief meeting with the cookbook committee would finalize the contents. But then Scone Wars had broken out. What to do?

"When you find yourself in a hole, stop diggin'" was another idiom from Aunt Cricket, and though I've found she borrows wisdom from others and edits to the situation, it is mostly still wisdom. Mostly.

I took a deep breath and tried to gather my thoughts. As I did, I inhaled the combined smells of hot coffee and fresh baked pies. No matter where you're from, food is a universal thing. But here in the heart of America it's absolutely baked into the essence of the people and the place. Whether a holiday celebration, a family dinner, or a potluck. It's infused into the joy, the grief, and everything in between.

Today I'd counted on food to bring together the St. Ignatius Founders' Day Committee. With the help of the Red Hen Diner, I'd assembled a mouth-watering spread of summer fruit pies. Cherry (my favorite), apple, and peach. Perfect flaky crusts, sweet fruit flavors, and fresh hot coffee. I'd placed my trust in food to bring the group together.

Instead I had a major fail on my hands. The mob was out of control.

Or at least two members of the St. Ignatius Founders' Day Committee were, and the rest of the group egged them on with their rapt attention. I looked around the chicken-themed meeting room with its bright red and white checked tablecloths. In a matter of minutes, the place had changed from a bright and friendly chicken-themed backroom at the diner, to a WWE smackdown ring, with two contenders and the rest of the committee craning their necks, and jockeying for the best view to see what was going down.

In one corner, we had Elsie "The Eliminator" and in the other corner, Bertie "The Rock of the Block." It had begun with jabs over whose recipe for scones should be included in the Founders' Day cookbook, and escalated to full blown insult-throwing. Both were now on their feet, red-faced and agitated, silver heads bobbing as they squared off.

The committee chair made eye contact with me from across the room. Petite and proper Harriet Hucklebee looked around at the roomful of people as if she wasn't sure whether she should call the sheriff or sell tickets.

"Ladies, ladies." I raised my voice in an attempt to be heard above the argument. "Let's talk about this. I'm sure we can come to some sort of agreement."

"You sure can, missy." Elsie Farmer whipped around toward me, her smart silver earrings jangling with the force of her turn. "*You* can take

Bertie's sad excuse for a scone recipe and toss it right in the garbage where it belongs."

"Come on, Elsie, everybody knows my scones put yours to shame." Bertie stomped closer to her opponent tightening the strings of her blue chambray apron with each step. "At last week's Ladies' Missions meeting, they were gobbled up. None left. You might have noticed if you hadn't been so busy flapping your lips."

"That must have been because people were taking them home to use for doorstops," Elsie shot back, her fists jammed on the waistline of the pink cabbage rose floral dress she wore. "If people knew ahead of time what you serve at your B & B, they wouldn't bother." She turned and addressed the rest of the committee. "I guess the 'B & B' stands for bad and…bad."

Not terribly creative insult throwing, but she spat out the last "bad" as if it were the foulest of swear words.

There was a collective gasp from the onlookers.

"You'd better watch yourself," Bertie bristled. She pushed up her wire-rimmed glasses and leaned in nose to nose with Elsie. "Don't you go bad-mouthing my business, old woman."

"What are you gonna do, *old woman?*" Elsie reached out a finger and poked it at Bertie's nose. "Do me in over a scone recipe?"

Oh my word, the two had plum lost their minds.

"Ladies—" I tried again to restore some civility.

"You." Elsie turned her finger toward me. "Sugar Calloway, you're the reason for all this fuss. You and your dumb cookbook."

Now all eyes in the room shifted to me. I didn't think it was the best time to point out that the "dumb cookbook" she referenced wasn't really *my* dumb cookbook. It was their dumb cookbook.

I looked to the other committee members for help. Poor little Harriet, bless her heart, looked ready to duck and run. Jimmie LeBlanc, head of the local historical society, ran a finger under the band of his bow tie like the bright red satin was about to strangle him. Tina Martin's bright fuchsia lips were frozen into a surprised "O." Dot Carson, the postmistress, leaned forward her eyes darting between Elsie and Bertie. And Lark Travers, jewelry store owner and project donor, suddenly found the ceiling of the room extremely fascinating.

Okay then, no help from the peanut gallery.

Turning back to Elsie, I took a deep breath.

She looked me up and down and lifted her chin. "When you're ready to see reason, you know where to find me." She walked to the door, and then turned back to the room. "Until this is sorted out, I will not support the Founders' Day project, nor will the Farmer family." With that, Elsie slammed out.

"Good riddance," Bertie called from across the room.

"Wow." I broke the silence that followed Elsie's exit.

And as if that had been the cue they were waiting for, everyone started talking at once.

Chapter Two

Holy guacamole, now what? How on earth did a short meeting to sort out a few details about a cookbook go from a pie and coffee to DEFCON 1 in a matter of minutes?

I did feel somewhat responsible because it wasn't news to me that a ton of emotion is often attached to a favorite recipe, but I'd never seen anything quite like this.

It would take the committee a little while to get settled down, which gave me a chance to gather my papers and my thoughts. The *St. Ignatius Founders' Day Cookbook* was tight on space already and truly didn't need two scone recipes, but there had to be a way to work this out. A great believer in the win-win theory (go ahead, call me Pollyanna if you like), I was sure there had to be a solution. A good one. I just couldn't put my finger on it at the moment.

What had ever possessed me to think the two would see reason? I guess I'd thought one of them would take the high road and volunteer to leave their recipe out. I'd even brought along alternative recipes each had submitted. Elsie's Pineapple Right Side-Up Cake sounded tasty and Bertie's Corny Casserole would be a great addition. But instead the two feisty seniors had gone at it like opponents at a sold-out rumble.

I looked around the table. With a break in the action, some had taken the opportunity to refill their coffee cups or take a restroom break. Others were headed back to their places, checking their phones or chatting with their neighbors. Most of the committee members had little interest in scones, or casseroles or cakes for that matter, but from what I could hear of the chatter the threat of Elsie Farmer's family pulling out had the group in a tizzy.

The Farmer family was a big part of many of the events. Farmer's Farm Feeds had the parking lot where the parade would start, Farmer Trucking would provide the flatbed truck that would serve as the stage for all the presentations and, most importantly, Farmer's Hardware was the sponsor of the Miss Iggy contest which would determine who would be crowned queen of the whole St. Ignatius Founders' Day Celebration.

Who would have thought that a dispute over a scone recipe would threaten to derail so many things?

I reached for my sheaf of papers and handed draft copies of the book's table of contents to Tina Martin, local real estate agent, who sat on my right.

"What do you want me to do with these?" She waved the papers in the air. Her hot pink perfectly manicured nails matched her lipstick. In addition to being the town's most successful realtor, Tina was also the local cosmetics maven. If she hadn't tapped you yet to host a Looking Pretty party, trust me, she would. I think I'd escaped thus far because I was newish in town and didn't know enough people to garner a big order.

"Just pass them down." I handed a few more to a young woman on my left who I had just realized I didn't know. "I'm sorry, I don't think we've met."

"You probably don't remember me." She took one of the sheets and handed the rest to her neighbor. "We met at last month's Dilly Dally Dayz. I'm Minnie. Minnie Silberhorn. I'm the new secretary of the Founders' Day Committee. I think they just picked me because I'm good at taking notes. And because Kenny Farmer volunteered me." She straightened the pens beside her tablet, one red, one blue, one green, lining them up equal distance apart on the table.

Her light blue eyes met mine and a twinge of guilt shot through me because I *had* forgotten meeting her. I prided myself on remembering names and faces, and usually tried to pair a person's name with something about their appearance so the name would stick in my memory. But Minnie was so quiet, both in dress and manner, nothing about her really stood out. It wasn't that she was homely; it was simply that she sort of blended into the background.

"We really appreciate your note-taking, but I'm sure you're good at a lot of things." I gave her what I hoped was a reassuring smile. "Are you any good at herding cats? Because I'm afraid that's what it's going to be like, trying to get this group back on track." I waved my hands at the room.

She gave me an odd look and straightened the red pen I'd just bumped out of alignment.

Okay then. Not everyone appreciates my sense of humor.

I watched my table of contents papers make their way around the table. Dixie and I had organized the recipes into the usual categories. Appetizers,

Main Dishes, Sides, and Desserts. I really had to get the categories signed off on today because I needed to get photos done for the sections. Add to that, I needed to get a photographer lined up.

Also, because the purpose of the book was not only to celebrate local fare but also to commemorate the town's founders, I'd suggested some snippets of history mixed in. I needed those today as well.

Harriet Hucklebee slipped into the space between Tina and me. "I know you told us we'd have a limited amount of space for town history, but Jimmie has put a few ideas together." She lifted her eyes heavenward. "Lord help us, I think he's written a novel."

I stared at the two-inch thick pile of papers she'd laid in front of me. Jimmie LeBlanc hadn't just written a novel. He'd penned *War and Peace* St. Ignatius style.

"In order to keep within the budget for printing costs, we have to stay with the number of pages we planned." I tried to give her my no-nonsense-I-mean-business look but it's hard to take a tough line with a woman that looks like Marian the Librarian. Dixie and I had been very clear with the committee on page count when we'd looked at options more than two months ago.

"I know, but you know Jimmie." She pushed at the sleeves of her soft blue sweater set and shrugged her shoulders. "You'll just have to be firm with him."

Me? So in other words, no one on the committee wanted to tangle with the retired history teacher turned local history fanatic. The truth was I was fascinated by Jimmie's stories, but the charming old guy had not even a passing acquaintance with the concept of brevity. Bottom line, we had to keep costs down or the cookbook would end up being a money pit rather than a fundraiser.

Harriet patted the back of my hand. "I know you'll help him to understand." She smiled and stepped away. "I'll work on getting the group back in their places so we can get on with our agenda."

I glanced at my cell phone to check the time and saw I had missed two calls. One of them from my landlady.

"Greer," I said under my breath.

"Did you just growl at me?" Tina took a swig of her ever-present energy drink and looked at me over her bright purple rhinestone-studded reading glasses.

"No." I laughed at her offended look. "I missed a phone call from Greer and..." I glanced back at my phone. "...from someone else I don't know." The other number was a different area code and not one I recognized. It wasn't my Mama Dearest's number nor the right area code to be any of my extended family.

"Oh, how is Greer?" Tina rolled her eyes and tucked a strand of perfectly highlighted blond hair behind one ear. I have no idea how the errant strand had escaped because her whole head of hair had been hair sprayed within an inch of its life.

"Doing well." I glanced back at my phone. "She probably just needs something from the attic or shed."

I was fond of Greer, who had rented me her well-kept Victorian at a great price when I moved to St. Ignatius. The darling eighty-something had decided a move to The Good Life, the town's senior living center, was in order and made me a great deal on the rent. The only caveat had been she wanted to leave some things behind until she decided what to do with them. However, with increasing frequency, Greer had been calling with various things she wanted me to look for in the many boxes and trunks.

"It's ridiculous she expects you, a renter, to do that." Tina shook her head. "Most people would simply sell their house and be done with it."

It could be as a real estate agent Tina had more than a passing interest.

"I think it's hard for her to let go and face no longer having her home to go back to." Whatever the reason, Greer wasn't ready to sell her house and I wasn't yet in any position to buy, but I hoped by the time she decided to put it on the market, I'd be able to swing the mortgage.

"Hmmpf." Tina leaned back in her seat, removed her purple glasses, and eyed me. "You know, Sugar, I have a Plum Passion eye shadow that would be stunning with your dark hair and gray eyes. Just stunning." She fumbled in her bag and I hoped she wasn't going to apply Plum Passion right then and there. "Not that you need help. Those classic cheekbones, that porcelain skin, and the contrast of your gorgeous dark chocolate hair. Still, it doesn't hurt to ice the cake, you know." She gave me a wink and handed me a business card.

"Thanks, hon." I took the embossed card though I was pretty sure I had one already. "We'll talk later." I would call my cheekbones angular, my skin type, pale and guaranteed to sunburn, and though I liked chocolate, I thought plain old dark brown better described my hair color. I wondered if Tina's real estate ads reflected her penchant for colorful descriptions.

Picking Greer's number from the recent calls, I started to step away and hit redial. Clearly Tina didn't think much of my arrangement with my landlady. It was a good thing Greer wasn't counting on her for help. I'd heard Greer had a son who lived in Minneapolis, which was not much of a jaunt, but he'd not been to see her in a long while. Not in all the time since I'd known her anyway.

"Let's get back to the business at hand," Harriet clapped her hands to get everyone's attention.

I dropped my phone in my bag. I'd have to call Greer back after the meeting and then I could also check to see if the other caller had left a message.

By the time order was restored and we'd taken care of all the other details, it was more than an hour later than what I'd planned. I thanked everyone, gathered my papers, shut down my laptop, and headed for the door.

I assured everyone who stopped me, and most did, that I would talk to Elsie and Bertie and we'd come up with a solution. I spotted Jimmie LeBlanc headed my way and I have to admit I ducked out as quickly as I could before he could corner me about his history tome.

"One crisis at a time," I muttered to myself as I piled my things into the back of Big Blue, my dark blue Jeep. The Jeep had been my last big purchase before I left corporate land and I knew I probably should downsize my vehicle like I'd downsized other things in my life but I liked the car and if Sugar and Spice Publishing could make a go of it, I might not have to. I slid behind the wheel and headed back to the office.

Now "the office" sounds way larger and much fancier than the little room in the back of the storefront on the town square that was the whole of Sugar and Spice Cookbook Publishing.

It had been a café once upon a time, but sat empty for long enough that the building owner was willing to offer the space at a discount. A big discount. Though small, it allowed Dixie a kitchen area for beta-testing and me both a small office and a sizable workspace for shuffling recipes and looking at layouts. The low overhead was key because this was our very first and only paying project. We'd fixed up the reception area without spending a lot thanks to chairs Dixie had unearthed from her family's second barn aka storage unit. Bright red gingham curtains dressed the front windows and I'd decorated the walls of the outer office with some vintage cooking utensils I'd collected from a series of estate sales.

The business would grow. I knew it would. I had a meeting later in the week with a quilting guild the next county over, and one the following week with a breakfast club in town. But before all that, I had to get two iron-willed ladies to meet in the middle on scone recipes.

I could do it. I had to. If I couldn't negotiate a truce, the *St. Ignatius Founders' Day Cookbook* was down for the count.

Chapter Three

Dixie could not stop laughing.

"Dixie Spicer, I don't think it's funny at all and you wouldn't either if you'd been there." I attempted a glare but the rosy-cheeked redhead is an awfully difficult person to be mad at.

"Well, thank goodness I wasn't because I would've thought it was hilarious, which would have irritated the living daylights out of my aunt." She guffawed again as she thought about the scone stand-off.

Oh, one thing I forgot to mention earlier, Bertie Sparks aka Contender Two, who ran the Jefferson Street Bed & Breakfast, is Dixie's aunt. The B & B was well-known across the midwest as a high-quality establishment, and Bertie worked hard to keep it going. I could understand why she had gotten so upset when Elsie Farmer had dissed it.

"I've got to fix this and fix it fast." I plopped down at the desk and flipped through my notes.

"Good luck with that." Dixie pulled her deep red hair into a ponytail as she talked. "Those two have been rivals as long as I can remember and they're both about as pig-headed as they come. Last fall, we had..." She paused for effect. "Walnutgate."

"What?" I looked up from my papers.

"There was this contest at church to see who could sell the most fancy walnuts during the Ladies' Missions annual food pantry fundraiser. Elsie and Bertie were neck and neck, and then Elsie got a humongous order from out of town and left Aunt Bertie in the dust. Bertie claimed Elsie bought them herself to inflate her sales, but she couldn't ever prove anything."

"You might have mentioned that little tidbit of knowledge before I stepped smack dab in the middle of the Game of Scones. Now the committee is in an uproar over Elsie's threat of her family pulling all their support for the Founders' Day celebration. And if we don't get this cookbook to the printer in the next six weeks our one and only paying gig is kaput."

"Not to mention, we both have bills to pay." Dixie suddenly turned serious. "I can't ask my brother to bail me out again and my mom will just start bugging me to sell my house and move in with her."

Dixie's family had been very supportive when she'd lost her husband in a farm accident a year ago, but she wanted to stand on her own two feet. When she'd contacted me with the idea of starting a community cookbook publishing business, the timing had been perfect because I'd just found out I was about to be unemployed.

She'd put her husband's life insurance settlement into the business and I'd invested my severance payment. We had to make this work. Our independence depended on it. Dixie didn't want to have to move in with her mother and I wanted to stay as far away as possible from mine.

Not that I don't love my mama. Of course, I do, but I had tired of not only my mother, but her well-meaning but beyond bossy sisters trying to run my life. So, when I got a job offer that took me out of their reach, I'd jumped at it.

I have to tell you there were times lately when it felt a little like I'd moved halfway across the country only to find myself in the same situation. Not that the aunts followed me to Iowa. Oh no, they were still in Searcy, Georgia sipping their sweet tea and telling anyone who would listen that Sugar would come to her senses soon and move back home. And marry that nice Danny Kindell who was such a good catch.

Not happening. And, frankly, Danny wasn't such a good catch. Unless, you had a penchant for philandering idiots.

My father had been from Iowa and though his kin was all gone it felt like I had some unexplored roots here. It was an added bonus that the opportunity to go into business with Dixie had also included a chance to leave the city life behind. I loved my newly adopted hometown and its "everyone-knows-your-name" atmosphere. Though lately it seemed everyone not only knew my name, they also knew my business. And at least half the town had a grandson, nephew, cousin, or friend they were interested in fixing me up with. Also, not happening.

But I did like living in St. Ignatius and if I wanted to stay here, and I did, I needed to get our project back on track.

"Okay, Dixie help me out. You've lived here all your life." I pulled out a notebook. "What am I going to do to get Elsie Farmer and your Aunt Bertie to stand down?

"Elsie Farmer is never going to stand down, so your best bet is my aunt. She's poured her heart and soul into her business, that B & B is everything to her. Maybe we could feature one of the Jefferson Street B & B signature dishes. That might win her over."

"Do you think the Farmer family will really pull their support for the Founders' Day if Elsie doesn't get her way?" I asked. I'd been in town long enough to understand just how much power a prominent local family can wield.

"I don't think Kenny will let it go that far." Dixie straightened her apron. "But come to think of it, her hubs did cave when she wanted Joey Waters fired. Claimed he backed into her Cadillac. Truth is he probably did, but it had nothing to do with his work."

Dixie and I strategized a bit and by the time I left the shop to head home, I felt much better about my chances with the two competitive cooks. After all, this wasn't about winning blue ribbons at the county fair. It was about simply having the best mix of recipes for the *St. Ignatius Founders' Day Cookbook*. We all wanted the same thing, a quality cookbook that would sell lots of copies and benefit the town. I just needed to remind them we were all on the same team.

I turned Big Blue toward the tree-lined older part of town, looking forward with a sense of calm to a quiet evening with my couch, my cat, and a good book.

I adored my little rental home. A well-kept white house on a big lot with a maple tree that would turn crimson in the fall, and a big yard edged in lilac bushes, it was a welcome sanctuary after the day I'd had. The house was a Queen Anne Victorian that had been updated. Greer said she had redone the kitchen and bathrooms, but tried to keep the feel of the house. In my mind, she'd succeeded. I loved the gingerbread on the front, the high ceilings, the oak woodwork, and the claw-foot tub.

It had been a heck of a day and all I could think of was how much I enjoyed the calm of being home.

Hold that thought, because the calm didn't last long.

As I parked and grabbed my things from the car, I noticed my next-door neighbor outside. I thought about making a run for it. Mrs. Pickett invariably had a complaint, and all my attempts at being friendly were met with indifference.

I lifted the tote bag I'd loaded with paperwork and slung it over my shoulder. Moving away from the car, I noted she'd moved closer to our shared fence line.

Oh, no. This did not bode well.

"Hello, Mrs. Pickett." I called. I knew her first name was Jean but she'd never given me permission to use it, and I'd been raised that you waited until invited to call someone, who was your senior, by their first name.

"Ms. Calloway." She nodded in my general direction. "Come here." She crooked a finger.

Now what.

I approached the fence and she pointed at the grassy area. "Do you see that?"

I peered over the fence. "See what?"

She sighed and pointed again. "Those leaves."

"Yes," I answered. The stiff wind from a couple of nights ago had blown some of the leaves from the tree rooted in Greer's side yard from the branches.

"Your leaves have fallen in my yard." She punctuated the "your" and the "my" with a jab of her spindly finger.

"But—" I started to explain that I didn't think a neighbor was supposed to chase after all the leaves that fell from their trees, but she'd already turned and walked away.

"Even though you're a renter, you'll need to take care of that," she commented over her shoulder.

Well, for crying in a bucket! She couldn't possibly think it was my responsibility to rake leaves that had fallen on her side of the fence. And she'd said "renter" with such derision that it sounded like I should have a scarlet R on my chest.

Last week it had been that she didn't like me putting my trash out the night before it was collected. The week before that it had been something else, I couldn't remember what. I think it boiled down to the woman just didn't like me. I wasn't sure why, but there it was. Probably she and Greer had lived next to each other for a long time and she didn't like the change.

Greer. Oh, gosh. I suddenly remembered I'd forgotten to call Greer back.

Unlocking the door and entering the foyer, I dropped my bags on the gleaming hardwood floor and grabbed my cell phone from my purse.

I hit re-dial and Greer picked up right away.

"Well, there you are, Sugar," she said, without a greeting. "I thought maybe you were out of town or something."

"No, just busy with this cookbook." I kicked off my shoes and continued down the hallway to the kitchen.

"You got my Garbage Cookie recipe, didn't you?" I could picture her whipping up batches of cookies at the very counter where I stood. Her snow-white hair, her narrow, stooped shoulders, her quick smile. A small stepstool still stood propped at the end of the cabinets because the top cabinets had been out of her reach.

"Yes, I did." I tried not to get choked up over the picture in my head. I hadn't known my own grandmother, but if I were picking one out, I'd pick one just like Greer. She insisted she wasn't sentimental about the house, but why else would she want to continue to store things. And why was she unwilling to sell the property.

"If it's not too much trouble," she began, which was how it always started. "It's not a rush or anything, but when you get time there's a frog figure I need from that box in the attic that's labeled 'Knick-Knacks.'"

I remembered the box. Mostly because it was actually marked 'Nic-Naks' which drove me crazy every time I saw it. My fingers itched to get a marker and fix the spelling. I guess once an editor always an editor. But the boxes weren't mine to mess with and so I resisted.

"It's no problem at all." I opened the refrigerator door and peered inside realizing I probably should have stopped at the grocery store on the way home. Ernest, the handsome six-toed tabby who'd appeared on the front step the day after I moved in, padded in to stand beside me. Together we stared at the empty shelves. I'd asked around the neighborhood and put up signs, but no one claimed him. So, I'd decided to keep him.

"He's a little green froggie figurine about yea tall." I was sure Greer was holding her hands up to show me. "I was telling Nellie Kaufmann today at cards about him. She saw a similar frog on that antiques show on the TV and she thinks he might be a collectible."

"I'll look this evening." I told her. "And if I can find froggie, I'll bring him by tomorrow."

"That's great. You're so sweet to keep bringing my things to me."

"Truly, it's no trouble." It seemed like the least I could do for the sweet thing. I hoped when I was eighty someone would do the same for me.

"Well, I won't keep you. They're having pot roast in the dining room tonight and I've been looking forward to it all day." And she was gone without further ado.

Ernest and I eyed the interior of my fridge. Nothing resembling pot roast in there, but I didn't want to go back out to the grocery store. Lazy, I know.

"It looks like something out of a can for both of us." I patted his head. "I know you're hoping for tuna sandwiches."

Right now, I was all about fixing something quick and easy, changing into my favorite t-shirt and yoga pants, and escaping into the pages of one of the books I'd picked up at the library.

Later, I'd make the trek to the attic, ignore the misspelled writing on the boxes, and search for Greer's frog figurine.

And tomorrow, I'd clear my head, strap on my diplomacy, and do battle with the two scone contenders.

Chapter Four

The next morning I was up early and raring to go, and I had decided to start with Elsie Farmer.

She was, after all, the one I needed to convince the most. I would simply tell her we were planning to include her scone recipe and then I'd hope she was okay with there being two recipes in the book. If not, my next stop would have to be to chat with Dixie's Aunt Bertie and find a way to convince her the inclusion of her Corny Casserole would be a much better representation of the Jefferson Street B & B instead of a silly scone recipe.

Divide and conquer.

I parked Big Blue on the street in front of Elsie's house. It was a large well cared for turn of the century Victorian a few blocks from the town square. I climbed the steps to the veranda on the front and knocked. A profusion of flowers in colorful pots stood out against the bright white of the house. I took a deep cleansing breath and inhaled the smell of the blossoms. The light scent of lavender from beside the steps mixed with the bright notes of hyacinth and pinks.

I smoothed my skirt and rehearsed my pitch in my head. I'd put on a sleeveless classic red dress, a leftover from my corporate days. A power color. I'd start with the initial offering of assurance that her wonderful scone recipe would definitely be included. Hopefully that would head off the fight. But if the rivalry was as longstanding as Dixie described, it might not be enough to include Elsie's. She might insist that Bertie's not be included.

I knocked again. Where on earth was the woman? I'd phoned to make sure it was okay to drop by and she'd grudgingly agreed. I think in the end the idea of skewering the new girl in town and watching her squirm proved irresistible. I also think she would have preferred a public skewering.

Knocking again, this time even louder, I glanced around. Big windows faced the veranda. It felt a little improper but I peered inside.

"Mrs. Farmer?" I tapped on the glass and waited. Nothing. No Elsie. Now what?

I had been specific about when I'd be there, but maybe she was in the back. I went down the porch steps and walked around the side of the house. There was a detached garage in the backyard and the garage door stood open. Elsie's car, a white Cadillac, was parked inside. So she *was* home.

"Hello," I called. "Is anyone back here?" As beautiful as the flowers had been out front, the backyard garden was even prettier. One section surrounded by a miniature picket fence seemed to be devoted to different colored roses. Roses are my favorite.

I caught a movement out of the corner of my eye and turned just in time to see a figure slip between the tall bushes at the back. "Hello," I tried again, but whoever it had been was gone. Stepping into the backyard I noticed a brightly colored pile of clothing on the ground. Maybe Elsie had been hanging out laundry and that's why she hadn't heard my knock. You'd be surprised how many people in St. Ignatius still hung their laundry out on a clothesline. My house (Greer's house) had one and I loved it. There was nothing like the smell of fresh line-dried sheets.

I wandered further into the garden. Once I was close enough to the pile of clothing, I realized my terrible mistake.

A scream rose in my throat but no sound came out.

What I'd mistaken for a pile of clothing was Elsie, her body prone, her glasses askew, her eyes open but sightless, a scone clutched in her outstretched hand.

* * * *

I have to be honest, it's a bit of a blur to me what happened next. I remember checking Elsie's pulse but it was clear she wasn't just taking a nap there on the ground in her backyard. I do remember I fished in my purse for my cell phone and called 911. Then I stood there flash-frozen in place until the police arrived. It seemed like forever but I'm sure it was only a few minutes before Sheriff Griffin and two uniformed deputies showed up.

The sheriff is handsome in an all-American boy sort of way. I'd met him before but I couldn't recall exactly where it had been.

The sheriff leaned over the body and then turned to speak to his deputy. "Cancel the ambulance and call the coroner."

"Ms. Calloway, if you could move back please." He touched my arm.

I guess I must have been standing there like my feet were glued to the ground. I guess I also must have given him my name at some point. I moved off to the side.

The other deputy stood at the garden gate, holding back onlookers. I'd heard the sirens when the sheriff arrived. A welcome sound, but I imagined one that also brought out neighbors up and down the street to see what was going on.

Suddenly Dixie careened around the corner of the house and slammed into the deputy who held his arm out to stop her. She ignored him, ducked under his arm and headed my way.

The sheriff moved to intercept her but she gave him a look I'd seen her use on her twelve-year-old nephew and trust me it had don't-mess-with-me superpowers. Sheriff Griffin stopped in his tracks.

Dixie wrapped me in a hug. "What happened?"

"I don't know." I repeated what I'd told the sheriff. "I just found her back here."

"She can go now, right?" Dixie addressed her question to the sheriff.

"We have more questions—" he began.

"Come on, Terry," Dixie shot back before he could finish. "She's just found a dead woman. You can ask your questions later. Come on, Sugar."

I guess they knew each other. Not unusual, Dixie knew everyone, but there was definitely something between the two of them. I couldn't quite put my finger on it but there was something odd. I tried to think if I'd ever heard Dixie mention Sheriff Griffin before and couldn't bring an instance to mind. They were about the same age so maybe they'd gone to school together.

Two deputies were stringing that yellow crime scene tape you see on TV from the veranda to the picket fence and shooing people behind it. The front yard was crawling with more people as others joined the assembled crowd.

Luckily we went pretty much unnoticed as we made our way down the street to Dixie's pickup. Big oak trees that lined the street shaded the sidewalk protecting us from the heat of the sun as the day came awake.

"What do they think happened?" Dixie fell into step beside me. "A heart attack or stroke?"

"I don't know. No one said. The sheriff cancelled the ambulance and had them send for the coroner. I guess, there wasn't any hope." I swallowed threatening tears. "She was already gone when I f-found her." My voice quivered and I felt my insides do the same.

"Let's get you home." She clicked open the locks on her truck and I climbed in. "We'll worry about getting your car later. There's no way you'd be able to get through that crowd right now."

"If it's all the same to you, I'd like to go on to the office." I settled into the seat. "I don't think I can stand to do nothing right now. It would be better to be busy."

"I understand." Dixie started the truck and carefully pulled out. Several people waved as we drove away.

The town square was only a few blocks away. It was quiet in sharp contrast to the neighborhood we'd just left. A few shoppers wandered along the sidewalk, and the parking surrounding the courthouse was full as usual with people paying traffic fines and renewing car titles. St. Ignatius was the typical midwestern small county seat with a town square of quaint shops arranged around a historic courthouse. The St. Ignatius version was a late 1800s Italianate revival style complete with clock tower that gave it an almost castle-like feel.

I inhaled a deep breath and filled my eyes with the idyllic square, the brilliant green grass, the park benches, the bright red pansies, hoping it would block out the picture in my head of poor Elsie Farmer lying dead in her backyard.

Dixie pulled into the alley behind the section of shops where our office was located and parked in the back. We trudged inside and dropped into the chairs where yesterday we'd sat talking about Elsie and Bertie and scone recipes. After a few minutes of silence, Dixie got up, filled the electric kettle with water and pulled out a couple of mugs. She reached into the nearest cupboard and dropped a couple of Tetley tea bags into the cups.

I wished for something stronger.

The small bell over the front door of the shop signaled someone out front. Dixie and I both jumped. Our business wasn't exactly a walk-in type of production so we didn't get many visitors. We did unlock the front when we were working, just in case, but it was usually one of the other merchants on the square.

"I unlocked it when I got here and then forgot to lock up when I heard about Elsie," Dixie noted. She poured hot water into one of the mugs and handed it to me and then went to investigate.

"Oh, it's you," I could hear her say.

"Yep, me." I recognized Sheriff Griffin's voice. "Is your partner here?"

"Sugar," Dixie called out. "would you come out here for a sec?"

I was already out of my seat and headed to check out what the sheriff wanted. He probably had lots of questions and I had a few of my own.

"Hello again." He directed his serious brown gaze in my direction. "I failed to get a phone number so we could contact you with additional questions."

I rattled off my cell number, the only number I had, and he jotted it in his notebook. "Did Elsie have a heart attack?"

"Why would you have 'additional questions' for Sugar?" Dixie made quote marks in the air with her fingers and her tone of voice clearly tacked on, "Are you an idiot?" to the query.

He leveled her a look and then turned toward me. "We don't know. It will be a while before we have cause of death."

Death. The word shattered the calm I'd thought I had. A picture of Elsie flashed into my mind. Prone, sprawled in the grass, lifeless.

"Wh-what if," I stuttered, my voice shaking, "I'd gotten there sooner?" The question had been haunting me ever since we'd left Elsie's. What if I'd arrived sooner? I'd stopped to pick up a coffee. Maybe if I'd been a few minutes earlier I could have gotten help. I'd read that minutes mattered with heart attacks and if I hadn't waited so long before looking in the back for Elsie, I might have made a difference.

His expression said he'd like to be reassuring but couldn't bring himself to lie. "I'm sorry, Ms. Calloway, we just don't know." He flipped shut his little notebook.

"Call me Sugar," I gulped.

"Sugar, you told me before you had called to say you were coming over, right?"

"That's right. She was reluctant, but she agreed. Which is why I was so surprised when she didn't answer the door. I mean she knew I was coming."

"What time did you call?" he asked. There were side glances at Dixie when he thought she wasn't looking but I didn't know how to take them.

"Around eight." I answered.

He made a note. "And what was the nature of your business with her?"

I hesitated and looked toward Dixie for help. In light of this morning's events it seemed trivial. "Well, we're working on this cookbook for the St. Ignatius Founders' Day and there'd been a little disagreement of which scone recipe was to be included. I was stopping by to see if I could convince her to be okay with the committee's decision to have more than one scone recipe in the book."

"I understand from talking with several people things got a little heated yesterday at the committee's meeting."

"They did." I sighed. "Recipes don't seem very important right now."
"They are to some people." He turned to look at Dixie directly. "My next stop is to talk to your Aunt Bertie."

"What are you saying?" Dixie's face flamed red, as red as her hair. "Is this a murder investigation? You think my aunt had something to do with Elsie Farmer's death?"

"We have to—" he started.

"For crying out loud. That's a new low, even for someone like you, Terrance Griffin," Dixie interrupted and then turned on her heel and walked out, headed to the backroom.

Whoa. If I'd thought there had been an undercurrent before, this one had boiled to the surface.

"We have to treat every death as a suspicious death until we know more," Sherriff Griffin finished. "I'll be in touch." And with a curt nod, he left.

No sooner had the sheriff slipped out than the bell over the door jangled again.

"Hey, Sugar." It was Disco, the guy who owned Flashback, the records and memorabilia store a few shops down from us.

"Hey there, Disco." His real name was Dick Fusco but everybody called him Disco and it seemed appropriate because the guy was stuck in the 70s. At least his fashion sense was.

"What's going on?" His loud pink and orange paisley shirt had puffy sleeves and wide cuffs and a big gold chain shifted on his thin wrist as he removed his sunglasses. As Disco stepped through the doorway and came farther into the shop, his eyes scanned the counter top. I figured he was looking to see if Dixie had any test dishes left over. We were pretty sure business wasn't booming at Flashback and I feared Disco was having some problems making ends meet. We were happy to share sample dishes after they'd passed muster, but I worried things must be really bad if Disco was cruising for leftovers this early in the day.

Dixie came out from the kitchen and offered our visitor some cheese puff appetizers she'd been in the middle of making when she'd heard about Elsie and rushed out. He munched a few and then happily headed out the door with the to-go bag Dixie had put together for him. He'd been gone only a few minutes when the bell jangled again. Then it became a steady stream of people who stopped by to see us with one excuse or another but who really wanted to know about Elsie Farmer. By the time the place cleared out, I'd told the story so many times I felt like I was on continuous play loop. Hello. Yes, I found her. Yes, she was dead. Clearly dead. Police came. No, I don't know any more.

There was a break in the visitors and Dixie flipped the lock on the front door and motioned me to the back room.

We heard a tap on the front window but we both ignored it, gathered up our things, and headed for the back entrance.

"Come on," Dixie held the door open. "You've had quite a day. Let's get your car picked up so you can get home and see if you can catch a break from answering questions about finding Elsie."

"I don't think I'll answer my phone." I ducked out and headed toward Dixie's truck.

Chapter Five

The street was thankfully deserted and I was able to pick up my Jeep without having to chat with anyone.

Bright yellow crime scene tape fluttered on the posts of the veranda and a length stretched from there to the garden gate. How awful for Mr. Farmer to face not only his wife's death, but then to top it off to have to look at crime scene tape strung all over his home. I hadn't seen him at the house earlier. I assumed they'd called him at work and broken the news about Elsie.

Did Sheriff Griffin really believe that Dixie's Aunt Bertie had something to do with Elsie's death? Like maybe the stress caused her heart attack? Poor Bertie, her harsh words to Elsie had to be haunting her. Though Elsie had gone on the attack first and had certainly given as good as she got, I'm sure that didn't make Bertie feel any better about it right now. I had no doubt Sheriff Griffin was kind when he talked with her, but still it had to be upsetting to be questioned by the police.

I drove home quickly and parked in the drive hoping Mrs. Pickett was inside. I didn't think I could take one of her petty complaints today.

As I entered the house, the frog statue I'd dug out of the storage box for Greer greeted me. It had taken me a while to find him because he was tightly wrapped in a soft bath towel, probably to prevent breakage. Bright green-glazed ceramic, he was less than a foot tall and stood upright with one leg bent at the knee in a jaunty pose.

I'd placed him on a book shelf near the front entry so I wouldn't forget to drop him off. That would be a good task for this afternoon. I'd brought home editing work for the Founders' Day Cookbook, but suddenly the thought of being alone didn't seem very attractive. I'd work for a while and then a visit with Greer would make for a nice break.

Ernest sauntered into the room and greeted me. He sniffed at my tote and peered around it as if to note, "What? No cat treats again?"

And he was right I still needed to make a trip to the store both for cat treats for Ernest and food for myself. Yet another reason to get out of the house. An hour or so of editing and then I'd make a list, gather up the frog statue, and check those two things off my list. It was a plan.

"This afternoon, I promise." I bent and rubbed his head. Big trusting green eyes looked up at me and I knew I'd better remember this time. "I promise."

I changed my clothes, tossing my red dress on the bed. I was glad to opt for comfort over fashion. One of the perks of no longer working in a corporate environment. I pulled on jeans and a deep purple cotton sweater which reminded me of Tina and her Plum Passion eye shadow recommendation. I wasn't sure how long I could hold her off on a Looking Pretty party. I'd begged off before because as I explained, being new in town I simply didn't know enough people to invite. The cosmetics were sold via home parties. You know the drill, don't you? You have a get-together in your home, serve food and drinks, and the consultant demonstrates: food items, jewelry, plastic containers, or in this case, cosmetics.

First things first. Once changed, I brewed a cup of tea and settled down with my first draft of the introduction to the book and my trusty red pen. If I could get the stories nailed down for each of the sections, I'd tackle the stack of pages about the town's history and see what I could pull out to add a little flavor of St. Ignatius's past to include in each part of the book.

After a couple of hours of work, I was ready for a break both mentally and physically. I stacked up the papers I'd been working with and took my pen and paper to the kitchen and in short order had a grocery list. But first a stop to take a ceramic frog to my landlady.

The Good Life senior living complex where Greer lived was on the edge of town, actually almost at the city limits. From what I understood, it was fairly new but had filled up quickly with seniors in the community who either couldn't handle taking care of a house or simply didn't want to anymore.

I pulled into the parking lot and found a spot in visitor parking without any problems. I'd called to let Greer know I planned to stop by and she'd said to come on ahead as she was free for about an hour. I smiled at her and her schedule. I swear the little lady was involved in most activities the senior center offered. Bingo, bridge, yoga, a trip to the casino, whatever. She was game.

The complex was made up of individual one-level apartments, some one-bedroom and some two, but all nicely appointed. They were brick but the entire front of each unit was a patio complete with flower boxes and planters. Most residents had also added outdoor furniture and decorations which gave each apartment a more personal feel.

Greer had decorated her patio with a profusion of colorful flowers and plants as well as bright white patio furniture with yellow and white striped cushions. She sat perched in one of the patio chairs waiting for me. As I approached she slipped off her reading glasses, put down the book she'd been reading, and smiled.

"A good book?" I asked.

"An okay book, a little too tame for my taste." She held up the hardback so I could see the cover, a bright beach scene with pastel umbrellas. "Women's fiction it's called. Don't know how that's any different than men's fiction, but I'd prefer a good thriller. This is the one we're reading for book club. The group voted."

"Maybe next time they'll pick a thriller." I pulled the towel wrapped frog statue from my bag and handed it to her. "Is this the guy you were thinking of?"

Greer pulled back the swaddling. "That's him, alright." She placed him on the table and gazed at the whimsical frog figure. "I hope he's collectible like the one on TV."

"I hope so, too." I smiled at her enthusiasm.

"Do you have time to come in for a minute? I've made cookies and coffee." Greer pushed herself up to stand and I moved forward to take hold of her hands to help. "I'm fine." She waved me away. "You take care of bringing in Mr. Froggie."

I picked up the frog figurine and tucked the towel around it. Opening the door to her apartment, I waited for Greer and then followed her inside. Each time I visited I was struck by how homey she'd managed to make her space. The antique furniture she'd brought from the house was mixed with new complementary pieces and the result was very comfortable and relaxed. The earth-toned colors were warm and inviting and like Greer herself, put together well but not fancy.

"I understand you found Elsie Farmer dead in her backyard this morning." She took Mr. Froggie from me and placed him on her dining room table.

As always, you could count on Greer to get straight to the point. No grass growing under this lady's feet.

I filled her in on going to meet with Elsie and finding her in her backyard. She questioned me on details as she laid out cookies and poured coffee.

The plate she handed me already had one of her Garbage Cookies on it. "Who do they think offed the Wicked Witch of the West?" she asked. I nearly choked on my cookie.

"I'm sorry." Greer took a bite of her own cookie. "I believe in telling it like it is. I'm too old to pretend in the name of making nice. She was mean to people and full of herself and there's many a person in town who would've poured water on her if it'd made her melt away."

"That's different from actually killing someone, though." I recovered my composure and took a careful bite. Wonderful cookies. Raisins, chocolate chips, walnuts. Oh, my.

"Maybe." She blotted her lips with a napkin. "You never know what pushes someone over the edge though. Makes them snap." She snapped her fingers. "Just like that."

I described the heated words at the committee meeting, and she leaned back in her chair.

"Those two have been going at it for as long as I've known them." She dunked her cookie in her coffee and took a bite.

"That's what Dixie said." I nodded. "I understand there was some big disagreement over sales of walnuts for their church."

"That's the most recent but it was just one of many disagreements over the years." Greer shook her head. "Before that it was some jam or jelly competition. Like I said, always something with those two. Been that way since forever."

"What a shame." I thought about how much time and energy the two had spent on such unimportant things. They could take a clue from Greer who never seemed to let anything get under her skin.

"Enough of that," she said. "Tell me what you've been up to."

We had a nice chat about nothing in particular and I felt the tensions of the day fall from me. Greer had that effect. I kissed her cheek when I left and promised to come by again soon to talk. Maybe I'd take her out to lunch next time.

A quick stop at the grocery store for a few things (cat treats included) didn't take long. I'll admit I hurried through, not really making eye contact, and not inviting conversation. Rude, I know. Still, a couple of people stopped me to comment, and the lady at the checkout wanted to know if I knew any more than what she'd heard at the car wash. Mostly though I was able to get through quickly. I think I may have lucked out with the time of day, because the grocery store wasn't all that busy.

Soon I was back home, my groceries put away, and ready to tackle Jimmie LeBlanc's tome of town history. I brewed a strong tea, gave Ernest a few treats, and settled in.

Hours later I surfaced, realizing I was hungry. I had in mind a fresh salad with some greens I'd picked up at last week's farmer's market and chicken I'd bought at the store today. Not very imaginative, I know. But like I've said before, Dixie's the cook in our cookbook business. And thank goodness for that.

By the time I'd cooked, eaten, and cleaned up I was beat and ready to call it a night. My head hit the pillow and I didn't awaken until a furry paw tapped me on the nose just a few seconds before my alarm went off. Who needs an alarm when you have such a reliable feline alert system?

* * * *

After all of the curiosity yesterday around Elsie's death with folks coming in the office and the people who stopped me at the grocery store, I should have been prepared, but I guess I'd thought interest would wane. Or at least the intensity of it.

But when I swung by the Red Hen Diner on my way to the office, I couldn't take two steps without someone stopping me. The diner is across the town square from Sugar and Spice, so it offered a similar yet different view of the courthouse and green space. On this side, there was a charming white gazebo to provide some shade for residents taking a little break. The courthouse was already busy, many of the shops were just opening their doors, and the parking spots in front of the diner were filled with cars and trucks. For such a small restaurant it did a good steady business.

There was a cluck as I entered, the Red Hen Diner's take on a door chime. The atmosphere was nothing like the day the Founders' Day Committee had met in the backroom. There was a subdued vibe as if everyone had been affected by yesterday's tragedy and I'm sure they had been. In a small town like St. Ignatius everybody knows everybody in one way or another.

As the cluck announced my entrance and I stepped through the doorway, all eyes turned toward me.

Oh, man. I immediately wished I'd just gone on to the office. Dixie always had coffee brewing and sometimes, like Disco, I enjoyed the results of her beta testing of various recipes. But right now, she was working her way through the side dish submissions, so I hadn't thought there was any chance there'd be breakfast-appropriate type food for tasting. Besides, I loved the diner's blueberry muffins.

"Hi, Sugar." Toy George, the proprietor, wiped her hands on her red and white chicken-themed apron and bustled to the counter.

Toy was toy-sized at least in height and rounded in a Mrs. Claus sort of way. She always wore an apron and a smile.

"Good morning. I'd like a—"

She'd already reached for a to-go bag and dropped in a blueberry muffin. Now, I'd like to tell ya'll I'm not that predictable but the truth of the matter is, I am. I mean, why would I vary my order when the blueberry muffins are to die for?

"Sad about Elsie, huh?" Toy folded the top of the bag and handed it to me. "Heard you found her."

Suddenly the ambient noise in the restaurant dropped to nothing. Well, almost nothing. Old Wally Nelson kept talking because he was hard of hearing and didn't realize everyone else in the place had gone silent. I'd been told he was called Old Wally not just because he's old, but mostly so folks don't confuse him with his son. Any guesses at the son's name? Yep, Young Wally.

In any case, except for Wally, all eyes were on me. Great. Just call me the Dead Body Finder.

"Yes, I did." I had apparently in one day's time morphed from "Oh, you're the new one in town." To "Oh, you're the one that found Elsie Farmer dead." I wondered how long the new label would last.

The silence continued. I could hear the clatter and snick of dishes in the kitchen but the restaurant area had gone still.

I reached in my purse to pay Toy. "She didn't come to the door. I knocked, but no one answered. And so I went around back and I saw her car was there and then I saw her and…" I suddenly realized I was babbling. "Here you go." I handed over some wadded-up bills and jammed the muffin in my bag. "Just keep the change. I've got to go, I'm really late," I called over my shoulder as I pushed open the door nearly knocking over the poor guy who was trying to enter.

"Cluck," the door announced. "Cluck."

"Oh, I am so sorry." I grabbed the man's arm to right myself. It was a nice solid arm. I glanced up at the jaw and followed the line of it up and to bright intelligent blue eyes. "Sorry."

"Are you okay?" He grabbed the doorjamb to steady himself. His rough voice matched his scruffy chin.

"Fine. I'm fine," I answered. "Just late." I fumbled for my keys and left him standing there as I rushed out.

"Don't look back, don't look back," I told myself. "That would be so uncool."

Of course, I looked back.

Blue Eyes stood in the doorway watching me.

Possibly not a St. Ignatius resident. I'd not met everyone in town, but almost and I was sure I'd have remembered meeting him. I tossed my things on the passenger seat of the Jeep and climbed in.

When I looked back this time, he was gone.

* * * *

The Sugar and Spice Publishing office was truly just minutes away across the square. When I entered from the back, I called out so Dixie would know I'd arrived. She was in the middle of testing three side dishes. I'd been right, none of them would have had the right breakfast type of flavor.

"What's cooking, girlfriend?" I reached into the cupboard where we kept a collection of coffee mugs, chose the Wonder Woman one, and poured myself a cuppa.

Dixie's little dog, Moto, was with her today. He stirred from his bed and sauntered over. Moto was a mixed breed from the local rescue, but I was pretty sure one of his parents was a cairn terrier. The feisty little guy knew I was a soft touch. I reached in my bag and slipped him the dog treat I'd tucked in earlier. (Don't tell Ernest.)

"We have Emmy Lou's Parmesan Peas, Edna Utterhofen's Sweet and Sour Cabbage, and Betty Bailey's Broccoli Gratin." Dixie set the final dish on the counter with a flourish and turned to begin the clean-up process.

"Here, let me help." I shoved a bite of muffin in my mouth and took a gulp of coffee.

"No, no, just sit down and finish your breakfast." Dixie waved me away.

Moto took his treat and headed back to his bed. I slid onto one of the strategically placed stools and reached for a napkin. The trip in my bag had destroyed the muffin's look but the taste was mouth-watering. The blueberries tart, the texture of the cake light but firm, and the smell...I inhaled. The smell made you feel all warm and cozy.

"Are you gonna eat that or just sit there smelling it?" Dixie piled bowls in the sink and began running water to rinse them.

"You've got me analyzing everything I eat." I lifted the muffin in salute. "Never again will I simply scarf down food without thinking about it."

"Good." She nodded. "As soon as you're done with that, you can taste our first round of side dishes."

"Great. Before this cookbook is done I'm going to be as big as a barn."

"As if." Dixie turned back to the sink. "I eat so much as a cupcake and I might as well slap that puppy on my thighs. Not you. You got curves in all the right places and you never seem to gain an ounce. It's not fair. I'd hate you if you weren't so darn nice."

"Right." I made a face at her.

I worked hard to keep from packing on the pounds and was mostly successful in my efforts. I also worked hard at being nice, sometimes not so successfully.

"You're the nice one." I pointed my cup at her. "You just don't want anyone to find out."

"See what I mean? You see the good in everyone. Even when it's not there." She handed me a spoon and pushed the casserole dishes towards me. "Taste."

"Okay, boss." I tried each of the dishes. The peas, not my favorite, but good. I'm just not a huge fan of peas. The sweet and sour cabbage was tasty and unusual. A nice change but it would definitely need to be served with something that would balance the flavor. The broccoli gratin was my favorite. A different take on a standard, but a great combination.

"Well?" Dixie handed me a note card.

"They're all good." I made a couple of notes. "What's the seasoning in the broccoli thing?"

"It's not seasoning, it's the Gruyère cheese you're tasting. Nice, huh?"

"Ahh, that's it." I slid off the stool and carried my spoons to the sink. "Have you decided which side dishes we're going to picture?"

"I have a couple of ideas for you and I think I found us a photographer." She picked up a sticky note from the counter and handed it to me.

"Max Windsor," I read. "Where'd you find him?"

"Hirsh gave me his info. He does mostly nature shots, but he's been doing other things too. My brother said this guy did the high school track team for the newspaper and apparently got some great shots."

"But does your brother know whether he can do food? Not much need for action shots here." I posed in a running stance.

"We can find out. He's going to stop by sometime today."

"If not, I can find out if any of the staff photographers from my former employer are doing freelance work."

Dixie finished her clean-up and left with Moto to run an errand. I washed my hands and got busy with my layout work. The editing I'd done yesterday at home would help me better plan the copy placement or, in this case, recipe placement. I liked the overall look and feel. I'd planned to meet with our graphics person, Liz, later in the week. We'd already discussed the project and what we were going for. She'd tell me if I was on the right track or not. Liz was a straight-shooter and I loved her for it.

The bell on the door jingled. Much better than the "cluck" at The Red Hen Diner, but I was beginning to hate the sound.

"Hello," a vaguely familiar male voice called. "Is anyone here?"

"Be right there." I carefully put my piles of recipes aside. The categories were shaping up nicely.

I stretched my legs and made my way around the piles of files and out to the front.

The guy from the diner.

"Hi, what can we do for you?" I stepped around the front counter. "I'm sorry I was so abrupt this morning. I didn't mean to run you over."

"No problem. Are you Dixie or Rosetta?" He walked toward me and I noted a slight limp I hadn't noticed when I ran into him at the Red Hen.

"Well, I'm not Dixie, but I don't answer to Rosetta either. My friends call me Sugar."

"I'm not sure if I count as a friend. Yet." He grinned. "I'm Max Windsor. Dixie Spicer left me a message about a cookbook you're working on. Her brother said you needed some photos taken."

"Oh, right." His eyes were unusual. A vivid Paul Newman–ish blue. A piercing blue. Striking, with his dark lashes and slight stubble. His dark hair was a bit on the shaggy side and, on closer inspection, shot through with streaks of silver, though he didn't appear to be that much older than me.

Max Windsor looked around the room and then his gaze landed back on me, and I realized I'd been staring.

"If you'd like to come on back, I can show you what we had in mind." I motioned toward the back, suddenly aware I probably looked a mess. I'd twisted my hair into a sort of bun to get it out of my way while I worked with the layouts. I'd worn black jeans because I didn't have any appointments, and I'd thrown on a faded gray Lake Okoboji sweatshirt that had seen better days. My mama would be appalled. She'd raised me better.

He followed me to the backroom, and I tried to pull the elastic hair band out without drawing attention. "Have you ever done any food photography?"

"Not really." He shook his head. "A few ads for local businesses. I'm mostly a nature photographer, but since I moved here, I've done a variety of things from high school football games to senior pictures. No weddings, though."

He seemed adamant about the weddings and I wondered if it was fear of Bridezillas or if he had something against matrimony.

"No weddings or even wedding food involved here." I dropped my hand from the elastic band which had only ended up more tangled, and reached for the layout mock up I'd been using to plan the categories. "We're looking at photos for each section, a few others scattered throughout, and then a cover shot."

"Will you make the dishes to be photographed or will the individuals who submitted the recipes make them?" He perused the papers.

"I won't be making anything. Dixie's the one with the cooking talent. She'll make the food and stage it."

"Sounds straightforward enough. I hoped taking the photos didn't involve going from house to house." He smiled and handed the pages back to me.

"Because it's for the town's Founders' Day I'd like to include some of these historical photos." I opened the file where I'd placed the early St. Ignatius pictures the committee had provided.

Max stepped closer to pick up one of the photos. "Some of these are great." He picked up the stack and flipped through the photos slowly, stopping to look more closely at some of them.

"I particularly liked that one." I reached over to point out a photo of a limestone home and as my arm brushed his I was suddenly very aware of his nearness.

"Me, too." He pulled it from the stack. "You've got a good eye."

I stood quietly as he held a few closer to the window light. I love it when someone is really into what they do. He had much the same look Dixie got when she was working on a difficult recipe.

"I'm not sure what to do with them." I noted. "Some are in fairly good shape and not bad quality for that era picture, but they may publish poorly in comparison to your high-resolution photos of the food."

"I could probably help you with sharpening up the images when you're ready for that." He closed the file and placed it back on the work desk.

"Hello…" The back door rattled as Dixie breezed in. "Don't forget that photographer guy is coming by."

Max and I looked at each other and smiled. I could hear Dixie sliding grocery bags on the counter.

"He's already here."

"What?" She poked her head through the doorway. "Oh, he's already here."

"You must be Dixie." Max stepped forward and held out his hand. "I can't believe we've not met before. Hirsh says you know everyone in town."

"Apparently not. I don't know you." She took his hand and then slid onto one of the stools. "Have you two reached an agreement?"

"I shared with Max our ideas for the layout and also showed him the old historical pictures. He may be able to help us out with those."

"Whatever you think." She waved her hand. "I'm the cook. Sugar is the brains of this operation."

"Stop it." I turned and gave her a hard look. Dixie was forever putting herself down and it needed to stop. "This whole venture was your idea."

"Well, in any case, it's Sugar you need to negotiate with as far as prices." She got up and headed back to the storage area bags in hand. "I've got to get some of these things refrigerated."

I shook my head. "She never stops moving."

"I'll get a quote to you." Max moved to go. "I'm sure we can work something out."

"What about your time frame?" I was a bit taken aback at his lack of interest in the payment. "We've got a pretty tight schedule. Are you available to do this with your other work?"

I was concerned about conflicts. The last thing we needed was to have a problem getting everything together and to the printer on time.

"I can work it in." He handed me a business card. "Call me if you have questions."

And he was gone.

Dixie came from the back munching on a carrot stick. "What's up, Doc?" She looked around. "Your photographer gone already?"

I ignored the "your" comment. "Yeah, he's going to bring a quote sheet to us. We'll see what it says. We're not committed to anything. I'd like to see his work and his prices first."

"From what I understand he does a fabulous job and is pretty reasonable." Dixie popped the rest of the carrot into her mouth. "I'll bet he's less expensive than any of those fancy food photographers you know."

"Maybe. We'll see." She was probably right. The photographers I'd worked with at Mammoth were very much in demand and could easily name their price.

"Looked like you two were pretty cozy." She smiled. "He's single, you know."

"No, I didn't know." But I wasn't unhappy to hear it. "We talked pictures of food, not dating eligibility." I went back to sorting the recipes into categories.

"Just saying." Dixie tapped me on the shoulder as she went by. "It wouldn't hurt for you to date once in a while."

"Look who's talking." I jabbed back and then immediately regretted it when a shadow passed over her face. "Oh, honey, I'm sorry. My mouth gets away from me sometimes." I crossed the room and gave her a hug. "I know you're not ready."

"Don't be silly." She hugged me back. "I'm not upset. I'll probably date someday. Though who I'd find to date in this place I don't know."

"Maybe you should hook up with Max Windsor."

"Not my type."

"Not mine either," I pronounced.

"Liar," she shot back.

The rest of the day went by quickly and when we locked up and headed home at the end of the day, I felt as if we'd accomplished a lot.

Categories sorted. Check.

Photographer interviewed. Check.

Dixie had beta tested two more recipes and I'd made good progress on the tome of historical information from Jimmie LeBlanc. As I'd suspected it was valuable background, but to cut it down and decide which pieces to use would be a major undertaking.

I'd packed it in my bag to take home. If we were going to stay on track and keep to our deadlines, I had to make some decisions quickly. It looked like my evening was planned.

* * * *

The next morning, Dixie was already at the office and busy cooking by the time I arrived. I'd skipped my trip to the Red Hen Diner knowing the questions about Elsie would start as soon as I stepped through the front door. I'd instead opted for a bowl of cold cereal and a glass of orange juice at home.

The aroma of fresh-brewed coffee hit me as soon as I walked in, and I made a bee-line for the coffee pot.

"What's cooking?" I asked as I filled my cup.

"Homemade biscuits," she answered over her shoulder.

"Man, I wish I'd waited." I pulled up a stool and settled in for a chat before starting on the next phase of recipe organizing. "You need to test those, right?"

There was a tap on the glass of the front door of the shop.

"I hadn't unlocked the door yet." Dixie turned, her hands covered in flour.

Dixie and I looked at each other. "Disco?" we said in unison.

"Do you think he's looking for breakfast now too?" I put my cup on the counter and went to answer the door.

It wasn't Disco. The sheriff was back. I opened the door and let him in.

"Come on back." I motioned for him to follow me to the kitchen. "Dixie's elbow deep in a new test recipe, and I'm sure she'll also want to hear whatever you have to say."

"I wouldn't count on it," he muttered.

"What are you doing here?" Dixie turned as we entered the kitchen area, wiping her hands on a towel.

The girl seemed bound and determined to be rude to the guy, and I didn't understand it. So far, I thought he'd been kind and as upfront as he could be. But something about him seemed to rub her wrong.

"Do you have news on what happened with Elsie Farmer?" I asked. "Was it a heart attack? Or what?"

"We still don't have autopsy results." He rubbed his eyes. The poor man didn't look like he'd slept since we last saw him. "Those take a while, but we do have something else."

"What?" I didn't like the look on his face which I didn't think could be any more serious.

Sheriff Griffin shifted from one foot to the other. Dixie and I waited.

"Well, go on," she finally snapped.

"The thing is," he rubbed his jaw, "Doc Chestnut didn't think it looked like Elsie Farmer had a heart attack, and so we not only requested the state crime lab do a tox screen, we also gathered up things, uhm food, from her house to check for poisoning just in case." He paused. "We were able to get those lab results a bit faster. And, we found something."

"What?"

"The pastry she had in her hand was from a basket of the same in her kitchen. They probably killed her," the sheriff blurted out.

"She made poison scones?" I couldn't see Elsie as a suicide but it sounded like that was what he was saying had happened.

"No." The sheriff shook his head. "There was a note with the basket indicating the pastries were a gift."

"A gift?" Dixie asked. "Elsie Farmer was mean and full of herself. Who would send her a gift?"

"The note said, 'Mine have a special ingredient you'll never guess,' and it was signed, 'Your friend, B.'" He took a deep breath. "Dix, I just wanted you to know that we're on our way to pick up your Aunt Bertie."

Dixie made a sound that reminded me of an angry grizzly bear I'd seen on *Animal Planet* the other night. She dropped her towel and charged at the sheriff, but he was already headed for the door.

"I thought you'd want to know!" he said over his shoulder as he exited.

"You can't do that! My aunt is not a killer." Dixie yelled at the door as it closed behind him.

"Oh, honey, of course she's not." I crossed the room to give her a hug and to pick up the towel she'd dropped. "I'm sure the sheriff will get this sorted out in no time."

Dixie took a deep breath and sat down. "I know he will. It's just the idea that anyone would think Aunt Bertie..." her voice trailed off.

"There must be some explanation for it." I handed her the towel and patted her hand. "I'm sure Bertie will clear things up with Sheriff Griffin."

Dixie rolled her eyes.

"What is it with you two anyway?" I asked. "What's up with the antagonistic attitude? That's not like you. He seems like a genuinely nice man."

"Not everyone is what they seem, Sugar."

"I know they're not." I was admittedly a take-people-at-face-value person, but I wasn't so trusting that I didn't realize some people had a private persona that was drastically different from the public one.

"And some people are exactly what they seem." Dixie stood. "Like my Aunt Bertie. She may be outspoken and pig-headed, but she's also kind and honest. And—" her voice caught. "Not a murderer."

Chapter Six

St. Ignatius didn't need a newspaper, TV or radio, or telephones for that matter. Word of mouth was faster than any other form of communication and it worked quite well.

It was only a matter of minutes before the bell over the door jingled, and the first to hear the news arrived.

I have no idea how they'd heard, but they'd heard and shared. And for the second time in a matter of days the offices of Sugar and Spice Publishing became the meeting place for those seeking the latest news about Elsie Farmer. I looked around at the faces I'd come to know in my short time in town.

Krissie, owner of the bakery down the street, Lark Travers from Travers Jewelry next door, Sherona, who had the hair and nail salon at the end of the block, and, of course, Disco, who'd also come to see why everyone was there and if there was food involved.

Dixie continued to defend her aunt and those who'd collected in our place of business were in full support. I had no idea what to do to help my friend and business partner, or what to say to the people who stopped by, but it was clear no one thought Bertie Sparks had it in her to harm anyone. Not even her arch-rival, Elsie Farmer.

I decided in lieu of joining the chatter, I'd make refreshments. I made coffee and tea and then dug up some paper cups from the storage room. I also discovered a stash of cookies in one of the cupboards. They were store-bought which seemed somehow wrong, but really who was going to notice at a time like this? I put them out on a fancy decorative dish I'd found and washed.

Just as I was making a second round filling up coffee cups, the bell jingled again and I glanced up to see Max Windsor walk in. He stopped, just inside the door, a confused look on his handsome face.

His gaze met mine and he nodded. I nodded back and crossed the room.

"I stopped by with a price sheet and some ideas for you." He indicated a folder he held. "I didn't realize you were having a party. I can come back."

"No, no, it's not a party." I shook my head. "Dixie's Aunt Bertie is being questioned about Elsie Farmer's death."

He looked even more confused.

"As people heard about it, folks came by to ask Dixie if it was true." I pointed around the room. "You know how it is in a small town."

As I said the words, it suddenly occurred to me Max Windsor was the only person I'd come in contact with in the past two days who hadn't asked me about finding Elsie Farmer.

Lack of curiosity? That didn't seem to fit him. Or respect for privacy? Maybe. If so, I liked that about him.

"Let's step in the back room and you can show me your stuff." I stopped. My cheeks burned as I realized the words could be taken in an entirely different way.

He didn't seem to notice my embarrassment, or perhaps he was too much of a gentleman to take advantage of my slip of the tongue.

He handed me the folder he'd brought with him and moved to follow me.

Suddenly the bell jingled and the door opened again, but this visitor drew everyone's attention. The handsome Sheriff Griffin was back and, if possible, he looked even more harried than when he'd left to pick up Dixie's Aunt Bertie. Just as Max had, the sheriff stopped just inside the door, probably taken aback by the change since he'd been here no more than twenty to thirty minutes ago.

"What is it, Terry?" Dixie stepped forward from where she'd been talking to Grace from Graceland Winery. Dixie's cheeks were bright, and I don't think Grace had been slipping her any samples. Her eyes flashed with bring-it-on boldness but I could see the hint of fear beneath the bravado. "Well, let's have it." She squared her shoulders.

Sheriff Griffin swallowed. "I went to pick up your aunt for questioning, and…" He paused.

"And what?" Dixie demanded.

"And, she's not there," the sheriff finished.

"What?" That was Dixie but there was a collective gasp from the crowded room.

"No one has seen her since early this morning," the sheriff continued. "Have you heard from her?" He addressed his question to Dixie but then looked around at the rest and raised his voice. "If anyone has talked to her today, I need to know."

What? Was Dixie's Aunt Bertie on the lam?

Or worse yet, had something awful happened to her?

I looked down and realized I was clutching Max Windsor's forearm. "Sorry." I released Max's arm.

The sheriff made his way through the crowd toward Dixie, who looked like she'd been hit by a Mac truck.

I looked up at Max. I imagined I looked like I'd been smacked by the same truck.

What now?

Chapter Seven

The crowd was silent for a full beat before the chatter restarted and everyone started talking at once. The sheriff, like Max, seemed to be confused by the number of people in the office.

The chimes on the door dinged and I looked up to see Nate Berg, the *St. Ignatius Journal* cub reporter, burst in. The newspaper only has two reporters and usually Roxanne Price, the publisher, didn't let newbie Nate cover anything more than weddings, funerals, and grand openings. Maybe Glenn Page, the news hound, was out on another story.

The young man ran a hand through his hair, looked around at the crowd, spotted Sheriff Griffin and rushed over to him, pen and notepad in hand. Now in some places, the reporter's notepad has been replaced by electronics but not here in St. Ignatius.

"What can you tell me, Sheriff?" I could hear him ask.

Nate's dishevelment was a stark contrast to Sheriff Griffin's sharply pressed uniform.

"Not much, Nate." He put his hands on the young man's shoulders and turned him. "I'll let you know when we have a statement."

"But something's going on here." Nate looked around at the people who stood chatting and sipping coffee. "I was just at the Red Hen and Toy George said everyone was over here."

"Like I said, I'll let you know."

I scanned the room myself and suddenly realized I couldn't see Dixie anymore. I caught a glimpse of bright blue slipping into the backroom and followed.

"And just where do you think you're going?" I asked as I caught up with her as she snagged her purse and fished in it for her car keys.

"I've got to find my Aunt Bertie so she can clear herself. That inept excuse for a sheriff probably didn't even try." Dixie's blue eyes flashed anger.

"Not without me you're not." I grabbed my bag and followed her out the door.

"I'll drive." Dixie flung her bag into the pickup, and I jumped in the passenger side.

I was very aware we were leaving our business full of people and unattended. Which I never would have done back home, but in small town Iowa I was pretty sure someone would keep an eye on things. And after all, the sheriff was present.

Dixie peeled out of the parking lot and then hopped over a block and headed south toward her aunt's bed and breakfast, which was only five blocks away. Parking in front of the stately gray Victorian, she was out almost before the truck was in park. The lawn was perfectly manicured and baskets of pink pansies made the entrance both elegant and welcoming. Dixie stomped up the front stairs, crossed the wide veranda and flung open the door.

The girl at the front desk looked up. Liv, according to her name tag. "Hi, Dixie. Your aunt's not here."

"Where is she?" Dixie demanded.

"I have no idea." Liv shook her ponytail. "She left a note that said she had to go out of town and I should stay until Ilene gets here."

"Where's the note?"

"What?" Liv snapped her gum and looked puzzled.

"The note." Dixie gestured. "Where is it?"

"Oh, the note from Bertie." She smiled showing braces. I was pretty sure she wasn't supposed to be chewing gum with that metal work. "I gave it to that cute sheriff."

"He's—" Dixie stopped herself and looked at me and sighed.

I shrugged. "Maybe when this Ilene comes, she'll know where your Aunt Bertie went."

"Ilene is Aunt Bertie's new business manager," Dixie explained to me and then turned back to Liv, her patience wearing thin. "What time does Ilene come?"

"She comes at different times. It depends. Did you want me to give her a message?"

"What's her phone number?" Dixie demanded drumming her fingers impatiently on the counter.

I heard a cough behind me and turned. A young couple with suitcases stood behind us, obviously waiting to check in. "Does your aunt have an office? Maybe it's in there." I nudged Dixie and tilted my head toward the hall.

"Oh, sure." She caught on right away. "We'll just get Ilene's number there."

"Welcome to the Jefferson Street B & B." I could hear Liv greet the couple as we moved away.

Dixie and I hurried through the kitchen where a young man appeared to be in the middle of lunch prep. The owner's absence didn't seem to have any effect on the operations, and the smells were divine. Some sort of sauce simmered on the big commercial stove and he was just taking warm scones from the big oven.

I inhaled the butter and cinnamon warmth. They looked delicious, but I'll admit it would be a while before I'd look at scones in the same way.

We slipped through the door to Bertie's office. I wasn't sure if the untidiness was the usual state of things or if the piles of receipts and papers were perhaps due to the fact that Bertie had left in a hurry. Dixie sat down at the desk and dropped her face into her hands.

"What would you like me to do?" I asked.

She pushed a Rolodex my way. "See if you can find Ilene's phone number."

"Wow, I haven't seen one of these in years." I flipped through the cards. Clearly Aunt Bertie was not into managing her contacts (or her receipts for that matter) on her computer. "Do we know Ilene's last name?"

"What?" Dixie looked up from a receipt she was looking at. "Oh, uhm, I think it's Jorkins. Try that."

I turned the circular file card holder to J but no Ilene Jorkins was listed. "No luck."

"Try the I's" Dixie looked up from the pile of papers she was sorting. "My aunt often is creative in her filing. I used to work for her part-time when I was in high school. It was always a challenge to try to figure how her mind worked."

I flipped to the I section and sure enough there was an Ilene Jorkins listed. "Here we go." I pulled the card out and handed it to Dixie.

"Super." She grabbed it. "Let's see what she knows." She punched in the numbers, held the phone to her ear, and waited. "No answer."

She handed the card back to me, and I put it back in its place. "Maybe she's already on her way here."

"I've got to help Bertie get better organized. This desk is a mess." She picked up one of the receipts she'd been sorting. "Wait, what's—"

Suddenly the door burst open and Sheriff Griffin and one of the deputies I'd met at Elsie's place, strode in. "What do you think you're doing?"

"I'm trying to figure out where my aunt is, and if she's okay." Dixie stood and as she did I could see her slip the receipt she'd been holding into the pocket of her jeans. "Did you ever think that maybe she didn't do anything wrong? And maybe she's in danger?"

"I've issued a BOLO." Sheriff Griffin, aka The Cute Sheriff according to Liv at the front desk, held the door open. A clear hint we should use it to exit.

"I don't even know what that is." Dixie stood arms crossed.

"It's a 'be on the lookout' alert, ma'am," the young deputy explained.

"Well, you should be out there looking for her." Dixie stepped forward a little closer to the two of them. "And by the way, this is private property. My aunt's property. So, I don't have to leave just because you think I should."

"Jeeze, Dix, give me a break. Of course, we have people out looking for your Aunt Bertie." The handsome sheriff rubbed a hand over his face. "You're not helping things by going all ballistic on me."

"You've searched the B & B?" she asked.

"No, we haven't." He paced back and forth. "She left a note."

"What's going on?" A thirty-something woman, dressed in shorts and a bright pink Jefferson Street B & B polo shirt, looked in.

"Hi, Ilene," Dixie greeted her. "My aunt is missing. She's just up and disappeared, which is not like her at all."

"Hmmm, I wouldn't worry." Ilene's expression was neutral. "She's been talking about taking some time off. I understand she left a note with Liv."

"She's a person of interest in a murder investigation," Dixie said evenly. "At least according to these two." Her tone of voice implied these two bozos, but at least she didn't say it out loud. I thought we were making progress.

"You left your shop full of people with no one there to keep an eye on things at all," Terrance noted. "So, I'm not sure you should be lecturing me on thinking through things."

It probably wasn't the best idea to walk away from your place of business when it's full of people. Still, we knew all those people and probably our biggest problem was that perhaps Disco had eaten today's taste test.

"They're all good people." Dixie took a deep breath. "I'm sure it was fine." I couldn't tell if she was reassuring the sheriff or me.

"I asked Max Windsor to call your brother, Hirsh."

"Thank you," I said. I wasn't sure Dixie could bring herself to do it. "We'll be going now." I tugged at Dixie's arm.

"Are you here to search the premises? Do you have a search warrant?" she challenged Sheriff Griffin.

"I don't have one, but I can get one if I need to." He stood at full height, apparently done being nice. "Right now, I'd just like to talk to your aunt. If you know where she is, you'd better tell me."

"You'd better watch yourself." And with that Dixie slammed out.

I nodded to the sheriff and deputy and followed her.

* * * *

Well, that didn't get us anywhere. I hopped in the truck, and we pulled out onto the street and headed back to the town square.

"So, what did you put in your pocket."

Dixie's expression was grim. She pulled a piece of paper from her jeans pocket and handed it to me.

I looked at what appeared to be a receipt from a hardware store in Des Moines. A store a good thirty some miles from St. Ignatius. It was for a case of rat poison.

Oh, boy.

"This doesn't look good."

"No, it doesn't." Dixie shook her head. "I know my aunt is not a killer. But what was she doing buying rat poison out of town?"

She pulled into the lot behind our building and jammed the truck into park. She laid her head on the steering wheel. "I've got to find her before the police do and figure out what's going on."

"We'll find her." I patted her arm. "She couldn't have disappeared into thin air. Someone knows where she is."

"I hope you're right." Dixie raised her head. "I hope nothing bad has happened to her."

We entered Sugar and Spice Publishing from the back door not sure what we'd find, but all was quiet. Then I heard a slight sound from my office.

"Hello," I called.

"Hello," a voice answered. Max Windsor sat behind my desk, his long legs propped on one corner. One finger marked his place in Jimmie LeBlanc's tome on the history of St. Ignatius. He had read quite a way into it.

"Oh, my word. Thanks for staying." The man looked pretty darn comfortable. "You sure didn't need to."

"No problem." He dropped his legs from the desk and stood placing the pages back on my desk. "I called your brother, Hirsh," he addressed Dixie, "but he was busy at the farm. I said I could stay until you got back."

"Thanks."

"He wants you to call him."

"Sure thing." Dixie was already pulling out her cell phone. She walked into the kitchen area, and I could hear her telling him about going to the B and B. I wondered if she'd tell him about the rat poison.

"Thanks again." I thought it said something really nice about Max that he'd waited around. "Dixie was hell bent on talking to the staff at the bed and breakfast, and I thought it best she not interrogate on her own."

"Well, I've got some photos to do before I lose the light." He gave a little salute and then headed out the back door.

I wandered out front where Dixie was cleaning up the remains of the refreshments. The cups and plates had been gathered up already and placed in the large trash can by the door. Which meant either we also owed Max an additional thank you for cleaning up, or our uninvited guests had been thoughtful and cleaned up after themselves. Dixie carried the last of the cookies back to the kitchen, and I followed.

Someone had rinsed out the coffee carafe and placed it in the sink. I ran some water and squirted dish soap. Dixie stacked napkins neatly in the supply cupboard.

"So what now?" I asked.

"I'm going to call Ilene and find out what she knows." Dixie shut the cupboard with a click. "She didn't seem very concerned about Aunt Bertie being gone. I think she knows more than she's saying."

"I wondered about that." I'd finished the coffee carafe and other dishes in short order and began drying and putting away.

Dixie pulled out her cell phone and punched a number. She settled onto one of the stools and waited for an answer.

"Ilene, it's Dixie Spicer." The call must have gone to voicemail. "I'd like to talk to you a little more about my aunt. Please call me as soon as possible." She gave her phone number.

"Now what?"

"I don't know." Dixie shrugged her shoulders.

"Someone has to know where she's gone." I pondered the possibilities. "If she left this morning, she may not even know that something has happened to Elsie."

Dixie looked up.

"Do you know if there are other B & B owners she keeps in touch with? Or suppliers?"

"I know she belongs to some association."

"Bingo." I stood. "Let's go back for that address card thingy, and I can begin making calls. Who in your family might know something? You could start by calling family members."

"You are brilliant." Dixie jumped up and hugged me. "I didn't even think about calling my cousins or my other aunts."

"Sounds like we have a plan."

Dixie grabbed her purse and keys and headed out the back door. "Be right back," she called over her shoulder.

I sat for a few minutes thinking about how fast things change. One day your biggest problem is which scone recipe to put in a cookbook, and two days later you're dealing with a possible murder and a missing person. While I waited for Dixie to return, I'd might as well do some work. We still had a cookbook to get done. I picked up the pages Max Windsor had been reading. I still had to get through them myself.

I was knee deep in early St. Ignatius when my phone rang. I looked at the time. It seemed like it was taking Dixie an inordinate amount of time to grab the address thing and get back. Maybe Ilene hadn't wanted to give it up.

I glanced at the display. It wasn't Dixie, it was Greer. I pushed the button to answer.

"Hello."

"Hello, hon. Are you busy?" She got right to the point.

"Just reading through Mr. LeBlanc's tome on the history of St. Ignatius."

"I'm sorry." Greer chuckled.

"Some of it is really interesting. It's a shame we can only use a small amount for the cookbook."

"You'll just have to give it to him straight," she advised.

"I guess so." I sighed. No one seemed to think that anyone other than me would be the one breaking the news to Mr. LeBlanc.

"Say, I know you're really busy what with the *Founders' Day Cookbook* and investigating Elsie's murder and all, but do you think you could come by this evening? I have something for you."

Sad to say, I had no plans for the evening, and so I promised to stop by on my way home.

I had hung up and started to call Dixie and make sure everything was okay when she came in the backdoor. She was carrying a box and on top of the box was the Rolodex from Bertie's office.

"Wow. I had begun to worry about you." I jumped up to hold the door for her. "That looks like a little more than just grabbing the addresses."

"I realized I needed to go through her papers, and so I just packed them up and brought them here."

I knew Sheriff Griffin was not going to like the idea, and I wondered what Ilene thought of it. Hopefully she didn't need any of the paperwork that Dixie had packed up.

"I called my father while I was there. Though he wasn't much help." Dixie rolled her eyes. "Mostly my dad talks in 'uh-huh' or 'huh-uh' so I didn't get much out of him."

"Did he have any idea where Bertie might be?" I lifted the Rolodex off the top of the box and set it down on the table.

"No, and he was not very concerned about her." Dixie sighed. "Said he'd been trying to get her to take time off for a while."

"But wouldn't she let him or someone know where they could reach her in an emergency?" I couldn't imagine that Bertie had just up and left town. Though I didn't want to alarm Dixie, I was worried something awful had happened to her aunt.

"Yes, if not my dad, at least Ilene." Dixie placed the box on the floor and slid it under the table and out of sight. "I pressed for family members and he did mention a couple of cousins that live in Nebraska. He's going to try to find phone numbers for me."

"Well, that's worth checking out." I flipped through the cards in the address keeper. There were a lot of vendors and other contacts in the listing. We'd have to think about how we wanted to tackle this.

"I know we've got to get back to working on the cookbook." Dixie looked around at the disarray caused by our sudden exit. The recipes she'd been working with were laid out on the counter where she'd been in the midst of making a list of supplies. Her face was pale and her shoulders drooped.

"We do, but right now the most important thing is to make sure your aunt is okay."

"Thanks, Sugar." She crossed the room and gave me a hug. "I wish our inept law enforcement felt the same way."

"All right, what's the deal with you and Sheriff Griffin?"

"Nothing." She walked away.

"Okay, I get it." I followed her. "You don't want to talk about it."

"I don't," she agreed. "Ever."

Okay then, this went deeper than I'd realized.

The place was soon set to rights and Dixie's list was made. I started making a list of potential friends and business acquaintances to call from Bertie's contacts. We wanted to be careful not to cause any problems for the business.

"You know some of these are people who are also part of the cookbook, so I can use that to make the contact and then see if I can draw out any other information they might have."

"See. You're good at this." Dixie smiled. "Besides people are always telling you things. You'll probably get way more information out of them than me."

"Yeah, sometimes things I don't even want to know." I cringed as I thought about my conversation with Tina at the committee meeting.

"I am starving. How about you?"

"I am too." It had been a long while since the cold cereal and juice earlier. "What do you say we lunch at the Red Hen? There's bound to be all kinds of chatter there. Maybe we'll pick something up."

"Sounds like a great idea." Dixie grabbed her purse and headed toward the front.

I followed.

As we stepped outside, Disco approached from his shop two doors down. My guess was he was on the lookout for lunch too, but had been hoping for a free lunch courtesy of the Sugar and Spice test kitchen.

"Hi, Disco," I greeted him.

"Any news from your aunt?" He addressed Dixie.

"None so far." Dixie kept walking.

"See you later." I waved to Disco and then hurried to catch up with Dixie who had continued down the sidewalk. "That was nice of him to ask," I commented once I'd caught up with her.

The short walk to the diner would be good for me; I'd been hunched over reading at my desk for too long. We stopped at the corner and were almost mowed down by Tina Martin who sported fuchsia spandex, a blond ponytail, and a sheen of sweat from her workout. We'd apparently gotten in the path of her power walk.

"Oh, sorry." She stopped, breathless, and took a swig of her ever present red energy drink. "This is my last lap. Can't chat." She waved as she walked off, arms pumping and ponytail swinging.

Now I felt completely wimpy about calling my walk from the shop to the diner exercise.

At least if she was on a mission to complete her walk, she hadn't had time to ask us about attending a Looking Pretty party.

We crossed the street and made it to the Red Hen Diner without further mishap.

"Cluck." The chicken over the door announced our entry, and the smell of warm food reminded me of just how hungry I was. "Cluck."

All eyes turned in our direction.

I felt Dixie stiffen, but she kept going. We headed for a booth against the wall. Chicken décor tracked from the rooster tiles lining the wall to the black and white checkered placemats that sported a red silhouette of a chicken, to the little ceramic baby chicks salt and pepper shakers; the Red Hen Diner took the chicken theme to the nth degree.

The wood tabletops in the booths were decorated with old *St. Ignatius Journal* newspaper articles that had been sealed under glass. I'd be willing to bet some of the stories were about people who were having lunch there today. In fact, sometimes when I ate at the diner alone, I entertained myself with reading articles and trying to guess who some of those folks might be. My favorite was a regular column, "Notes from Memory Lane," that gave snippets of things that had happened ten, twenty, fifty, and hundred years ago in the town. I guess the newspaper had been around a long time.

Toy George, attired in a bright red apron with "Head Chick" embroidered across her chest, bustled over with two glasses of water and two bright red menus. "What can I get for you two?" she asked. "Sugar, you're an iced tea this time of day, right? What about you, Dixie?"

"I'll take an iced tea, also." Dixie opened the menu. "What's your special today?"

"Ham balls." Toy pointed to a chalk board with the day's special lunch and the soup of the day.

"I'll have those." I was quick to choose.

"And I'll take the tenderloin." Dixie handed her menu back to Toy.

I almost changed my mind. The Red Hen Diner tenderloins are legendary. A pork loin hammered thin and then coated in bread crumbs and deep-fat fried. A quintessentially Iowa sandwich. Not exactly your healthiest food choice, but so tasty. The locals were probably immune to their draw, but I'd tried one when I first arrived in the state and had been addicted ever since.

"You got it." Toy dashed off to put in the order and then returned with our iced teas.

She slid them on the table and then slid into the booth next to me. "Any news on Bertie?" she asked Dixie.

Dixie shook her head.

"I figured we would have heard if she'd showed up." Toy shook her head. "I know you're without a doubt worried about her."

"I am," Dixie agreed. "Very worried."

"Well, I guess it isn't the first time, but still..." Toy stood. "Sorry, I'm short-handed again. Your food will be out in a jiffy." Toy hurried up front to the cash register to take care of her waiting customer.

Dixie and I looked at each other.

"Not the first time?" I looked at Dixie. "What does she mean?"

"No idea." Dixie took a sip of her tea, her forehead furrowed.

Our food arrived, and the ham balls were delicious. Dixie's tenderloin looked good too, but was huge. Any good midwest diner offers a variety of fried food, and any decent Iowa diner has a pork tenderloin on the menu. If you're lucky enough to attend the Iowa State Fair, your fried food is on a stick, but that's a whole other story.

Dixie cut her tenderloin in half. There was enough for another meal.

I could see she was barely tasting her sandwich as her eyes followed Toy George around the restaurant. Looking for a chance to catch her.

"I can't believe she'd just say that and then walk away." She nibbled on the edge of the bun.

"She said it like she thought you already knew." I took another bite of the tangy ham balls.

We'd been so focused on the tidbit from Toy that we'd forgotten we were there to plan out our next steps and listen to the gossip. We listened to the buzz at the nearby tables but from our place in the back it was hard to pick up much more than the occasional word here and there.

Old Wally Nelson stopped by the table. I wondered if the guy ever ate a meal at home. He was in the diner nearly every single time I'd been in it.

He leaned on the table and shouted, "Don't you worry, Spicey." He was so loud the people in the booth behind us jumped, and probably the people at the antique shop next door heard him. "Your aunt is fine. She's just gone…" he paused, apparently realizing mid-sentence that he had no idea where she'd gone. "…somewhere," he finished grinning at her.

"Thanks, Wally." Dixie patted his hand.

He walked away smiling and Dixie rolled her eyes.

"He means well." She took a sip of her tea.

I smiled.

"What?" She put her glass down.

"See, I told you." I smiled. "You're the nice one."

"Ha," She smiled back. "Hardly."

The diner was busy. No sooner would a booth or a table open up than it was filled again as hungry patrons continued to come. It was clear Toy was not coming back to our booth. The same harried waitress who'd delivered our food, stopped by to offer drink refills and leave our bill.

"I'm sorry." She shifted the dirty dishes she held. "I should have been over here before now, but we're short-handed since Katie left. Can I get you anything else?"

Dixie asked for a to-go box for the rest of her tenderloin. I'd like to say I asked for a to-go box too, but I have to tell you I'd finished off the last of those yummy ham balls.

I wiped my hands on a paper napkin. I wanted to lick them but I restrained myself. Then I picked up the check. Dixie started to protest.

"No, let me get it." I shook my head. "It's a business lunch."

"Yeah, more like monkey business." She slid along the vinyl booth and looked around for our waitress.

Toy was at the cash register, and I hurried up before she could walk away again. I handed her the check and two tens. Yes, in St. Ignatius two lunches still add up to under twenty bucks with change left over to tip your waitress well.

"What you said earlier about it not being the first time," I asked, trying to keep my voice low. I motioned to Dixie to join me.

She stuffed the half-sandwich into the cardboard carton and hurried over.

Toy looked over her half-glasses at the two of us. "Bertie has left town at least two other times. That I know of," she added.

"Left? As in just up and left?" Dixie asked.

"Uh huh." Toy confirmed. "But don't ask me. Ask that manager of hers, Ilene. She's not from here, you know."

The look on Toy's face told me she'd suddenly remembered I wasn't local either.

"Sorry, Sugar. No offense." She smiled. "I feel like you've become one of us."

"None taken." That was high praise. I understood that no matter how much I loved St. Ignatius I was still from somewhere else, but apparently I was making progress.

"Well, I don't know what that has to do with anything." Dixie was quick to take offense on my behalf.

"Just saying, that Ilene, she's a different one. Got fancy ideas for the B & B." Toy handed me my change. "Gluten-free scones. Sugar-free pie. For cryin' out loud, it's a bed and breakfast not a health spa."

I dropped the change in my purse and fished out some tip money. I might not be a native, but I wasn't going to be accused of not properly tipping the waitress.

"But what about Dixie's aunt?" I asked. "She just up and leaves town from time to time?"

"That's what I heard, but as for why? I figure that's none of my business." Toy motioned to the guy in overalls standing behind us and he reached around me to hand her his check and his money.

She straightened her "Head Chick" apron and punched some buttons on the cash register. Clearly, she was done talking.

"Cluck," the door said as we exited. "Cluck."

Chapter Eight

"How could Toy George know my aunt has gone missing before and me not know anything about it?" Dixie shifted her bag on her shoulder and pushed her copper colored curls off her neck.

"And why didn't Ilene Jorkins mention it when we were at the B & B?" I hurried to keep pace with my agitated partner. "Was she there when you went back to get the Rolodex?"

"No, she wasn't around." Dixie shook her head. "Just that ditzy teenager we talked to earlier. I guess Ilene might have been there somewhere. It's a huge house."

"I wonder if she mentioned your aunt's previous disappearances to the sheriff." I reached for Dixie's arm to stop her before she stepped off the curb. St. Ignatius does not have stop lights on all sides of the square. The main thoroughfare on the east side that takes you to each end of town does have, but the western edge of the square has none. Foot traffic mixes with vehicles and crossing the street safely depends on the good manners of the drivers and the attentiveness of the pedestrians.

We waited for a car to pass and then the next vehicle, a pickup, waited for us.

"It sure makes the fact that she's gone less worrisome, doesn't it?" I let go of Dixie's arm.

"In a way, I guess, yes." She shaded her eyes. "It looks like Disco is having a sale."

In the time we'd been at lunch, Disco had pulled a couple of clothes racks out on the sidewalk in front of the big window.

"Are you in the market for a T-shirt?" I asked. "It looks like he's got several."

I flipped through them as we passed. Unfortunately, the shirts were all alike and the front splashed with the name of a group I'd never heard of. Not saying they're bad, or unpopular, just that I'd never heard of them.

I fished in my purse for the keys and opened the front door to the shop. It was eerily quiet in comparison to the noise of the diner. In comparison to the noise we'd had at the shop earlier for that matter. It seemed like days had passed since the first visit from the sheriff this morning to now.

Dixie slung her purse on the table and plucked her cell phone out of the bag. "First things first." She pushed buttons. "I'm going to call Ilene and see why she didn't mention that Bertie had done the disappearing act before."

Back at my desk, I pulled out a tablet and began to flip through the Rolodex making a list of people we could call to see if they had seen Bertie in the past couple of days. I could hear Dixie's voice out front. It sounded like Ilene had answered, but with only one side of the conversation I couldn't tell if Dixie was getting anything useful.

From the sound of her boot heels, I could tell she paced back and forth. And finally said, "Okay, if you hear from her tell her she needs to call me right away."

"No luck?" I asked as she stepped into the office.

"She said, yes, Bertie has been gone without much notice before. But, she hasn't ever asked her about it because she figured if Bertie wanted her to know where she was going she would tell her."

"That doesn't sound like your aunt. She's passionate about her B & B."

"Ilene says she's always been able to reach her with any questions on her cell. This is the first time she's been completely out of communication."

I had been going through the cards in the Rolodex. "I've made a list of vendors and other out of town numbers for you to look at. Maybe you'll recognize some of them."

"I don't want to cause any problems for the business with my questions but I can't just sit idly by while the Sheriff's department does nothing."

"If Elsie really was murdered, and it seems they are definitely thinking she was, that means not only do we need to find your aunt and clear her, but the real murderer is still out there."

"And likely someone we know," Dixie added.

A sobering thought.

"I've got a couple of errands to run and then I'm going to stop by and see Greer."

"Not something else from her attic again?" Dixie pulled the notepad toward her and perused the list I'd started.

"Not this time," I answered. "She called while you were gone this morning and she has something for me."

"I have some errands too." She headed back out front to get her bag.

I interpreted that to mean she had some arms to twist. Look out Spicer family. If anyone knew anything, they'd better be ready to come clean.

We locked up and went our separate ways to take care of our errands. I hoped we could figure something out soon. If this project went belly up, I might be applying for that waitress job at the diner. Somehow that seemed more appealing than heading back to Georgia and the Sugarbaker sisterhood that had plans for my life.

* * * *

I made short work of my stops and then headed to The Good Life retirement center to see what it was that Greer had for me. She wasn't on the patio today so I knocked and she opened the door and invited me in.

"So, how's the cookbook coming along?" She settled into her chair and indicated I should have a seat. Greer always wanted to know what progress we were making on the project and I appreciated her interest. I wished I had more to report.

"It's going well." I sat down on the couch across from her.

"I hear that handsome Max Windsor is taking the pictures for you."

How on earth did she know this stuff? I'd only just met with Max and had barely had enough time to review his proposal.

"He's given us a quote," I explained. "We haven't come to any sort of arrangement yet."

"He's not from here, you know."

I did know that. Several people had mentioned it to me. Seemed we had that in common. Most of the people had grown up in the town, or if not in St. Ignatius at least somewhere within the county. There were a few, like me, who moved here for business or other reasons and stayed because we loved it. At least that was true in my case.

"I'd say he's a man with a mysterious past." Greer smiled at the thought.

"Really? What makes you say that?"

"Well, no one knows anything about his past." She wrapped her sweater around herself. "Old man Weaver left his place to his daughter who had no interest in it at all. Olivia Weaver could not wait to get out of St. Ignatius, and she made it clear she was never coming back. She must have sold it to Max sight unseen. Next thing we know, he showed up in town. None of us had ever seen him before then."

"I guess that is kind of mysterious," I agreed. "Still there must have been a reason. They must have been friends or at least had something in common."

"Or something." She scratched her head. "Ollie never said. And Max Windsor isn't saying now. Then there's that slight limp."

"Hmmm." I didn't encourage that line of thought. It seemed to me a bit too personal.

"Some think he might have been in the military or a spy or something."

Or something.

"Say, something I wanted to ask you about." I settled back on the couch and changed the subject. "Dixie and I had lunch at the Red Hen Diner and Toy George mentioned that Bertie Sparks had disappeared before. You know everyone. Had you heard that?

"Bertie?" Greer raised her brows. "I can imagine she might want to, but I never heard of it. That lady has lived here all her life, never married, worked for the bank for a long time, and then when she retired bought the house on Jefferson and turned it into a B & B. Think she does okay. It's always busy anyway. Nice addition to the town."

"So, she has always lived here?" I filed that knowledge away.

Greer nodded. "St. Ignatius High School Class of...well, I can't remember what class she was in but several years after I graduated."

"Elsie, too?" I asked. "Did they know each other in high school?" I wondered how far back the rivalry had gone.

"Oh, no. Elsie came from Mars. I don't remember her maiden name but a well-to-do family, to hear her tell it anyway."

"Mars, huh?" I pictured a town with UFOs everywhere. I knew that Riverside, Iowa was purported to be the future home of *Star Trek*'s James T. Kirk, but I'd never heard of Mars. "How did she and Bertie get sideways with each other?"

"I'm not really sure what started it, but I think Bertie just got tired of Elsie always holding her position in the community over everyone."

"I can imagine."

"And I think it peeved Elsie that Bertie wasn't at all impressed by her."

"Wow, so like you said, this has been going on for quite a while?"

"Yes, usually Harriet Hucklebee is the one who has to wave her magic wand and calms the troubled waters. She and her husband play cards with Karla Farmer, Kenny's sister, and she can usually get her to let it go."

She sure hadn't helped me out at all the day of the Scone Wars. I wondered why she'd stood back and let me take all the heat. I needed to talk to her about the next steps for the committee. Maybe I'd call her and see if I could slip in a question or two.

"No news on Elsie's cause of death?" she asked.

"Not anything the sheriff is sharing anyway." I still hoped there was some mistake and Elsie really had died of natural causes and the town could get back to small worries. Like parking around the square, the Red Hen Diner being understaffed, and why the one stoplight in town was so darn slow.

"He's got a good head on him. I bet Sheriff Griffin will figure things out."

I really wanted to ask her about Dixie and the sheriff and if she knew why there was such tension between them, but it didn't feel to me like that would be playing fair. Dixie would tell me. I knew she would. But in the meantime, not knowing was killing me.

"Well, I'd better let you get to dinner." I stood. "Are they serving something good tonight?"

"Chicken Cacciatore." She tapped her tummy. "That George they have in the kitchen is a great cook. I hope you have one of his recipes in the cookbook."

"I'll have to check. What's his last name?"

"George Amaro."

"It sounds familiar, but I'll check tomorrow to make sure." I headed for the door.

"Oh my gosh, wait a minute," Greer exclaimed. "I forgot about why I asked you to stop by. I'd forget my head if it weren't attached."

I turned back.

"Here you go." She handed me a small tissue-wrapped book.

"What is this?" I asked.

"It was mine when I was small, and I'd like you to have it."

I folded back the tissue paper and uncovered a cookbook. It said, *Mary Frances First Cookbook,* and it was in great condition but very old. I opened the front cover and checked the copyright. It said 1912.

"Are you sure?" I asked. "You might want to hang on to something like this."

"I didn't get it new. I'm not that old," she chuckled. "My mother knew I loved cooking and gave it to me because it has recipes and stories in it. I'd apparently packed it away with some of my mysteries and thrillers, and when I was looking through some boxes today I found it. No arguments. I want you to have it."

"Oh, Greer." I hugged her. "Thank you so much. What a wonderful gift."

My eyes misted as I carefully rewrapped the book and tucked it into my bag. Greer was a gift herself, and I was so touched by her thinking of me.

"Say, no rush about this," Greer began. "But if it's not too much trouble, I wonder if you could check up in the attic for a pair of cruets I think are in the box that says, 'Kitchen Items.'"

"Cruets?" I asked.

"Yes, there are two little white ones. There's a bunch of strawberries on the side. I used to use them for various things but most of all for oil and vinegar salad dressing."

"I'll see what I can do," I promised.

"Thank you, Sugar." She beamed. "If you don't find them it's all right, and whenever you have time. Like I said, there's no rush."

"I'll bet you have plans for the night." I checked the time.

"I am going to the old folks' buffet with Bunny and Alma. The food's not all that good, but I enjoy their company so much that I go anyway. Alma still drives and so I've got plenty of time.

Saying good-bye and thanking her again for the gift, I stepped outside and walked toward the parking lot. Greer seemed so happy at The Good Life that I couldn't imagine her ever wanting to move back home. And yet there was the reluctance to actually sell her house and the ongoing requests for items from the attic. As I reached my car and looked back at the place, I could've sworn I saw Disco walking between the buildings. He was hard to miss in his psychedelic colors. What would he be doing at The Good Life? I didn't know if he had family in town. Maybe he had a grandparent living in the retirement village. I made a mental note to ask Dixie about his family.

* * * *

Pulled out onto the street and heading toward home, I smiled thinking of how perfect Greer's gift was. I loved the uniqueness of it and the history behind it. Did the lady know me or what? I would have to do some digging on the origins of the charming little book.

But first I had to use my research skills to help my friend find out where her aunt had disappeared to and who might have wanted to kill Elsie Farmer.

Parking in my driveway, I called Dixie's number. She picked up right away. "What are you doing?"

"Pulling out my hair," she answered.

"But it's such beautiful hair," I laughed.

"Figuratively." She laughed. "No one seems to know anything at all about Bertie taking off before this."

"She must have wanted it that way." Bertie was not flighty by any stretch of the imagination so there had to be a reason.

"What kind of family are we?" The question was, I believed, rhetorical. In any case, Dixie didn't wait for an answer. "Our unmarried aunt may be in trouble, and no one was interested enough to keep tabs on her."

"Some would think that was a good thing." I was thinking of my family back home and how overbearing too much togetherness could be.

"I feel like I've failed as a niece." She let out a big sigh.

"Do you have plans this evening?" I thought Dixie could use a distraction. "If not, why not come on over for dinner at my house."

"You're cooking?" The surprise was clear in her voice.

"You don't have to act so shocked. I'm not totally inept." Okay, maybe I was. "I thought we'd order pizza."

"Pizza sounds wonderful." She sounded sincere.

"Okay. Any preferences?" I had favorites but nothing I dislike so strongly it was a no go.

"None. I'm game for anything."

"All right, I'll order."

I carted my things in, happy my neighbor was busy elsewhere and not conveniently outside. It was hard not to feel that she often laid in wait for me, hoping to catch me in some violation of her code of conduct for living next to her.

Dixie showed up promptly at six. The pizza was not quite as prompt. It hadn't arrived yet. She carried a grocery bag.

"What's this?" I motioned her in. "You didn't need to bring anything."

"I brought the wine." She handed me the bag.

"Fantastic." I carried it through to the kitchen, found a corkscrew and handed it to Dixie.

"You open, I'll find some wine glasses." I knew I had some but it took me a few minutes to locate them. Nice crystal glasses my mother had gifted me with on my last birthday. I didn't think I'd ever used them. The wine was a Chianti which would be great with the pizza flavors. I poured a glass for each of us.

"Nice pick." I held out a glass.

No sooner had we each taken a sip than the doorbell rang. I hoped it was the pizza.

A teen with a sad attempt at a goatee stood on the front porch. I paid him, added a tip, and took the pizza box from his hands.

"Thanks, lady." And he was off and running toward his car.

I quickly carried the box to the dining room table. The pizza was still really hot so the delay hadn't been on his part, more likely a backup in the restaurant's kitchen.

I'd put out plates and we dug in.

"Any luck with anyone who might know where your aunt is?"

"None whatsoever." She waved her piece of pizza. "The woman has simply vanished."

"When I stopped by Greer's she mentioned that Harriet Hucklebee is often the one that smoothes things out between your aunt and Elsie. Apparently, Harriet and her husband play cards with Kenny Farmer's sister, Karla, and her husband."

"I can see Harriet being the peacemaker. It's Elsie who always has her name on every committee but it's Harriet who's usually behind the scenes actually doing the work."

"That can't make her too happy." I wondered how long Harriet had been picking up the pieces. And also, what motivated her to keep doing it. Maybe it was as simple as a strong civic commitment. She'd certainly been the key player on the *Founders' Day Cookbook*, and though I'd been working with her on the project for months now, it occurred to me that I didn't really know her all that well.

"I'll admit that when I came up with this bright idea to publish community cookbooks, I thought it was going to be simple and straightforward." Dixie took a sip of wine. "It never occurred to me we'd find ourselves in the middle of this kind of a mess."

"Of course not." I laid my hand on her arm. "There will always be some issues to work out but this is extreme."

"That's the understatement of the year." She refilled her glass and took another piece of pizza.

"We'll get it figured out. It's still a great idea, we have a strong business plan, and the right stuff to do this." I'm often accused of being too much of a look-on-the-bright-side person, but I didn't think I was being overly optimistic in this case. I really believed we had the right stuff.

She looked at me like she wanted to believe me.

"We just need to get this murder figured out so we can get back to the work at hand."

"I know." She set her glass down. "I'm sorry. I'm so worried about Bertie."

"That's natural." I snagged another piece of the pizza. "I'll call Harriet tomorrow and see if I can find out anything. You keep going through those numbers."

"All right."

"We'll find her and get this straightened out. And you can tell me what's up with you and our handsome sheriff." I paused hoping she'd fill in the gap for me.

Dixie gave me a pointed look and shifted gears. "Let's talk about something else. What did Greer want to give you?"

"It's the niftiest book." I got up and retrieved it from my bag. "Take a look."

She wiped her hands and carefully took the book from me holding it with the tissue paper. "It's very old."

"Nineteen-twelve the copyright says." I had thumbed through the book when I got home and it had wonderful children's stories about the recipes. "The young girl in the stories wants to cook for her family. Her mother has taken ill but has written instructions for the girl to use in a little cookbook. The cooking utensils come to life, helping the girl who is unsure of herself, and creating a fun story."

"I love it." Dixie gently turned the pages. "And what a perfect gift for you. I take back almost all the mean things I said about Greer."

I smiled at her. "Almost?"

"I still think she takes advantage of you." She laid the book aside. "Always wanting something from her attic. I noticed a cup by the door. Is that another case of an object she must have?"

"In this case, it wasn't in the attic but in the garage." I laughed. "Which reminds me, I wanted to ask you if Disco has family in town. Maybe at The Good Life?"

She shook her head. "Not that I know of."

"I saw him there today, or I'm pretty sure it was him, and I realized I couldn't remember his last name. I was on my way out so I didn't get a chance to ask Greer."

"His last name is Fusco."

"I didn't remember that." I polished off the last of my slice of pizza.

"He used to have family here but I don't think he does anymore." Dixie stood and began cleaning up. "I think when his folks moved away, he stayed behind."

Chapter Nine

I'd cleaned up before hitting the sack and gotten coffee ready to go, so all I had to do the next morning was push the button. As I waited for the coffee to brew, I repacked my bag of papers and fed Ernest.

He ate a few bites and then watched me as I went through my morning routine.

"Planning a big day of lying in the sun by the window, are you?" I asked as he followed me back downstairs. "Or maybe you'll change things up and sleep in your cat bed?"

He meowed as if in answer and jumped to the arm of the couch. I scratched the top of his head and picked up my things. Stopping by the kitchen to pick up the wine bottle from last night, I tucked it under my arm and took it outside with me.

Heading out to my Jeep, I opened the recycling container by the side of the house to add the wine bottle. When I turned I was startled to see Mrs. Pickett swaddled in a fuzzy pink bathrobe and standing between me and my car.

"Oh, my word." I clapped a hand over my mouth. "You scared me."

"Had quite a party last night, didn't you?" She raised a silver brow.

"What?" I had no idea was she was talking about. "What do you mean party?"

"Apparently a pizza party from the looks of the pizza flyers littered all over my yard."

I looked over at her front yard and sure enough, not just her yard but the one the other side of hers, had Pizza House flyers scattered around. They must have blown out of Goatee Boy's car and he hadn't noticed. Or hadn't cared.

Way to get me in trouble, kid.

"I did have a pizza delivered but it certainly wasn't a party." I wondered why I felt the need to correct her misconception about my having a party. It wasn't really any of her business, but she'd made me feel defensive. I wanted to be a good neighbor. "Though it wasn't me that littered, I'll see that those are picked up."

I took my bag to the car and proceeded to gather up the two-dollars-off-a-large-pizza coupons that were still being tossed in the breeze.

Mrs. Pickett went back to her house and disappeared inside shutting the door with a click. But I'd be willing to bet she still watched from her window to make sure I didn't miss any flyers.

Once I'd collected all the papers and disposed of them, I called Dixie explaining why I was late.

"I don't know how you put up with that woman, Sugar." She had no patience for difficult people. "I'd have told her off by now."

"I needed to go to the post office so I'll just do that on my way." I had to pick up some paper samples that had been shipped to us by one of our paper suppliers. The mail person had tried to delivery it yesterday, but we'd been closed when she came so she'd left a notice.

"Sounds like a plan. I've got some notes for you on the first section."

I went back in for a second cup of coffee and then headed to the post office which was only a block from the square. I could have parked at the office and walked. But this would be easier with everything I had to carry.

Dot Carson, the postmistress, was behind the counter, her short dark hair curved around her angular face.

"Good morning, Sugar," she greeted me. "Here to get that package from The Paper Mill?"

"I am." I dug in my bag for the notice. "We weren't at the office when Pat tried to deliver it, and I'm sure it wouldn't fit in the mail slot."

"I guess you were probably out investigating." She raised a drawn-on eyebrow. "I hear you and Dixie have been asking questions all around town."

"Dixie is understandably concerned about her aunt," I defended my partner.

"Oh, everyone knows Bertie didn't kill Elsie." Dot scoffed. "I mean, why would she? Over scones?"

"Right." I wondered if Sheriff Griffin counted in that 'everyone' she referenced.

"Plenty of other people with reason to do the deed, though." She blinked a couple of times.

Before I could ask her what she meant, the door opened to a young mother with a baby in a stroller. She held the hand of a toddler and attempted to wrestle the stroller through the door.

"Here let me help." I held the door while she lifted the wheels and got the stroller inside.

"Stay right there," she directed the toddler. "Hello, Dot. I've got some more packages to mail."

"Be right with you, Jan." Dot shifted paper on the counter. "First I've got to get Sugar's package for her." She disappeared into the back.

"How old are you?" I leaned down to speak to the little girl.

"I'm three, but my brother is only one." She pointed at the baby. "I'm the big sister."

"Wow, you are," I exclaimed. "I'll bet you're a good one too."

"You've got a great little helper here," I said to the woman and straightened.

"That's right." She shifted the box of envelopes from her hip and slid them onto the counter.

Dot returned from the back with my package. It definitely would not have fit through the mail slot. I order almost everything online, but with paper I've got to be able to feel the texture and the weight when making decisions so I really needed these samples.

"Thank you." I picked up the package and turned to go. "You take care of that little brother now." I smiled at the girl.

"I brought you a sample of that perfume you like," I heard the mom say to Dot as I went out.

I'd parked in the post office parking lot. As I headed to the Jeep, I nearly ran down Jimmie LeBlanc.

"Here let me help you with that." He took the box from me. "Is that your car?"

"Yes, the dark blue Jeep." I pointed it out. "Thanks for your help." I was thankful for the help but I knew what was coming next.

"Have you had a chance to read through the St. Ignatius history that I supplied for the cookbook?"

"I have." I opened the back, and he set the package inside. "It's very good, but—"

"Thank you." He brightened. "I worked very hard on it."

Oh, man, I hated to disappoint the guy. But we really couldn't afford any more than three pages of history. I had to find a way to tell him.

"Here's the thing—"

"Sugar, come quick!" Just as I was about to break the bad news, I was interrupted by Disco who ran up, his yellow bell bottoms topped with an orange turtleneck and a heavy gold chain. He looked like an ad for citrus fruits.

"Spice and the Sheriff are going at it," he paused as he tried to catch his breath, "and I think he may arrest her if you can't get her calmed down."

Good grief. What had happened now?

I excused myself to Jimmie and got in the Jeep. I hoped Dixie didn't get herself in so much trouble that she really did get charged with something. Something like assaulting a police officer.

I pulled my car into the parking lot and entered through the back. I could hear yelling when I opened the door.

Sheriff Griffin was warding off blows from Dixie who was bashing him over the head with a piece of cardboard from some supplies we'd unpacked the previous day.

"You need to put all those papers back where you found them." He ducked as she struck again.

"I have every right to look through my aunt's papers." Bam. She came at him sideways.

"Not before I do." He got out between smacks. "I have a search warrant."

"Whoa." I stepped between them and got bashed on the head with the cardboard for my efforts. "What's going on?"

Neither acknowledged my presence.

"Dixie!" I shouted in my best speak-to-a-crowd voice.

She stopped.

The sheriff took a step back and crossed his arms.

Dixie's face was as red as her hair. "I am not going to give Aunt Bertie's papers to him until I've finished looking at them."

"I went by the bed and breakfast." The sheriff straightened his tie. "I have a search warrant to search Bertie Sparks's office. Looking for information on where she might have gone," he explained.

"Dixie, he's trying to help find Bertie too." I knew it would be hard to turn over her aunt's papers, but I really didn't think she had any choice.

"Sure he is. So he can hang her." She glared at the sheriff.

I thought that might be a pretty extreme exaggeration. And I didn't think there'd been any hangings in Iowa for decades. But I got her point. Though I did believe that Sheriff Griffin was trying to help find Bertie.

"Come on, Dixie." The sheriff stepped forward and Dixie raised the cardboard weapon again. "You can either give me the papers now or I'll have to go back and get another search warrant. One for this place. Given the circumstances, I won't have any problem getting one."

"Fine." She dropped the cardboard on the floor. "Go ahead. Take what you want."

She stepped back from the table where she had begun making stacks of the papers.

I happened to notice the front window. At least a dozen faces peering in. So, that was how Disco had known what was going on. We'd collected a crowd.

The sheriff followed my line of sight and seeing the crowd at the window shook his head. Striding forward, he pulled open the front door of the shop and motioned for people to move along. Stepping outside to his patrol car, he said something to the deputy who waited there.

In the short time he was gone, Dixie opened the lid to the metal trash can that sat at the end of the counter and dropped in the Rolodex.

The sheriff returned with the deputy and the two of them made short work of boxing up the papers. Mostly invoices and correspondence from the look of things, but a few letters. I wondered how many of them Dixie had a chance to get through.

"That it?" he asked as the deputy carried out the last box.

Dixie nodded.

I knew it wasn't. I knew the receipt for the rat poison was tucked away in her wallet. And I knew the Rolodex was in the trashcan beside Dixie. What to do?

Wondering what the penalty was for withholding evidence and convincing myself that I was pretty sure it wasn't hanging, I stayed silent. My love for my friend overrode my judgment and my fear of repercussions.

"Dixie—" Sheriff Griffin began. Then seeing her set expression, he stopped. "Never mind." He turned on his heel and walked out the door.

I stepped forward and flipped the lock on the door. The last thing Dixie needed right now was a bunch of well-meaning snoops. When I turned around Dixie's eyes were pooled with tears and she bit her lip to keep from crying.

"Aw, honey." I put an arm around her shoulder. "I'm so sorry."

"I can't believe I just did that." She opened the trash can and fished out the Rolodex.

I handed her some paper towels to wipe it off. "I can't either."

"I'm going to put it in the cupboard in the back in case the Terminator comes back." She picked it up.

I glanced out the window to make sure our onlookers hadn't returned. No faces at the window, but it looked like we were in for a summer storm. The sky was heavy with dark clouds.

I went to check on Dixie who I found pacing back and forth in the backroom. "Come on, let me show you these paper samples." I hoped a discussion about something other than the murder and her missing aunt would serve as a distraction.

We went through the paper stock samples and I showed her the one I thought would be best. It was a good weight, durable, and wouldn't break the bank as far as cost. After we'd agreed on the choice, we each moved on to our various projects and the day went quickly.

It was still looking stormy went I got ready to leave and so I made sure all the windows were closed before I left.

When I got home I grabbed my mail and hurried inside, hoping to get inside before the downpour. And also not wanting to have to deal with Mrs. Pickett and her complaints.

Ernest was always happy to see me, unlike my neighbor. I gave the required belly rub and then put on water to boil for a pasta salad. Something quick and easy seemed like the right choice after a long day.

Chapter Ten

After cleaning up my dishes and setting up my laptop at the dining room table, I decided to make the trip to the attic before I forgot. Although Greer had said there was no rush, if I found the two cruets, I could take them to her and also take the opportunity to ask her about some other things.

The attic stairs were steep and creaky and not all that well lit. I stepped through the doorway, always surprised at how clean the place was. After my father died, my mother and I moved a lot, each place fancier than the previous, but none with any sense of history. And definitely none with an attic. And so probably my expectations on what attics looked like came from watching movies where there was always a coat of dust on everything. Always an old trunk crammed with clothing, toys, and sometimes a treasure map. Not Greer's. There were boxes and boxes of various cast-off household things.

It took some time moving boxes around, but I finally located the large box labeled Kitchen Items. I tore off the tape and opened the top. Everything in the box seemed to be wrapped in newspapers. The local *Journal* was mixed with the *Des Moines Register*, but each of the items had a newsprint wrapper. This was going to take a while: I should have brought a water or some tea up with me.

I carefully plucked out a few things and set them on the floor. Then I pulled up a small wooden stool and started folding back the paper. The first few things were casserole dishes of varying sizes. I was surprised Greer hadn't taken some of them with her. There were also some random coffee cups. One was from the St. Ignatius Centennial which had been held a few years back. I rewrapped it and set it aside. It might be worth looking at what the town had done for a centennial celebration as I tried to figure out what to do with Jimmie LeBlanc's historical tome.

I unwrapped a few more items but found no white cruet with strawberries on the side. The wind had come up and the old house creaked. As I stood and reached into the box for another round of objects, the rain began. I could hear the hard strike of water on the roof as the rainstorm began. The state was known to have tornadoes this time of year, but the weather forecasters hadn't predicted any severe weather. Just rain.

I looked around at the space. No leaks that I could see. That was a good thing as Greer had replaced the roof just a couple of years ago. If I were able to purchase the house, it would be fun to use the attic space as something more than storage.

I unwrapped the next round of kitchen items. An old coffee maker, some mismatched spoons, a set of measuring cups.

Suddenly there was a big clap of thunder and the lights went out.

I felt around to make sure I didn't step on anything and then slowly made my way in what I believed was the direction of the door. There was a small window at the peak of the ceiling but the street lights must have gone out too. It was absolutely pitch black.

I crouched down on the floor, berating myself for not bringing my cell phone up with me. I moved slowly trying to be careful. I knew there were candles downstairs. All I needed to do was get to the foot of the stairs and I could feel my way the rest of the way.

Thinking I must be close, I stood and reached my arm straight out hoping to touch a wall or the door. Instead I touched what felt like a shelf. I pulled my hand back and reached out in the other direction. Just as I did the lights came back on and I found myself face to face with a glass clown mask. I screamed and slapped it off the shelf.

Not a dainty scream either. A shriek that probably scared poor Mrs. Pickett right out of her pretty pink bathrobe.

Once my heart rate returned to normal, I picked up the mask. I hoped I hadn't broken the scary thing. I took a better look at the mask. It was a decorative glass piece and looked like it was meant to be hung on the wall. I can't imagine why anyone would want to, but I suppose with the bright primary colors it might have been meant for a child's room.

As I turned away, I noticed a white box on the shelf beside it that said "Salad Set." On the off chance it might be the cruets, I opened it. Sure enough, there they were. White and with strawberries on the side, just as Greer had described. Simply not where she thought she'd packed them.

They had also been cushioned by newspapers and I decided I'd just take the whole box downstairs.

I went back to where I'd been dragging things out of the kitchen box. I had a lot of things to put back.

"Sorry, Greer." I said aloud. "I am done for the night. I'll set things to rights tomorrow."

I cautiously made my way down the steep stairs, carrying the white box with the strawberry cruets. I set them on the counter in the kitchen and carefully unpacked them. Placing them in the sink, I thought I'd wash them before taking them to Greer.

Locating my phone in case the electricity went out again, I also tracked down the flashlight I'd put in a kitchen cupboard and checked to make sure it worked. Candles were in the sideboard in the dining room and I set out a few. Again precautionary, I hoped.

I flipped on the television which had a scroll about thunderstorms but they seemed to be running their regular programming. The rain continued to come down. I went to the front door and watched it pour. The street lights were all back on and so you could see the sheets of rain.

※ ※ ※ ※

The next morning my fright over the clown mask seemed silly. Your mind can play such tricks. After last night, I was better prepared for a power outage.

As I waited for the coffee, I washed Greer's cruets and set them on a paper towel to dry.

At the office, we continued laying out plans for the cookbook. I picked up where I'd left off, plowing through Jimmie LeBlanc's history of the town. Dixie worked on recipes and made phone calls.

Disco showed up looking for free food.

In other words, it passed for what had become our usual day.

Chapter Eleven

Elsie's funeral was planned for Saturday at ten o'clock at the St. Ignatius Lutheran Church. Most of the town was expected to attend so they had brought in two large screen televisions for the overflow crowd which might have to be seated in the church basement. So many flowers had been ordered from Glee's Flowers and Gifts that the shop had run completely out of carnations.

The announcement about services had been placed in the *Journal*. A light luncheon would be served at the church after the service. All the arrangements had been made. There was only one problem. No Elsie.

The state medical examiner's office was so backed up they were not going to get to Elsie's autopsy for at least another week. Maybe two.

Kenny Farmer had thrown a fit. Or at least that's what we'd heard. According to Dot at the post office, he'd called his state senator, he'd called the governor's office, but to no avail. No one was able to move the wheels any faster and so that's how we found ourselves on our way to a funeral without the guest of honor.

We were early but the church parking lot was already full.

"Do you want me to let you out?" Dixie glanced at my high heels.

"No, I'm fine." I answered. "We might as well have walked from the office." I peered down the side street which was already filling up with cars. At least we'd carpooled. It looked like everyone else in attendance had driven their own car.

Dixie found a spot not too far away and I carefully eased out of the truck. I was out of practice with dresses and high heels. It had been my daily attire when I'd worked in publishing, but since we'd launched the company, I'd gotten used to dressing for comfort, not for style.

I pulled down the hem of the little black dress hoping I hadn't flashed the crowd of silver-haired ladies that had just passed. The bevy of flowered dresses hurried past without even glancing our way so my modesty was preserved.

I'd covered the sleeveless black shift with a deep gray shawl. Textured gray heels and silver jewelry and I was set. I leaned toward the side mirror and checked my teeth for lipstick.

"You look fabulous." Dixie motioned for me to catch up. "So, fabulous you make me sick." She grinned.

"You clean up pretty good yourself." I smiled back at her. She'd worn a yellow linen sundress that set off her fabulous red hair and she carried a matching yellow shrug.

"I think I wore this for my brother's graduation. That's how old it is." The sound of car doors slamming shut as others parked and piled out drew her attention and she grabbed my arm. "Come on, we want a good seat."

We hurried to the church and picked up a folded brochure as we entered the sanctuary. The brochure had a picture of Elsie Farmer on the front and the inside listed the details of the services. It didn't mention her absence.

The pastor would talk, Kenny Farmer would say a few words, the mayor would also say a few words, Tina Martin would sing "Amazing Grace," and then the plan had been to take the trip to the cemetery for internment. But I guess that wasn't happening.

We settled into a pew about midway. The sanctuary was filling up fast. I assumed the flyer had been printed before the news had come about the autopsy delay.

I read through the names of the pallbearers. Their duties were not needed today.

"I imagine you know all of these people." I pointed to the pallbearers' names.

She looked at the listing. "All guys who work for Kenny in some capacity."

That's kind of sad." I grimaced. "No family friends or relatives?"

"She wasn't nice to people." Dixie waved her hand at the crowd. "Still they're all here, aren't they? And I'll bet half of them have a better reason to kill Elsie than my aunt."

I glanced around at the room. The front of the room was filled with floral tributes, from green plants, to colorful mixed arrangements, to vases of deep red roses.

The roses reminded me of Elsie's garden and finding her lying there among her rose bushes.

I probably should have ordered roses instead of the peace lily I'd selected. I'd liked the idea though of a living plant that could be kept by a family member. There were so many flowers across the front that they had also begun to line the outside walls with flowers. My gaze followed the flower arrangements and I turned my head to see how far back they went. A group was just entering and appeared to be filling the last of the available seats. I spotted Greer in the group, attired in a dark burgundy dress and a straw hat with a ribbon that matched. She saw me and waved. Greer had told me earlier in the week that the Good Life was bringing anyone who wanted to attend in their van. It looked like many had wanted to attend.

I also caught sight of Sheriff Griffin out of the corner of my eye. He leaned against a back wall, arms crossed, watching the doorway. I wondered if he was watching for Dixie's Aunt Bertie. Wherever she was, she was missing a big event.

"Good grief," Dixie muttered under her breath.

I turned to see what had caused Dixie's comment. A man in a dark suit, who I assumed was the funeral director, was setting up an oversized photo of a smiling Elsie Farmer amongst the flowers. I don't know that outside of a museum I'd ever seen a portrait that large.

Kenny Farmer was ushered in by the same dark-suited man. He seated Kenny in the first pew at the front of the room. I glanced around at the rapidly filling pews. No one else sat in the front row with Kenny.

"Did they not have children?" I whispered to Dixie.

"No. I don't think by choice," she whispered back. "One of them couldn't. I don't remember which one."

The interior of the church was beautiful. A ceiling with wooden beams came to a peak and a simple cross at the front hung over the altar, surrounded by gorgeous stained-glass windows.

The sanctuary had filled to capacity and it appeared they were now funneling new arrivals to the overflow room in the church basement. It took a while but finally the stream of people was down to just a few stragglers.

The minister stepped to the podium. "Let us pray."

We all bowed our heads.

After the prayer, Tina Martin entered from the side and took her place at a microphone that had been placed by the church organ. She closed her eyes, smoothed the arms of the choir robe she wore, and proceeded to sing "Amazing Grace." The woman was not half bad. I was so relieved. Not to be a music snob, but sometimes friends and family singing at weddings or funerals can be iffy.

When she concluded, the minister introduced Kenny who was to read Elsie's eulogy. I wondered if that was a good idea. I'd also seen that go badly. He climbed the stairs to the podium.

"Thank you all for coming," he began. "We're here today to remember Elsie Louise Farmer."

I'd wondered what Elsie was short for and I guess it wasn't short for anything. Elsie's eulogy was brief and to the point. She was born Elsie Banks, met Kenny Farmer at a high school track meet, they'd married, she'd moved to St. Ignatius and lived here ever since. They had no children and she had no Banks family left. She was chair of the local Garden Club, a board member of the St. Ignatius Historical Society, a St. Ignatius Library Foundation board member, a member of the Ladies Auxiliary, a member of the Quilters Guild, and of the St. Ignatius Founders' Day Committee.

Wow. Elsie had been one busy woman.

The minister approached the podium again. "If anyone else would like to say a few words about Mrs. Farmer, please come forward at this time."

The silence was deafening. No one came forward. Most of the congregation seemed motionless like students in a classroom that fear being called on.

"Perhaps you'd like to share a memory." He paused.

Still nothing.

Finally giving up, the minister cleared his throat.

He looked to Kenny Farmer who nodded.

"Let's end with a prayer."

After a short prayer, the minister announced that refreshments were available in the church basement.

Dixie and I waited for the crowd to clear a bit before making our way to the back and then downstairs.

After that uncomfortable service, everyone seemed to be talking at once as they went through the line and filled their plates with food that had been provided by the church luncheon committee.

I bypassed the sandwiches and went straight for the pie. There were several varieties to choose from and all looked homemade. I finally settled on a French Apple and then looked around for a place to sit down.

Dixie was caught up in a conversation with Dot Carson. It sounded like the postmistress had embarked on a guessing game about where Bertie Sparks might be holed up. Spotting a table with coffee I grabbed a cup and found a folding chair off to the side. Hoping against hope that no one thought this was an appropriate occasion for me to recount the finding of Elsie Farmer's body, I took a bite of my pie. I wondered how much longer it would be before the State Medical Examiner finished the results of the autopsy.

Attendees milled about and more kept coming. The large television that had been set up for the overflow crowd had been switched to a video with pictures of Elsie. I shifted to a chair that was closer to watch, curious about the woman who no one had been willing to memorialize with a story or anecdote.

There were a few older photos of Elsie and Kenny at various functions. In those her expression was still unsmiling but less severe than the Elsie I'd known. Then there was a series of photos that appeared to have been taken at more recent events. Two ladies perched on folding chairs in front of me offered a running commentary on the photos.

"And that's the Winterfest where she got her knickers in a knot over her name being misspelled in the program," said the one with the pill box hat.

"That's right, and that one," the other one pointed as the picture changed. "That's the New Year's Eve party at the Country Club when she had a cow because the toasting glasses were plastic."

A younger woman sitting in front of them turned around and chimed in, "And this one—" She pointed at the screen. "Was the library craft fair, where she made Suzie LeGrande, the new librarian, cry."

Wow. I wondered who had picked the pictures.

In addition to the unflattering anecdotes they sparked, not one of the photos was flattering to poor Elsie. Either a sour expression, or a frown, or the photographer had caught her mid-sentence or, every woman's worst nightmare, mid-bite.

I watched the loop of pictures begin again. Really? Could no one have found a nice picture of the poor woman? A happy Christmas, a dinner with friends? Many of them seemed to be at either company events or events in the community. Kenny Farmer was in some. I noted the woman from the committee meeting, Minnie, in a high percentage of the photos. I imagined as the Girl Friday she took care of the details at many of the events so was probably required to attend.

Dixie slid into the chair beside me balancing a slice of pecan pie and a coffee. "I finally escaped."

Like me, she'd gone straight for the dessert. "What did Dot Carson have to say?"

"She was full of ideas about my aunt Bertie." Dixie took a bite. "She did give me some useful information though. She said Bertie had been getting mail from an address in Minnesota on a pretty frequent basis."

"Do you think that's odd?" I asked. "It could just be a family member or a business contact."

"We don't have any family in Minnesota," Dixie mused. "It's possible it's a business contact but Dot said the correspondence was addressed by hand."

"Did she remember an address?" I wasn't sure Dot was supposed to share information about someone else's mail. Even with a relative.

"No, she didn't. But she did remember the town was Winona."

"Maybe a road trip is in order."

"I don't know where in Winona we'd look for her but it may come to that."

"Here I'll take your plate," I offered. "Did you want anything else?" I really wanted another piece of pie but restrained myself.

"No, I'm ready to go whenever you are."

"Let me make a trip to the ladies' room. I've somehow managed to get sticky apple pie on my hands. I'd better wash it off before I get it on my one and only decent dress."

"It's down that hallway." Dixie pointed. "And to your left."

"Okay, I'll be right back." I slipped through the crowd, dropped off our plates and then headed down the hallway Dixie had indicated, but didn't see the ladies' room. I must have misunderstood. I backtracked and saw another hallway, but the arrow on the wall said it led to Sunday School classrooms. Maybe I was to go down there and then turn left.

No luck. I started back toward where I'd started when I heard a giggle. I peeked through the doorway on my right, which the sign on the door said was the Little Angels classroom. I could see a blond head and a white dress with big bright red cherries, but couldn't see the woman's face. She giggled again and then leaned into a man who stood just out of my sight. Oops, it didn't look like the occupants were little and they definitely were not angels.

None of my business. I started to turn away but then out of the corner of my eye caught a glimpse of the man.

It was Kenny Farmer.

What the heck? I let the curtain fall and got out of there. What was the supposed grieving widower doing with the blonde? Well, let me rephrase that. I could see what he was doing. But really? At your wife's funeral?

You know they often say that the first person you should look at in a murder case is the spouse. What if Kenny Farmer had seen an opportunity to get rid of his unpopular wife so he could move on to someone new?

When I got back to my starting place, I realized where I'd gotten confused. I had turned right instead of left. I have no sense of direction and am often lost, but not usually inside a building. I spotted the restroom. I hurried in and washed my hands and then headed back to the main area to find Dixie.

She stood by the stairs looking around.

"What took you so long?"

I didn't answer.

"You got lost, didn't you?"

I nodded. "We need to go."

"I can't believe you got lost on the way to the ladies' room." Dixie laughed. "I didn't even give you any north or south instructions. You do know your right from your left, don't you?"

"Let's get out of here." I took her arm and pulled her toward the stairs.

"Okay." She gave me a strange look.

"I'll explain when we get to the car."

We climbed the narrow stairs to the first floor and were headed out the door, when we ran into Harriet Hucklebee. Her gray plaid suit was neat and tidy like always, but her short gray hair which often reminded me of a bicycle helmet seemed nicely tousled today.

"Glad I caught you both. Together." She ran a hand through her hair and sighed.

That might explain the tousled look.

"Yes," I prompted.

"I'm worried about the cookbook project."

"We're making great progress on the recipes," Dixie noted.

"And we've got a photographer lined up," I added. "No reason to be concerned, we'll be fine on the timeline."

Though we wouldn't be if we spent more days like the last few, trying to locate Dixie's aunt.

"It's not the time that I'm worried about." Agitated Harriet ran fingers through her hair again. "It's the Farmer family. One of the committee members stopped me and she had heard that in light of Elsie's death the family is thinking it might not be appropriate to publish the cookbook."

"But the cookbook had nothing to do with Elsie dying."

"I know, but it was a sort of catalyst. Getting Elsie all riled up," Harriet was quick to clarify. "I can understand that they might have reservations."

"Kenny was a big supporter of the idea," Dixie noted.

"Well, we'll just have to see." Harriet sighed. "But I wanted you two ladies to know, just in case we have to call it off."

"Thank you, we appreciate that." I took Dixie's arm and steered her in the direction of the truck.

"But—but—" I ignored her sputters until we got out of earshot.

Once we were down the sidewalk and away from the church. I let go of her arm.

"They can't do that." She huffed. "We have a contract."

"Yes, we do."

We fell into step, her long legs and her agitation eating up the sidewalk.

"Dixie, I can't jog in these heels," I finally spoke up after trying to keep pace.

"They can't walk away. We've already put so much time into this project. That's why we had them sign a contract, right?"

"Yes, but do we really want to be the company that made the Founders' Day Committee pay up when there's been a murder of one of the committee members?"

"Well…no."

"So, we're going to have to convince them not to cancel."

Maybe the best way we could do that was to figure out who really killed Elsie Farmer. Greer had mentioned a disgruntled employee and I'd just seen Kenny playing kissy face with someone he was obviously interested in.

I filled Dixie in on what I'd seen at the church.

* * * *

When we entered the shop, I kicked off my heels. I should have taken Dixie up on her offer to take me by my house to change, but I wanted to get busy working on planning the remainder of our testing.

"Sugar…" Dixie stood in the doorway of my office.

I looked up from the history pages I was still trying to get through. I'd pulled out several interesting bits and had made notes on where I thought they might fit into the chapters.

"What is it?" The look on her face worried me.

"You know what Harriet said about the Farmer family wanting the committee to not do the cookbook."

"Yes."

"What if we can't find Aunt Bertie and what if we can't figure out the real killer?"

"What are you saying?"

"Well, maybe we should see if we can talk to them."

"I'm not sure how to go about doing that." I made another note. "Do you have an idea?

"Why don't we stop by Kenny's house this evening? Maybe take him some food."

"But not scones, right?" The minute that was out of my mouth, I couldn't believe I'd said it.

"Gosh, no. Like a casserole he can re-heat. It would give us a chance to see if we can find out anything about who he was playing Sunday School with. And we might also talk to him about continuing to support the cookbook."

"I like that idea. Did you want to make something here? Or did you want to do it at your place?" I just assumed Dixie would be the one cooking. And then I immediately felt bad about my assumption. It wasn't that I couldn't handle making a casserole, but when you're around a really great cook, you begin to rely on their superior abilities.

"I think I'll just go to my place to do it. I've got all the ingredients. And I've got a casserole dish there that I don't care if I don't get back. We've got all the fancy stuff here for staging."

"I'm happy to help with something."

"I'm good." She seemed calmer now that we had a plan of action. "How about you pick me up in an hour?"

"I can do that." Now I was kind of glad I hadn't changed clothes. What I had on would look much better for a condolence call, rather than the jeans I usually wore when we were working in the office.

Dixie gathered up her things and headed out the back to her truck. She'd only been gone a few minutes when I heard a knock at the back door. I hadn't opened the curtains of the storefront because we'd been gone. We didn't get many but it could be a delivery.

I opened the door to Max Windsor. Casually dressed in jeans and an untucked white shirt, he still managed to look crisp. And handsome.

"Hello," he said. "I wasn't sure if you were here, but thought I'd check. Do you have a few minutes?"

"Sure." I opened the door wider and stepped aside so he could come in. I led the way back to my office and offered him a chair.

He sat and studied me for a few minutes.

"A bit dressed up today," he noted, smiling. "You look very nice."

"Thank you. I felt my cheeks heat up at the compliment. "Dixie and I attended Elsie Farmer's funeral. I didn't see you there."

"I didn't know her." He shrugged. "Knew of her, of course, and the family. But I really don't know any of them."

"It was odd," I mused.

"In what way?" His blue eyes sharpened on my face.

"Well, first off. No Elsie," I explained. "Because they haven't finished the autopsy, they couldn't release the body, but Kenny had already made all the arrangements. So, they went ahead without her."

"That is odd."

I shifted papers to make some work space. "I don't know that I've ever attended a funeral without the deceased present."

"Hmmm." He moved his chair, the lone chair in my office, closer to the desk.

"And then there was the tribute video." I shook my head. "You could appreciate this, working with images as you do. I don't know who put it together, whether it was the funeral home or a family member, but there was not one nice picture of the woman in the whole thing."

"It can be hard to find candid shots that are flattering."

"I know. But literally not a single one." I'd not known Elsie well, and most of our interactions hadn't been warm and fuzzy. But still, I was offended on her behalf that no one had been able to come up with a nice photo. "Anyway, back to why you're here." I turned back to where Max sat watching me.

"Yes, I've done some work on the historical photos and think I can create something useable for you, but wondered if you had particular ones you'd thought about using."

"Interesting you should ask." I reached for the folder that held my notes. "Here are some of the items I've pulled from Jimmie LeBlanc's history tome."

I showed him my list.

"I thought that one was interesting." He pointed to one of the pages I'd marked.

I did too. Before its incorporation, the town had been a trading post. Like many other Iowa towns, it had been a stopping off place as settlers migrated farther west. But apparently some had decided to stay and take advantage of the rich farmland.

The town had been named by a Jesuit priest. Father Paul Nickless was a German immigrant and had moved west with a group of farmers. When he and many members of the party became ill, the rest traveled on without them. A log structure served as the first church. Though the log church was not still around, the second effort, a building made from local limestone, was.

There was also an interesting story about one of the other founders, W.L. Buckwald, who was well known for his stories about the frontiersmen of the times. Most were considered tall tales but were highly popular in their time. He became interested in the newspaper business and bought the *Constitution* which later became the *St. Ignatius Journal.* The home that he'd had built was still standing as well as the home of an Otto Styles, a chemist who had done groundbreaking work in the field of weed killers. Both homes were native limestone and pretty impressive.

We spent more than an hour pouring over the pages and Max made notes as to some of the locations. I looked up at the clock on the wall and realized it was almost five o'clock.

"My gosh, look at the time. I could easily get lost in this stuff. It's easy to see why Jimmie LeBlanc got so carried away." I turned to Max and suddenly became aware of how close he was. I mean it was simply so we could read the articles together, right. A matter of convenience. But realizing it made me blush like a school girl. Good grief, I was really out of practice.

Max offered to stop by in the next couple of days with some of the restored pictures and I promised to have a finalized list for him of the food pictures we'd need. That is if we could salvage the cookbook project. As soon as Max was gone, I grabbed my phone and bag and headed out to pick up Dixie.

Chapter Twelve

As I parked my Jeep on the street in front of the house, all that happened the day I found Elsie dead in her backyard came flooding into my mind. The veranda was still swept clean, the flowers were still in full bloom. And as we approached the house, their fragrance hit me again, just as it had that day. The crime scene tape was gone from the side of the house. The garage door was closed so we couldn't tell if Kenny's car, a Cadillac that matched Elsie's, was there. Surely he would be home by now.

We rang the doorbell and waited. Dixie had made a ham and potato casserole that smelled so good. I could hear a voice inside the house so someone was there.

"That's so thoughtful." I pointed at the instructions for reheating she'd taped to the top of the casserole.

"I just know lots of times people think they can microwave everything." She shifted the glass dish to the other hip.

The voices inside came closer. Dixie and I looked at each other. Perhaps Kenny had other visitors. I hoped it was the lady from the Sunday School assignation. I hadn't seen her face, but I thought I'd recognize the bright cherry-dotted sun dress.

I glanced at the cars on the street. My Jeep right in front, a brown-ish Corolla, down from that a rusty gray Ford van that may have once been blue, and behind that a shiny silver Lexus. The person—guy I thought—in the Lexus ducked down suddenly as I surveyed the street. The person in the van also slipped out of sight, and then popped back up, and pulled the person in the passenger seat down with him. This time I really couldn't tell if the driver was a male or female. It looked like that game. What was it called? The one where the animal keeps popping up in different places.

"Whack-a-mole," I said aloud.

"What?" Dixie face said she thought I'd really lost it this time.

Just then the door was pulled open. "Can I help you?" Minnie from the committee stood looking at us expectantly. She glanced at the casserole that Dixie clutched.

"We—" I began.

"Take a number." Minnie handed us a sticky note with a number written on it.

"What?" Dixie and I said at once.

"Take a number." She extended the sticky note. "So I can log your food in."

Ahh, I got it now. Minnie had a system. Of course, she did. How could I have forgotten that the secretary of the Founders' Day Cookbook Committee was also Kenny Farmer's administrative assistant?

I took the sticky note. It had the number twenty-one on it. Do you suppose Kenny had twenty dishes that had come through the door before ours?

"Hello, Minnie." I wasn't going to make the same mistake I had before and forget the poor girl's name. "We just stopped by with this casserole for Kenny. Is he here?"

"He is." She didn't move from the doorway. "Put your address on this card along with your number. That way it will make it easier for Mr. Farmer to send thank-you notes and return dishes."

"Okay." I fumbled with my purse. "Do you have a pen?"

Dixie took advantage of Minnie's distraction in helping me and barged through the doorway. "I'll just take this through and set it in the kitchen for you," she said over her shoulder as she headed into the house and down the hallway to the kitchen.

"But, but…" Minnie was flustered. Kenny may have asked that she make sure he not be overrun with well-meaning visitors in addition to helping him keep track of the casseroles, pies, and other assorted dishes.

But Dixie was not going to be deterred. I could see her disappearing down the hallway and toward the back of the house.

Minnie looked over my shoulder and I turned to see a tall slim woman with short gray hair holding a plate of cookies.

"I'm so sorry." I smiled at the woman and then at Minnie. "I'll just go see if I can help."

"Take a number," I heard Minnie say.

I couldn't fault her, it was a great system. And would make sure that thank-yous were sent and dishes returned to their proper owners. I headed down the hallway before Minnie could stop me.

Kenny Farmer was perched on a stool at the gray marble counter still in his suit from the funeral though he'd removed his tie. Whatever cologne or after shave he wore, a pungent green, he'd overdone. It reminded me less of a pine forest and more of one of those things you hang in your car.

Kenny had a plate full of food and was putting it away like he hadn't eaten in days. I guess grief had not affected his appetite.

"This is good." He shoveled another fork-full of some green marshmallow salad into his mouth. "Don't know what it is, but it's good."

"Watergate Salad," Dixie explained. "I'm not sure why it's called that, but it's pistachio pudding, crushed pineapple and Cool Whip. It's just a matter of stirring all the ingredients together."

Yes, she is a recipe snob, but I figure when you've won as many blue ribbons as her, you can flap your apron at those (like me) who don't go to the trouble to actually make something from scratch.

"I'm going to go ahead and put this in the freezer for you." Dixie held up the covered pan. "The instructions for heating it up are taped to the top."

"Thanks, Dixie. I'm sure if you cooked it's got to be good. Who are you?" Kenny suddenly zeroed in on me. "Do I know you?"

"This is my partner, Sugar Calloway," Dixie explained. "We're working on the Founders' Day Cookbook."

"You're the one that found Elsie." Kenny's eyebrows shot up.

"I am so sorry for your loss." I should have realized that he would recognize the name and have questions.

"The police are saying that it might not have been accidental. That someone might have meant to poison Elsie." Kenny took another big bite.

"My aunt…" Dixie's face got pink.

"Ah, hon." Kenny waved his fork. "Surely nobody really thinks that your Aunt Bertie would have poisoned my wife."

"Well, it seems our sheriff does."

"I've known Bertie all of our lives. She and Elsie fought like two wildcats. But it was just sport to them two." He started to take a drink from his coffee cup and then realized it was empty.

"Hon, could you refill me?" He handed me the cup.

Dixie looked away. But I knew she rolled her eyes even though her back was to me.

"Sure." I stepped across the big country kitchen to the coffee pot that sat on the counter. I felt it. It was still hot, so I filled it to the brim and returned it to Mr. Too-Good-To-Get-His-Own-Coffee Farmer. Maybe I was being too hard on him, he had been through a lot. But there was just something about his attitude that said this was his modus operandi.

"If not Bertie Sparks, then who?" I asked. "Can you think of anyone who would have wanted to harm your wife?"

"Can't say that I can." He took a slurp of the liquid. "Now, don't get me wrong. My Elsie could be irritating to people. But that was part of her charm. She was no nonsense. Got things done."

Believe me I knew all about no-nonsense-get-things-done women. That was my mother and my two aunts. Run a business? Run a political campaign? Run a charity dinner? They were your go-to women. But Elsie Farmer lacked the finesse the Sugarbaker sisters had. Still, maybe the way she'd done it had been just what was needed. Maybe I was expecting a gloss of southern charm over the get-it-done attitude and it wasn't always called for.

"The police do seem to be focused on Dixie's aunt," I commented. "But if not her, then someone else," I hesitated, "must be responsible." I really wanted to say, "must have wanted her out of the way." But that was probably going a little too far.

"Looks like you've had a lot of people stopping by with food," Dixie noted, surveying the dishes on the counter.

"That's true," Kenny agreed. "Thank the good Lord for Minnie who came by from the office to help keep it in order. This way I'll be able to give proper thanks."

I'd be willing to bet that the ever-efficient Minnie would be the one writing out the proper thanks.

"So nice of people to think of you, and these dishes all look great. I hope some of them are included in the Founders' Day Cookbook." I thought I'd see if I could segue into the reason we'd really come.

"Hmmm," Kenny agreed. Or at least I thought that was agreement. He'd moved on to a slice of cherry pie and had his mouth full.

"Harriet Hucklebee says your family doesn't want the cookbook project to go forward," Dixie blurted out, "given the tragic circumstances." She turned and looked at him.

"Can't see why." Kenny was quickly plowing through the pie. Clearly a stress eater. I could relate, although he didn't show any signs of outward stress. "The cookbook didn't have anything to do with Elsie dying."

"It started the whole thing," Minnie interrupted from the doorway.

"It did?" Kenny's eyebrow shot up. "How's that?"

"The fight over which scone recipe would be included in the cookbook was what caused the big fight between her and Bertie," Minnie explained.

"Oh, that's right." Kenny took his last bite of pie and licked the fork.

"Thanks for reminding us," I muttered under my breath.

"Except that my Aunt Bertie did not kill Elsie," Dixie huffed. "And so it had nothing to do with the scones. It must be about something else and it must be someone else. And that someone is still out there."

"Oh." Minnie's eyes got wide and she went pale. Okay, paler.

I appreciated Dixie standing up for her aunt and all, but I don't think it had occurred to Minnie that there was a killer on the loose. Now, she'd frightened the woman who was probably already scared of her own shadow.

"We were thinking maybe a tribute page in the cookbook," I suggested. "You know, to highlight her community involvement and her support of the Founders' Day celebration."

Dixie frowned at me. We hadn't talked about it. For one big reason. Mostly because I'd thought it up just now. I could make it work. I'd have to take out something, but I could fit it in. Probably I'd have to eliminate one of those interesting historical tidbits that Jimmie LeBlanc had written. But if it helped the project to move forward, well, the homestead of the author of frontiersman pulp fiction might have to go.

"That'd be nice." Kenny stood and took his plate to the sink. I was surprised he didn't hand it to me. "I don't know what Harriet was talking about. She plays bridge with my sister so it was probably just some off-hand comment that Karla made."

Great. Now I'd given away a page in the cookbook to help with a problem that didn't exist. A page for a tribute to a woman that no one really seemed to care a lick about. My mouth gets away from me sometimes.

The doorbell rang and Minnie headed to the front to answer it, sticky notes and file cards in hand.

We took our leave before Kenny needed more coffee.

After saying good-bye to Minnie, who stood at the door, file cards in hand, waiting for the next wave of people, Dixie and I walked to my car. I looked up and down the street where I'd noticed the cars earlier. The gray van was still there, as was the Corolla, the Lexus was gone. It had probably been my imagination that there were people in the cars. Or if they were, they probably had good reason. I have to admit to being a bit on edge with the current situation. I, like Dixie, was sure her aunt had not killed Elsie. Like I'd said to Kenny Farmer, if not Bertie then who?

I dropped Dixie off at her house and headed home. We made plans to contact Harriet Hucklebee the next day and see if we could clear up any concerns about the cookbook project.

Turning the Jeep onto my street, I drove slowly praying Mrs. Pickett was not outside waiting for me. I couldn't think what transgression I might have committed this time, but I was sure in her mind there was something. Leaves, flyers, something.

As I approached the front step, I noted someone had shoved several of the pizza flyers into my mailbox. I thought I'd gotten them all, but I must have missed a few. One guess on who had returned them to my porch rather than just putting the dang things in the trash.

I pulled them out, shoved the wad of papers in my bag, and put my key in the lock.

"Meow," I heard from behind me.

I turned. Ernest sat on the small bench by the door. He stretched his legs until he was upright and meowed again.

"Oh, no." I dropped my bag and scooped him up. "How did you get out?"

He must have slipped out as I'd left that morning. I didn't see how; I was always so careful. If I'd realized he was out I would have herded him back inside. I'd had a cat when I was a young girl who escaped so many times, my Aunt Celia said we should have named him Houdini.

"You sneaky thing." I rubbed his head. I would have to watch it even more carefully from now on. "Why would you sneak out like that? When you have such a grand life here?"

Still holding him, I turned the key and went in. I'd been remiss about getting him a collar and an identification tag because he never went outside. Tomorrow I would take care of it.

I searched the refrigerator for leftovers wishing for some of that casserole Dixie had made for Kenny. My nose remembered the smell of the ham and potatoes and I thought I'd detected a rich cheddar cheese. Maybe tomorrow I'd ask her for the recipe, but tonight it was warmed-up soup and a grilled cheese sandwich for me.

I sorted through my mail, while waiting to flip the grilled cheese. Bills and advertisements mostly. There was an envelope addressed to Greer with a Minneapolis postmark. Greer had forwarded her mail to the Good Life, and usually our delivery person was good about catching anything that had been missed in the sorting process, but this one had slipped through. I'd take it to her tomorrow.

I went to put it on the table by the door so I wouldn't forget to take it to her.

Wait a minute. Where were the strawberry cruets I had placed on the table? They were cute little white cruets with red stoppers and bunches of strawberries on the side. I could swear I'd put them there to remind myself. Obviously, I hadn't. I must have set them aside when I'd unwrapped the scary glass clown, but I was sure I'd come downstairs with them. I guess I'd been more rattled than I realized.

It looked like another trip to the attic for me.

Once I finished up my meal prep, I sat down to eat. As I did, my mind wandered to the time at Kenny's.

Small towns celebrate and comfort with food. It's a middle America tradition to bring food when someone has died. Kenny was smart to take advantage of Minnie's organizational skills to help him sort out all the different dishes. The man would not need to cook for at least a month.

He had seemed dismissive of the idea that Dixie's Aunt Bertie had anything to do with Elsie's death. I was sure he was right. But, the receipt that Dixie had taken from the B & B was for a large amount of rat poison. Why would Bertie need that much? And why wouldn't she have bought it locally? I remembered a lecture she'd issued at one of the committee meetings about using local merchants whenever we could. If she'd bought it for a good reason, and I had to assume she had, then could someone else have used it to kill Elsie?

The sheriff had said the scones had rat poison in them but he hadn't said how much. Come to think of it he hadn't actually said that was what killed Elsie. We couldn't know all the details, and the way Dixie treated the sheriff any details probably weren't going to be shared. So maybe we needed to concentrate on who rather than how.

Who were the other potential suspects? According to the group watching the video at the funeral, there was a long list of people Elsie had offended. I wondered if she really was as bad as they'd described. Even if those stories were true and she hadn't been well-liked, it was a big leap to kill her. There had to be more to the story. Something bigger than meanness.

I gathered up my dishes and took them to the sink. I missed having a dishwasher but living alone there were so few dishes, I couldn't complain about washing them by hand. I washed and dried the wine glasses Dixie and I had used and admired the sparkle of the crystal. They were quality glasses and a nice gift from my mother. No one could ever accuse Cate Sugarbaker of not having good taste. The *Southern Living* home, the designer suits, the best of everything. Her one fail at the high-class life was me. She blamed it (my low-class taste that is) on my late father.

The truth was lately I often used paper plates. I hoped my mama didn't hear about that transgression. An unlikely occurrence, as she'd made it clear she was never going to set foot in Iowa. As much as I loved her, that was okay with me.

Once I'd gotten ready for bed, I curled up with my book and Ernest to read for a while. But even the latest Lisa Jackson suspense, which according to Greer was a page turner, couldn't hold my attention. Finally, I pulled out a notebook and pen and jotted down a few thoughts in order to clear my head.

Tomorrow maybe one of those ideas would spark something.

* * * *

The next morning I overslept. Not surprising given the restless night I'd had.

"Where was my faithful cat alarm?" I scolded Ernest. "First you run outside without me knowing. And then you let me down, ignoring your wake-up call duties."

Ernest tipped his head and meowed. Tail in the air he padded down the hall and to the bathroom to wait on me. He likes to have his morning water from a running faucet and I confess I frequently gave in to his demands.

I hurriedly got ready for the day, threw on leggings, a bright multi-colored dress, and tied my hair back with a scarf. Not fancy, but it would do.

The great thing about living in a small town, one of the great things anyway, is no morning rush hour. Now, even when I'd been living in Des Moines, the rush hour there is more like a twenty-minute rush. Not an hour. Not like what I'd been used to growing up in the Atlanta area. But now I was really spoiled.

I hadn't taken the time to make coffee. I figured I could do that at the office. I gathered my papers and dropped them into my tote bag. After reading more on the history of St. Ignatius, I truly thought there might be a complete book in Jimmie LeBlanc's tome. I didn't have any experience with history books, but I could reach out to a few former colleagues from the magazine who might. Maybe I could steer him in the right direction.

"See you tonight," I said to Ernest as I closed the door. I know it's silly to say good-bye to a feline like they know what you're saying, but I'd forgotten to a couple of mornings ago and he had definitely pouted when I got home.

In a matter of five minutes I was at the shop. Dixie pulled into the back parking lot as I was getting out of my car. She had several bags of groceries. I thought we'd just done a grocery run but it seemed like there was always some ingredient we were missing for the latest test recipe.

I opened the door and then held it for her.

She stepped through the doorway and then screamed.

Chapter Thirteen

"What is it?" I dropped my tote, my purse, and the bag of groceries I'd taken from Dixie and rushed forward. "Are you hurt?"

I stepped around and then saw what or rather who had caused her reaction.

Dixie's Aunt Bertie sat on one of the stools at the counter. It appeared she'd been looking through some of the pictures I had been showing Max.

"Egads, Bertie!" Dixie gulped air. "How did you get in? You nearly gave me a heart attack."

"Sorry about that." Bertie pushed up wire-rimmed glasses. "I thought I'd better stop by and let you know I was back in town. I hear you were a little worried."

Uh-oh. I backed up.

"A little worried?" Dixie face flamed red. I watched her get control of her temper.

Bertie continued to flip through the pictures in silence.

"I'm glad you're okay." Dixie gave her aunt a hug. And then held her at arm's length.

"Where have you been?" she demanded.

"When I stopped by to see Sheriff Terry, he said you'd been worried," Bertie explained, not answering Dixie's question about where she'd been. "Of course, that could have been an excuse to talk to you. You know he's still carrying a torch for you, right?"

"Not true. Terry Griffin is not carrying a torch or anything else for me."

"Back when you two were an item..." Bertie began.

So I hadn't imagined it. Dixie and the sheriff did have a past.

"Bertie..." there was a warning in Dixie's voice. "Where did you go?"

"I went to visit a sick friend."

"Who was it?" Dixie asked. "Anyone I know?"

"No, not anyone you know." Again, only answering half of the questions.

"Why didn't you let someone in the family know where you were?"

"This third degree is worse than the sheriff." Bertie shook her silver curls. "I didn't know any of you would be looking for me."

"Well, it sure made you look suspicious."

"Suspicious? For Pete's sake, girl. You know I didn't kill Elsie Farmer."

"Of course, I do."

"So there you go. Nothing to worry about. Nobody's business where I was."

"Really." Dixie fished in her bag which she'd dropped on the floor when she came in. "What about this?" She pulled out what I was sure was the receipt for the rat poison.

Bertie plucked the paper from Dixie's fingers and looked at it. She tucked it into her pocket. "So the sheriff hasn't seen this?"

"No, but only because I took it off your desk when I went to the B & B to try to figure out where you were." Dixie sat on the stool beside her aunt.

"I'm sorry I worried you, dear." Bertie smoothed the skirt of her soft pink print dress. "This is really nothing to worry about. I don't know who killed Elsie. Probably a lot of people wanted to, but it wasn't me."

"What about the poison?" I asked.

"That's nothing to worry about either." Bertie crossed her arms.

"It's a lot of rat poison," Dixie noted.

"Can you think of anyone who had a reason to kill Elsie Farmer?" I asked.

"Like I said, plenty of people." She got down from the stool. "Listen I'm not being flippant. I'm sorry Elsie's dead. But I'm sure Sheriff Terry will figure it out."

Dixie stood also. She gave her aunt a hard look but then stepped forward and gave her a big hug.

"How did you get in by the way?" I wasn't sure I wanted to know.

"Key in the geranium pot." She held up a key tied to some green yarn.

"Dixie!" I had repeatedly warned my partner that we needed to get rid of that spare key and if we needed a backup, we could leave a key with one of our fellow merchants on the square.

She had the grace to look guilty. "I know I promised. But I keep forgetting my key and I'm usually the first one here..."

It was a bad habit a lot of people in town had of either leaving doors unlocked or leaving keys where it was very easy to find them. The town had a low crime rate, but the pharmacy down the street had a break-in not too long ago. There was no use tempting fate.

"Sorry." She looked sheepish.

Bertie stopped, her hand on the doorknob. "I guess I missed Elsie's funeral by a day, huh?"

"Yes, though she missed it too." Dixie explained about the medical examiner being backed up and Elsie not being able to make it.

"Was it nice?" She tipped her head.

"As funerals go, I guess so," Dixie answered.

"A lot of people?"

Dixie nodded.

"She would've liked that." Bertie stepped out and closed the door behind her.

"Wow," I said when she was gone. "That was a shock. I wondered how it went at the Sheriff's office. I'd have loved to have been a fly on the wall for that conversation."

"Me, too." Dixie picked up her bag and headed to the kitchen area. "Me, too."

We made short work of putting the supplies away while the coffee brewed and then we each got busy with our own tasks. I really wanted to ask Dixie more about her aunt's comment regarding Sheriff Griffin and her, but held back. If she hadn't been forthcoming under the influence of wine the other night, probably under the influence of coffee wasn't going to work. I would need to pick my time.

We each finished up our duties and then headed out to take care of other business. I had some things to mail and errands to run. Dixie had promised to help her mom with sorting out some things that had been stored in her former bedroom at the farm.

"You watch out for valuable things in that cleanout of your room," I cautioned. "According to Greer the idea that one man's junk is another man's treasure is true, and according to her sources, which I believe consists of reruns on that antiques TV show, you might find something worth thousands of dollars."

"I'll keep my eyes peeled," Dixie laughed. "But I'm afraid in this case, one woman's junk is still just another woman's junk."

I organized my things, headed out the door, and then stopped to make sure it was locked. I paused and checked the geranium planter to make sure my partner or her aunt had not put the key back.

Back in the office that afternoon, I stood and stretched. It seemed like I'd been on the phone all day, getting prices, confirming advertising. I'd been drinking water since I was talking so much but I'd also begun to get hungry. Of course, it might have had something to do with the smells coming from the test kitchen.

I wandered into the kitchen. "How's it going?"

"Really well." Dixie picked up her notebook and made a couple of notes.

"I've nearly finalized our advertising for the cookbook. I'm following up by phone to confirm and sending the ad copy to Liz." Liz was our graphics person.

"It feels so good not to be worried about Bertie." Dixie leaned against the counter.

"I'm sure it does," I agreed. "Though it still feels unsettling to know the police feel there's a murderer out there."

"I know." She sighed.

"I'm thinking about calling it a day." I glanced at my watch. "I need a break from the phone. Unless there's something in particular I could help you with?"

"Not really."

Suddenly the bell dinged out front. I went to see who it was.

"Thought I'd come in the right way this time." Dixie's Aunt Bertie had just stepped through the door. This time she was in her usual work clothes. Jeans and T-shirt, and a Jefferson Street B & B apron tied in front.

"What can we do for you?" I asked. "Dixie is in the back."

"Hey, there." Dixie rounded the corner and joined us. She leaned in and kissed her aunt's cheek. "I guess I'm going to forgive you for giving me gray hair."

"I'm sorry about that. Really I am." She sounded a sincere this time. "But that's not why I'm here. I'm trying to get some work done at the B & B and the sheriff says all my papers they confiscated I can't have back. They've given them to some state crime something or other. Terry said you had them and they took them from you. Can you tell me if my Rolodex was part of what they took? Sheriff Terry didn't seem to know what I was talking about."

"I might know something about that but I'm not sure I can be forthcoming when you're not open with me."

"About what?"

"About the rat poison, Berts."

"You always were too snoopy for your own good, Spicey. Even when you were a kid."

Dixie waited for a few minutes and then went to the cupboard and pulled out the Rolodex and handed it to her aunt. "I could put these addresses on the computer for you. It would be a lot easier to update."

"Thanks, hon, let's do that." She smiled innocently.

"And the poison?" Dixie stared her down.

"I have rats," Bertie finally sputtered.

"Oh, gosh, no."

"I bought it because I have a rat problem. I didn't buy it locally because if word got out that I had a rat problem no one would want to stay at my place."

"Did you tell the sheriff and the state people that?" Dixie asked.

"No. I did not." Bertie put her hands on her hips defiantly.

"Why not?"

"Did you hear what I just said?" She raised her voice. "Once they put it in a public record it's there for everyone in the world to see. I can't have that. The only ones who know right now are me and you two."

"But because you aren't telling them where you were they are going to continue digging and you are still a suspect."

"Yeah, having a DCI agent at the B & B this morning wasn't exactly good for business either."

"I imagine not."

"I know you guys have been asking questions while I was gone. What have you dug up?"

"I saw Kenny with someone—a female someone—at the church the day of Elsie's funeral."

"The one she didn't attend?" Bertie rolled her eyes.

"That's right." I chimed in. "He was kissing a woman in one of the Sunday School rooms. But I couldn't see her, only him."

"There've been some rumors about him from time to time. He's always been sort of full of himself."

We heard the bell ding again and again I went back out to answer it.

It was the sheriff.

This wasn't going to go well. Any fool could see the writing on the wall. Another Aunt Cricket expression.

"Come on back." I motioned to him. "The gang's all here."

"I stopped by the B & B and Ilene said you were here." The sheriff walked into the backroom. "The DCI agent who is looking in Elsie Farmer's death said you had asked to get your papers back."

"That's right." Bertie glared, her chin set. "Since I didn't kill anybody."

"If you have any evidence of any kind," the sheriff looked at Bertie and then at Dixie, "it is a crime to withhold it. Do you understand?"

Both stubborn heads nodded. Neither spoke up.

I escorted the sheriff back out. I guess just because Bertie was back in town didn't mean she was no longer a murder suspect.

After Bertie left, I took a break from phone calls and started the process of sorting names and recipes. I looked up to see Dixie leaning on the doorjamb of my office.

"What's up?" I asked.

"Well, I've been thinking." She rubbed her forehead with her hand. "I've tried to think of how we could figure out who it was you saw Kenny with at the church."

"I would recognize that dress anywhere," I offered. "I'll bet not one other woman in town has one like it. I, for one, wouldn't be caught dead in it."

Dixie gave me an eyeroll.

"Sorry, bad use of that expression."

"Anyways," Dixie continued. "Maybe we don't need to look for the 'other woman' at all. Maybe we simply need to watch who comes and goes at Kenny's house."

"Right," I followed her line of thinking. "Or rather who comes and stays. I like it."

We agreed to meet later that evening. Our thought was if the woman came to Kenny's house, she probably wouldn't show up in broad daylight.

"I'll pick you up," I called, as Dixie left.

"I'll bring snacks," she answered.

* * * *

I don't know how private detectives do it. I have to say that surveillance is the most boring work. There was the boredom and then also the discomfort. We sat scrunched down in the seat so that we wouldn't be easily seen.

In the suspense books Greer had loaned me, the police or private detective usually had stale coffee and terrible snacks to help them stay awake on a stakeout. Because Dixie is who she is, she'd brought great snacks. Tonight's snack was homemade oatmeal chocolate chip cookies. So, there was that. I'd brought a thermos filled with good hot coffee.

The first two nights we'd taken Dixie's pickup. Then the third night we switched to my Jeep. We were afraid the neighbors would notice if the same vehicle was parked down the street from the Farmer house night after night.

We were right. By the fourth night, there was a tap on the window.

"What are you two doing?" It was the sheriff.

I hit the button to lower my window. I had just crammed a cookie into my mouth, so Dixie answered.

"Just talking." She leaned forward to look at the Sheriff. "We're not parked in a 'No Parking' zone, are we?"

"No, but one of the neighbors called in a suspicious vehicle. Everyone else was busy with other calls so I said I'd check it out. I should have known." He bent down to see into the car. "What's in the bag?"

"Cookies," I answered, holding out the bag. "Want one?"

He reached in, snagged a cookie, and bit into it. "Wow, really good." He took another bite. "You make these?

I nodded toward Dixie.

"These are great." He reached in and helped himself to another. "Alright, you two. Move along. I don't know what you think you're doing, but if there's any need for watching the Farmer house, law enforcement will take care of it. You," he pointed at us, "are not law enforcement."

He ambled back to his car munching on a cookie. We sat in silence as he pulled away.

Once his headlights had disappeared, I started the Jeep. It looked like our watch was over for the night. All of a sudden Dixie was bouncing in her seat. She pointed at the Farmer house, the garage door had gone up. Kenny Farmer's white Cadillac backed out, and headed east down the street. At least I was pretty sure that was east. I pulled out and followed. He headed toward the square and then turned at the light.

I followed the Caddy as closely as I could without being seen. When he headed out of town, I glanced over at Dixie.

"What do you want to do?" I asked. "Should we stay on him?"

She nodded. "You bet."

He stopped at the edge of town and then pulled onto the main highway. Churchville, 8 miles, the sign said. I stayed with him but hung back. There was hardly any traffic on the road so it was easy to keep him in sight.

"I don't think Sheriff Terry would approve." I glanced at Dixie.

"I'm not looking for that man's approval." She leaned forward in her seat. "It looks like he's turning."

"Are you ever going to tell me what the deal is with you and your animosity toward the man? He seems really nice. He hasn't arrested your aunt even though she refuses..."

"Look." She pointed at the Caddy's taillights.

Apparently tonight was not going to be the night I learned about Dixie's history with Terrance Griffin. I could ask someone else in town. I imagined everyone but me (and maybe Max) knew, but that didn't seem to me to be fair play. If she wanted me to know, she'd tell me.

Kenny had pulled off the highway at a sign that said, Churchville, Population 193. There was a gas station which was open, a diner which was closed, and a small motel called The Weary Wanderer Motel, and, sure enough, there was a church. He pulled into the parking lot of the motel.

Bingo.

The gravel in the parking lot crunched like the sound was on loudspeaker as I pulled in. Or at least it seemed extremely loud as we were trying our best to be inconspicuous. I headed into an empty parking place that gave us a good view of the whole area. It was a white single-story structure with all of the rooms facing a small cabin-like building in the middle that said, "Office." Amazingly, there were other vehicles parked in the lot.

Kenny didn't go to the office. He approached one of the rooms and knocked. Though it was dusk and getting a little difficult to see, we had a clear view. The door opened and he slipped inside.

Dixie and I looked at each other.

"I told you he was having an affair." I slapped the steering wheel. "I knew it."

"Guess you were right." Dixie shifted in her seat and settled in getting comfortable. "Doesn't it seem strange though that he'd meet whoever it is at a motel? I mean, he doesn't have a wife at home."

"Maybe he wanted to keep it from the neighbors. Look how quickly they reported us, sitting in a car on his street, minding our own business."

"We weren't exactly minding our own business," Dixie pointed out. "Wonder how long we'll have to wait now. I should have brought more snacks."

"If we get hungry, I can run over to the gas station." I was sorry I hadn't paced myself with the oatmeal chocolate chip cookies.

"I'd bet they aren't open much longer." She pointed toward the station. Dixie was probably right. Even in St. Ignatius the local gas station was only open until ten o'clock. Though the town did have a convenience store that stayed open all night.

"What the heck?" I couldn't believe my eyes.

The door had opened and Kenny was leaving. He stood in the doorway for a couple of minutes, straightened his clothes, and then pulled the door shut. The light still shone through the curtains. I couldn't see anyone else. And then Kenny walked to his car, got in, and drove away.

"What do we do now?" I asked.

"Well we know he came here to see someone."

"Yeah, but that was awfully quick." I tried to be a grownup and not snicker when I said it.

"I couldn't see anyone else. Could you?"

"No, I couldn't see at all." I thought for a minute. "I guess we could ask at the office who's registered in that room."

"I'm afraid they probably aren't going to tell us," Dixie lamented. "Like the sheriff said, we're not cops."

"We could pretend to be. Or we could pretend to be lost. Or we could go to the room and rattle the doorknob, you know, like we've got the wrong room. Or..."

"Or we could go to the door and knock and see who answers."

Way less imaginative than my scenarios, but probably more honest and straightforward. And productive.

"Okay, let's go." I had my car door open already.

We crunched across the lot. Again, the gravel was extremely loud in the quiet of the place. The lot was well lit, and June bugs buzzed around the tall lights. There was no light on outside the room, but we could see from a gap in the curtain that there was a light on inside.

"What if the killer is Kenny, and he came to meet his lover, and now he's killed her too." I stopped in my tracks. "Finding one dead body was enough for me."

"If she's dead she won't be answering the door," Dixie pointed out. "If no one comes to the door, we'll go to the office and ask them to do a welfare check."

Good point.

We approached the door. Dixie took a deep breath and knocked.

No answer.

I was already imagining the dead body inside. In my mind, she still wore the dress with the bright red cherries. I'm sure the woman I'd seen with Kenny had changed clothes since that day at the church, but that's how I always imagined her because I didn't have anything else to go on. Now, I could picture her draped across the bed, clutching her throat from the poison she'd just ingested.

Dixie knocked again, this time a little louder.

The door suddenly popped open and a beefy arm blocked the entry. My eyes landed on the tattoo on his forearm, a knife stabbing a heart, and then traveled up to the scowl. I tried to speak but choked on my words.

"What do you want?" Tattoo Guy was in his thirties with short hair. Very short, think crew cut buzz with a couple of weeks of growth on it.

"We were looking for Kenny Farmer." I finally found my voice. "He was just here."

"No, he wasn't." His voice was sharp.

"Yes, he was." Dixie drew herself up to full height. "We saw him."

"You need your eyes checked, lady." He moved to close the door. "I think I'd know if he was here."

"Wait—" I started to say, but he'd already snapped the door shut.

Not what we'd expected. This was not some affair, Kenny was into something much worse.

Dixie and I walked back to the Jeep and quickly got in.

"Maybe Kenny used an alias or something." Dixie locked her door and looked at me.

"Wow. I don't know what to think." I also hit the lock and then started the Jeep.

"Do you think it's drugs?"

I hate to stereotype, but that's what had come to mind. Especially since the guy was so furtive, not opening the door, and denying that Kenny had been there.

I pulled out onto the highway. It was a quiet ride back and we were both lost in our own thoughts about what we'd seen. Soon we were back in St. Ignatius.

I pulled up in front of Dixie's place. "Do you think we should let the sheriff know?"

She didn't hesitate at all. "We don't breathe a word of this to the Sheriff."

* * * *

When I got up the next morning, I started the coffee then opened the pantry and got out cat food for my furry companion.

"Ernest," I told him, "For being two smart cookies, Dixie and I were really stupid last night."

"Meow," he agreed.

"You don't have to be so quick to chime in." I filled his bowl and sat down at the kitchen table waiting for the coffee to brew and thinking through all the bad choices.

Watching Kenny's house had simply been an effort to figure out who he was involved with. If we could figure who she was, and confirm that Kenny had a motive perhaps the Sheriff would follow that line of investigation.

However, bad choice number one, staking out Kenny's house. And bad choice two, following Kenny when he left town.

And then, here comes the big one, we could have called it a night, rather than knocking on the door of the room at the motel. It hadn't seemed like such a bad choice at the time. The truth was we had just expected a disheveled female to answer the door. Not dangerous. Instead a large scary-looking man had answered. Dangerous.

"Dangerous," I told Ernest. He looked up from his dish and I'm pretty sure rolled those gorgeous green eyes.

Once at the office, I got to work. I had made good progress but the clock was ticking to get this project completed and ready to go to print. I called Harriet Hucklebee and asked if we could meet for coffee to go over some things later that morning.

First, I had some details about the project I needed to discuss with her. Second, maybe I could figure out why she'd gotten the impression there was a problem with the Farmer family and the cookbook. It would be good to know if there was still an issue looming that might derail the whole thing. Third, I thought she probably knew more than she was saying about Kenny and Elsie. She wasn't a gossip (I liked that about her) but she might be more comfortable sharing something with me, rather than the sheriff, if it had to do with Kenny and his catting around. (Apologies to Ernest for the term.)

I had the sections separated. The recipes were labeled for each section and I'd planned a few backups in case there were any problems and we needed to make changes.

From the paper samples I'd picked up the other day from the post office, we had picked one in particular that we thought would work the best. It was clean and simple but sturdy enough for a cookbook that would become a keepsake. At least that was the hope.

Mid-morning at the Red Hen Diner was not as busy as breakfast or lunch time but a smattering of people sat at the tables and booths. Harriet was already there and sipping a black coffee while she looked at her phone messages.

She looked up as I approached the table and put her phone away. "Hello, Sugar."

I placed my bag on the extra chair and sat down. "I hope you haven't been waiting long."

"Not at all." She adjusted the scarf at her neck. "What do we need to cover?"

I'd hoped for a little chit-chat so I could work in a few of my questions but the lady was all business. Toy George showed up at the table with cup and coffee pot in hand. I looked up and nodded and she poured.

"I have a sample of the paper I'm proposing and a list of items we're still waiting on." I pulled a sample from my bag and reached in again for the list.

"I know nothing about paper so I'm sure you're right on that." She took the sample but then immediately handed it back.

"On the items we still need." I plucked a pen from the outside pocket. "Here's the table of contents. I'll adjust the page numbers when we have everything. And I'm working with Max Windsor on the photos."

"Ah, the handsome and mysterious Max." Harriet raised a brow. "I didn't know he did food."

"I don't know that he has before, but the work I've seen leads me to believe he's up to it." I didn't know why I was defending Max. "And his pricing was good." I didn't need to go into all the reasons he was such a good pick, that's what we were being paid to figure out.

"What else?" she asked.

"It had been suggested that we do some sort of a tribute to Elsie Farmer." I threw it out there.

She looked up from her papers. "Who suggested that?"

I had, but only to get Kenny talking. But now I felt like we needed to follow through. Even if he was a murderer. "I don't remember who first suggested it." I didn't look at her.

"The committee will have to give the okay to do that." She pushed up her glasses. "I'm not sure what they'll think. Elsie wasn't a popular person. But she and the Farmer family were big contributors to this project."

Here was my opening. "You said the other day at Elsie's funeral that the Farmer family were opposed to going forward with the cookbook given Elsie's death. But when we talked to Kenny a couple of nights ago about it, he was fine with it. He suggested talking with his sister. Do you know? Did she have a problem?"

"I said they were concerned." She folded her papers. "That's what had been expressed to me by several people."

"You're friends with Kenny's sister and her husband?"

"Not close friends." She tucked the papers in her bag. "We play cards together with them and some other couples once a month."

"Was everything okay between Kenny and Elsie?"

"I'm not sure what that has to do with the cookbook, but yes, they seemed okay. No different than they'd been."

No different than they'd been was not necessarily the same as everything was okay.

"The sponsors." I snapped my fingers. I'd almost forgotten. "Do you have that list? I need a complete list of all of the sponsors so I can get that formatted and ready to go into the cookbook. Are there logos we should be including?"

"You'll have to check with the secretary. She had collected all of those. I'm sure she has it handled."

"Minnie," I said. "Her name is Minnie."

"That's right." She gave me a funny look.

"Great." I made a note. That would give me a chance to talk with her and see what she knew about Kenny and his secret lover. The assistant always knows what's really going on.

I took my time walking back to the office. It seemed the problem Harriet had thought there might be with continuing the cookbook project might be with Karla Farmer and not Kenny as we had supposed.

Dixie was hard at work when I arrived at the office and I filled her in on my conversation with Harriet.

"I think we should just outright ask her." She sorted through cans and jars. "What have we got to lose?"

"Do you know her?" I wondered how difficult it would be to set up a time to talk to her.

"Not really. I think she has a daughter a few years younger than me, so I used to see her at basketball games."

"You played basketball?"

"I did." She pushed a curl off her forehead. "And I was good."

"I'll bet." I could picture that. The lady was competitive in most everything she did. Perhaps that was the secret to what had gotten her and the sheriff crosswise.

"So should we call the office and see if we can get in tomorrow to see her?"

"Great plan." She nodded agreement.

I called the number Dixie gave me and was surprised when the woman on the other end said Karla Farmer would see us first thing in the morning tomorrow. First thing for me meant eight or nine o'clock.

It turns out to Karla Farmer that meant seven a.m. Ugh.

* * * *

The Farmer family's business office was located at the edge of town on the highway we'd taken the night we followed Kenny. It's a plain metal building on the outside. A pole building, Dixie said it was called. It was tan and sort of blended into the corn field behind it, but the roof was a forest green. I noted the parking spots up front for the owners. There were signs that said, Farmer #1, Farmer #2, and Farmer #3. I wondered if there was an order implied or if the siblings handled it with a first to arrive system.

In any case, I didn't see Kenny Farmer's Cadillac in any of the spaces. We parked in the visitor-designated area and headed to the building.

As we walked in there was a reception desk which was manned, or rather womanned, by a young woman in a chambray shirt that said, "Farmer Industries" on it in bright blue thread.

"Hi, Phil." Dixie apparently knew the young woman. "We have an appointment with Karla Farmer."

"Have a seat over there." The girl pointed to a row of chairs. "I'll let her know you're here."

The interior of the place looked like any office. Tough slate-colored carpet, desks and cubicles. There were three doorways across the end to my left. (Don't ask me north, south, east, west. Remember that little directional challenge I have?) We were close enough that I could read the nameplates. Keith Farmer, Karla Farmer, and Kenny Farmer. The signs didn't give titles, but all of the doors were open except for Kenny's.

"She's ready for you." The young woman who'd greeted us motioned for us to follow her.

Minnie Silberhorn rushed in just as we were being ushered into Karla Farmer's office. She carried a stack of file folders.

"Hello, Minnie."

She looked up and then gave a faint, "Hello."

I would try to catch her after we'd met with Kenny's sister and ask about the sponsors' list. It would save me trying to get in touch with her.

Karla Farmer stood as we stepped through the doorway.

"Good morning." She had a firm handshake. "I assume you're here about the St. Ignatius Founders' Day celebration. I've already agreed to take care of the crowning of the queen and the flat bed for the stage. If you're selling advertising, Kenny handles that."

"Thanks for seeing us." I was in my element here. She was like many of the execs I'd dealt with in the corporate world. And their biggest interest was always time and money. And if you wanted their money, you'd better not waste their time.

"We know you're busy and we won't take much of your time." I got right to the point. "We're here about the cookbook."

"Cookbook?"

Yes, there's a committee putting together recipes from people in the community and compiling them into a Founders' Day cookbook. Your sister-in-law, Elsie, was on the committee."

I stumbled a bit as I noticed the change in her expression. Clearly not a fan, but whether of Elsie or the cookbook I wasn't sure.

"Harriet Hucklebee had indicated to us that the Farmer family might not support the project moving forward. When we spoke with Kenny, he said we should talk to you."

"I don't have any problem with the cookbook. Are we a sponsor?"

"Just initially," Dixie answered.

"The project is self-supporting. The sale of the cookbooks will cover the costs of producing them," I explained.

"Well, then." She stood. "Thanks for checking with me, but I don't see why we'd have any issue with it."

"We won't take any more of your time."

Dixie and I excused ourselves and headed out of Karla Farmer's office and toward the door.

"Wait." I stopped and turned back to the receptionist. "Is Minnie still here?"

"No, she's gone out on some errand for Kenny," the young woman replied. "Can I give her a message?"

"That would be great." And would save me a phone call. "Would you ask her to email the cookbook sponsor list? She has my email."

The receptionist made a note and promised to deliver it to Minnie when she returned. I thanked her and Dixie and I headed outside.

Once we were back in the Jeep, we looked at each other.

"So, I'm lost." I said. "You?"

She shook her head. "I have no idea what Harriet Hucklebee was talking about."

"Back to the office?" I asked.

She nodded. "Yes, let's get back to work."

We headed back to the office and picked up where we'd left off the day before. Still unclear on why Harriet had thought the Farmers had a problem going forward with the cookbook.

Chapter Fourteen

As I walked by Flashback, Disco's shop, I could see through the window and into the store. If Disco wasn't busy maybe I'd stop by and ask him about being at the retirement village where Greer lived the other day. It wasn't really any of my business, but I was puzzled by it and frankly feeling a little bad that I knew so little about him.

I stood and looked in the window. Disco stood behind the counter, his bright pink satin shirt a flash of color amidst the crowded racks of who knew what. There was a guy at the counter talking to him. I sure didn't want to jinx any potential sales. I could come back.

Wait a minute. I stopped in my tracks. It wasn't just any guy—it was the guy we'd seen the night we followed Kenny to the Weary Wanderer motel. What was he talking to Disco about?

I rushed back to the shop and yelled for Dixie. "Come quick."

"What is it?" She brushed flour-dusted hands on her apron.

"The big tattooed guy from the motel is in Disco's store." I tried to catch my breath. "I'm sure it's him. Come."

She followed me as we hurried down the block toward Flashback. Darn. The guy had just walked out and was leaving. He walked toward a gray van and got in the passenger side. I couldn't see who was driving as they backed out and then sped away.

Pulling open the psychedelic-colored door, Dixie and I entered Flashback. The Rolling Stones played in the background. Disco was on the phone at the register and so we waited.

I looked around the store. Had the guy been looking for something in particular?

I didn't think he seemed like the type for a life-sized E.T. or an unused Pink Floyd concert ticket, but the Shut Your Pie Hole button might be a possibility. Or the one next to it with a saying that was even more rude.

By the time Disco got off the phone, I was deciding between the "Chocolate doesn't ask silly questions. Chocolate understands." t-shirt and the "A balanced diet is chocolate in both hands" one. I hadn't realized he stocked new novelty items in addition to his memorabilia and I was impressed with the variety.

He moved aside a box that had been on the counter and as he set it on the floor I thought I spotted a frog statue inside that looked a lot like the one I'd taken to Greer the other day. He quickly fluffed the newspaper packing around so I couldn't see for sure.

"This is so cool," he said. "I can't believe you guys came to my place. Looking for something for your brother? This is rad." Grinning from ear to ear, he pulled out a vintage Chicago Cubs hat for Dixie to see. "Nineteen sixty-eight. Rare."

"Hirsh is a fan, but I'm not shopping for him right now."

"Too bad." His smile drooped a little.

"I'll come back closer to his birthday," she assured him. "Actually, we were wondering about that guy who was just in here."

"Guy?" He blinked and stared at us with a vacant look.

"Come on, Disco." Dixie had no patience. "The big burly tattooed guy who left shortly before we came in."

"Oh, that guy." He put the Cubs hat back in the display case.

"Yes, that guy."

"Dude wanted to know about some things I'm selling for Kenny Farmer."

"What kind of things?"

Disco stood for a while thinking, and I wasn't sure whether he couldn't remember what he had from Kenny or if he'd just spaced off for a bit.

"Mr. Farmer brought in some of his wife's things a week or so ago." He pulled at the sleeve of his hot pink shirt. "Collectibles, you know."

I didn't know, and I was sure Dixie didn't either.

"What kind of collectibles?" I asked. Elsie didn't seem the type for vintage records or unused rock concert tickets.

"She had these little figurines. Real little." He held his thumb and index finger about an inch apart. "Little bitty ceramic mouses, meeses, uh…"

"Mice," I supplied.

"Yeah, mice. A whole bunch of them." Disco cupped his hands. "I don't know much about those kinds of collectibles but I called my friend, Rik, up in the Twin Cities and he had a friend of a friend who does that kind of stuff. Turns out those crazy little guys are worth a bucket load of moolah."

"The guy who was just here doesn't seem like the type to be in the market for little mouse figures," Dixie noted.

Dixie's sarcasm was lost on Disco. "Nah, he was mostly fishing for intel about what Kenny Farmer brought in."

"What else did he say?"

Disco thought for a while. "He was kind of freaky-deaky, if you know what I mean. He wouldn't tell me if there was something in particular that he was after, something that he knew Kenny might be bringing in. I mean I could maybe find the item or items elsewhere you know."

"Did he give his name?" It would be a great breakthrough if he had.

"Nope." Disco shook his head. "No name. No phone number. I told him if I knew what he wanted, I could call him if it showed up, but he just said he'd check back. Do you know him?"

"No, but we've run into him before," I said. "Listen, if he comes in again, would you let us know."

"Sure thing." He went back to packing whatever it was he'd had on the counter when we came in.

I started to ask about the frog statue, but even if it was Greer's Mr. Froggie, it was none of my business.

Back at the office, I thought about what we'd seen at Disco's shop. If this guy was a drug dealer and he was stalking Kenny, we really should report it to the sheriff. And Disco had thought he acted suspicious. At least that was my interpretation of freaky-deaky. Disco had acted a little freaky himself, but with him it was hard to tell.

Still what could we say? "Say, Sheriff, there's this guy—we don't know his name, or where you can find him, or what he was doing at the motel, or why he was asking Disco about Kenny." Yeah, we knew little to nothing that would be helpful.

Dixie sat down to finish up making a list for me of which recipes would be highlighted. I could tell she was still preoccupied with the secrets her aunt was still keeping even though she was still a suspect. I guess we think we know someone and they still have secrets.

"Hon, I know you feel bad that Bertie didn't share whatever was going on with you, but we all keep secrets. It doesn't mean she doesn't trust you." I wanted to point out that she so far refused to tell me what the source of the friction between her and the sheriff was, but I wasn't going to harass her while she was down.

"I'm useless." She stood and started cleaning up. "I'm going home."

"That's a great idea." I picked up the list she'd left on the counter. "If you're okay with Max Windsor's pricing, I'm going to call him and let him know how many photos there will be. We should get him scheduled." I still thought he was underpriced, but who was I to say if he wanted to give us a deal. It could be that was his way of contributing to a civic project.

I hunted down his card which I'd put in the desk drawer. It felt good to move forward on some aspect of the cookbook. I didn't want to make Dixie feel any worse than she already did but we needed to keep moving forward if we were to meet the project deadlines.

"See you tomorrow," Dixie called out as she left. "I'll call you if I find out anything more."

I dialed the number on Max's card and he answered right away.

After explaining the reason for my call, I gave him the run down on the number of dishes we hoped to have photos of. He said he would stop by the next day and pick up the list, and I confirmed that would work for us. One of us would be in the shop. I kind of hoped it would be me.

As we hung up, the bell dinged and Minnie Silberhorn walked in.

"Is this a bad time?"

"Not at all. Can I get you something to drink? I'm afraid we only have coffee or water." I offered, thinking to myself that it might be just water if Dixie had cleaned the coffee pot before she left.

"No, that's okay." Minnie seemed distracted, her eyes staring at the wall behind me.

I turned and looked at the wall. No, nothing there but the various kitchen tools and gadgets we'd hung on the big hooks that had already been in place when we moved in.

"I haven't been in here since it was the pie place," she explained. "It seems about the same."

She was right. We'd done very little to the storefront. Cleaned, slapped on a coat of fresh paint, updated the kitchen, but that was about it. For us it was a workspace. I'd hoped to eventually create an area to meet with clients, but we'd never intended for it to be as public as it had been the past couple of weeks.

"Did you bring me the list?" I had hoped she'd send it via email but this would work too. If we were to stay on schedule, I needed to get busy making sure we had all the logos so I could get them to our layout person.

"Yes, I did." Her gaze shifted from the wall to my face.

She reached in her large tan bag and pulled out a spreadsheet and handed it to me. I looked it over.

"Hon, I'm sorry. This is the list of advertisers. What I need is the list of sponsors. I need to get them listed in the book and make sure we have logos and all that. Harriet thought you'd have the list."

"I do." Minnie brushed her bangs out of her eyes. "But the note said advertisers. I don't have the other list with me."

"That's okay. Maybe I can get it from you tomorrow." I had really wanted to get this done. "Now that I know where you work, I could stop by and pick it up."

She stepped around me and straightened the cheese grater so it hung straight.

"Do you like working for the Farmer family?" I asked. "It seems like a good job."

"It's okay." She gave me a funny look and then again shifted her gaze to the wall. "I don't really work for the family though, just Kenny."

"It must be hard for everyone right now with Elsie's death."

"I heard Karla Farmer telling you that things were fine between Kenny and Elsie and that the family thought highly of her." She eyed the tongs next to the grater as if they were next.

"That's not true?" I asked.

"It's not true at all. I mean Kenny couldn't talk about it yet, but they were getting a divorce."

"What?" I was floored. Now she really had my attention. "How do you know?"

"Well, when you work for someone you hear things."

"They talked about it in front of you."

"Not exactly, but I heard Kenny talking about it on the phone." She fidgeted with the handle of her purse. "That Elsie, she was a mean woman. And she was especially mean to Kenny. Always putting him down, always complaining, nothing was good enough for her."

"Do you think he might be involved with someone else?"

"What?" She stopped. "No." She shook her head again. "Kenny would never do anything like that. He wouldn't be with someone else while he was married. But I think he might have cared for someone. Maybe had someone else in mind, you know, after the divorce was final."

That made sense to me. If that someone was the one he'd been playing around with at his wife's funeral they may have been celebrating.

A shiver ran down my whole being at the thought.

"What is it?" Minnie looked at me.

"You don't think Kenny may have…" I couldn't bring myself to make the accusation without any proof. Especially since Dixie's Aunt Bertie had been falsely accused without any real proof.

"You think Kenny killed Elsie?" she gasped. "No way. He is the nicest, kindest, man. He could never do anything like that. But lots of people didn't like her. She was awful to people, got people fired, took credit for things other people did…" Her voice trailed off.

Yep, I'd bet Minnie had experienced that last one a time or two.

"But it's a big leap to go from not liking someone or hating the awful things they do, to killing them. There would have to be a bigger motive, I'd think."

"You think so?" She paused, her pastel blue eyes wide.

"I do."

Yes, Minnie, I do. And I think you might be working for a murderer.

She didn't say anything for a couple of minutes and I wondered if that thought had occurred to her as well.

I hadn't meant to scare her and I truly didn't believe she was in any danger. If Kenny *had* killed Elsie he'd probably gotten what he wanted. And what he wanted might have been a clear path to marry the woman he'd been fooling around with.

"Well, I'd better go." Minnie blinked and pushed up her glasses. "I can get the list of sponsors for you when I get to work tomorrow. Do you want me to bring it to you here or what?"

"Maybe I could pick it up from you?" She could email it to me but I thought going back to the Farmers' offices might give me the opportunity to find out more about Karla Farmer's take on Kenny and Elsie.

"Okay, it's in the files. I'll have it ready for you."

Minnie left as quietly as she'd come.

I closed the curtains before leaving and went to lock up, but as I approached the door Tina Martin tapped on the glass. Not wanting to be rude, I opened it to see what she wanted.

"I'm so glad I caught you." No fuchsia spandex today. She must have come from the real estate office. Her black and white polka-dot sundress looked snappy with bright red patent leather heels, but she still had her energy drink in hand.

"I was just getting ready to lock up." I hesitated. I didn't want to be rude and besides with her being in real estate maybe she knew something about Kenny and his plans for divorce. Or maybe something about this other woman Minnie had hinted about.

"This won't take long." She handed me an envelope with a red satin ribbon tied around it. "It's an invitation for you and Dixie to my house for a Looking Pretty party."

Oh, man. Now, I wished I'd been rude. I untied the ribbon and checked the date, hoping I had legitimate plans. It was a week away. I probably didn't.

"I don't know—" I began.

"Don't start with the excuses already." She wagged a bright red fingernail at me. "Hear me out."

I rubbed the glossy ribbon and waited. The woman was very persistent—you had to give her that.

"I know you're always saying you don't know enough people to have a party so this is the perfect solution." She smiled at me as if she'd just handed me the winning lottery ticket.

"This party is for the Founders' Day Committee." She raised her brightly manicured hands in a celebratory pose. "Everyone has worked so hard, and whether you liked her or not, what happened with Elsie has been hard on everyone. This is my way of sharing a relaxing evening with my fellow committee members."

I sighed. How did you say no to that? And when I thought about it, an evening with the group might bring forth some interesting tidbits. Though Kenny must have been careful, someone knew what the truth was. Was he having an affair? Did the man have a drug problem?

I was afraid it meant the purchase of Purple Passion eye shadow was in my future, but attending could be worthwhile. And, even if not for that, I didn't think as the company working on the cookbook, we got to opt out.

"Thank you," I said. "We'll be there."

Dixie was going to kill me.

"See you then," Tina took a sip from her drink container, waved good-bye, and headed down the sidewalk. I could only assume to drop off more invitations.

I locked the door and went out the back.

When I pulled into the drive it was a relief that Mrs. Pickett was nowhere in sight. But I'm afraid, in the words of my Aunt Cricket, I'd counted my chickens before they hatched because, as I approached my front door, there was a note tacked to it. And it wasn't an invitation to a neighborhood block party.

"Dear Ms. Calloway," it began. "I would very much appreciate it if you would remove the foul language from the side of your garage. It is disgusting and upsetting."

I left my bags on the front porch and went to look. Sure enough, the clean white clapboard side of Greer's garage had been used as a canvas. Red paint appeared to have been sprayed on in a hurry. I'd seen street art but this was far from that. It was a bunch of crude words and the vandals' rather graphic thoughts on school attendance. Given some of the misspellings of the swear words, they needed more schooling rather than less.

Well, I could see why Mrs. Pickett did not want to look at that. But she could have called the police, which was what I did as soon as I got back to the porch and located my phone.

The dispatcher at the Jameson County Sheriff's Office was very nice and said they'd send someone by to take a look. She said they wanted to see the graffiti before I painted over it because there had been some random vandalism in town. They would stop by tomorrow and take pictures and then give me the go ahead to paint.

I appreciated that she'd shared that intel. It looked like school kid stuff based on the content but it was still unsettling.

Sorry, Mrs. Pickett. You're going to have to look at it one more day. If you'd called me and let me know, we could have probably taken care of it today.

Although she was right and the graffiti was mine to take care of, I still resented the tone of her note. I debated about whether to knock on her door and let her know that I had to leave it until the sheriff's office had taken pictures, but before I could make up my mind my phone rang. I unlocked the door and stepped inside to answer.

"Sugar, honey, it's Greer." I was happy to hear her voice. She was always a welcome bright spot in my day.

"I'm so glad you called," I slipped off my shoes and sat on the couch. I explained to her about the graffiti and what the sheriff's office had said. "I'll paint over it just as soon as they tell me I can."

"There should be some white paint in the garage left from the last time I had it painted." Greer took everything in stride. "I hope they catch the little stinkers that are doing this."

"The sheriff's office said there'd been other incidents like this," I explained.

"I'd heard that," she said. "George in the kitchen said some car windows were broken out in his neighborhood."

"Seems like mostly kid stuff, but I agree, I hope they catch them." I propped my feet up on the coffee table. "But, I'm sorry, I just jumped in with the graffiti. You called me about something."

"Heavens to Betsy. Yes, I did." She laughed. "I wanted to tell you that I had a call from my son in the Twin Cities earlier today. You could've knocked me over with a feather. I thought something must be wrong but Spencer had just called to check on me. I told him about Elsie and all that. He said Kenny had called him about a month ago out of the blue and wanted to purchase life insurance on himself and Elsie."

"That's odd," I rolled my neck from side to side in an attempt to work out the kinks.

Ernest had come to stare at me. I think he thought he could telepathically direct me to the kitchen and his food dish.

"Why wouldn't Kenny have done that locally?" I wondered aloud.

"That's what I thought too." She stopped for a moment. "Unless he didn't want the local insurance agent telling tales. He knew Spencer from school and knew he was in insurance."

"That could be." I wondered. Could Kenny have seen the opportunity to have his cake and eat it too with Elsie out of the picture and a big check for him and his new honey?

"It seemed suspicious to me," she said. "I thought maybe you could share the info with Sheriff Griffin. Spencer didn't want me to. Didn't think I should get involved. I think the truth is he's afraid it will look bad if it comes from him. Like he talks about people's personal business."

I could kind of see his point, but if I told the sheriff I was pretty sure he would figure out where the information came from. "I'm afraid I don't have a lot of credibility with him, but I'm happy to try." I stood. "I assume if they 'found out' about this insurance policy that your son would be willing to talk to him."

"I'm sure he would," she said. "He wasn't hiding anything. It was simply no one had asked about it."

I could hear something ding in the background. "Is that your doorbell?"

"It's my oven, so I'd better let you go. Talk to you soon."

I put my phone down on the table and headed to the kitchen. It turned out Ernest *was* able to telepathically direct me to feed him.

He followed on my heels, meowing his irritation with my slowness to respond.

Getting cat food out of the cupboard and filling his dish, I mulled the idea of sharing the information with the sheriff. It seemed like it should have been Greer's son's place to do that, but if a tip would help to find the real killer, I was willing to try.

Chapter Fifteen

The next morning when I left, I glanced next door at Mrs. Pickett's house. I was going to drop by the office and then head over to the Farmer family's office to pick up that sponsor list from Minnie.

Dixie and Moto were already there and working when I arrived.

Let me clarify that, Dixie was working and Moto was sleeping. He lifted his head expectantly as I came in the door. I nodded and he trotted over for his treat.

Dixie shook her head. "You spoil him worse than I do."

"I know, but he's so darn cute." I patted his head. "And grateful. Don't get me wrong, I love Ernest, but he never looks at me like that. Demanding, yes. Grateful, not so much."

"I have coffee started." She pointed toward the coffeemaker. "I'm going to try to make up for lost time yesterday."

"I'll pour a cup when it's done." I got two mugs down from the cupboard. "I have a lot to tell you."

I carried my things back to the office and went to stand by the coffeemaker. I know, a watched pot and all that, but I was in desperate need of more caffeine.

When the coffee was ready I poured two cups.

"Okay, here's your fortification." I handed her one of the cups. "You keep working and I'll talk." I pulled up a stool.

I filled her in on the visit from Minnie and what she had told me about overhearing Kenny and Elsie arguing about a divorce. And then my phone call from Greer and the news that Kenny had taken out an insurance policy on Elsie shortly before she died.

"Wow," Dixie stopped kneading the bread dough she'd been working with. "I would hope that the sheriff's office would have looked into that possibility, but they've been so fixated on Aunt Bertie, maybe not."

There was a tap at the front door and I got up to see who it was. I'd been so focused on making sure I filled Dixie in on everything I hadn't thought to unlock it.

It was one of the sheriff's deputies. A young and serious one. I thought he looked familiar so he might have been there the day I'd found Elsie, but so much of that was a blur. I unlocked the door and let him in.

"You're Sugar Calloway?" he asked.

"I am." I nodded. "Can I get you a cup of coffee?"

"That's okay." He held up a hand. "I'm on duty."

I wanted to point out that I hadn't offered him a beer or a bribe. Just coffee. But he seemed so serious, I held my tongue.

"I've been by your house to look at the graffiti and have taken pictures of it for comparison to some of the other vandalism."

"And?" It hadn't seemed like the nasty comments were personal but I hoped for confirmation of that.

"We'll have to take closer look back at the office, but it looks like some of the other spray painting." His radio mic sputtered. "Anyway, you can go ahead and paint over that now. When I was there your next-door neighbor seemed to think I should. I explained to her we don't do that."

"Thank you for taking the time to stop by and let me know." I followed him to the door.

It was good to know I wasn't the only one not meeting Mrs. Pickett's expectations.

"What was that about?" Dixie asked when I returned to the kitchen. "I wanted to come out to see, but this dough was at a critical stage."

"I hadn't gotten to that part of my story yet." I refilled our cups and perched on the stool again.

I explained about coming home to the note from Mrs. Pickett and finding the graffiti on the side of the garage.

"I'd heard there'd been some problems." She expertly rolled the dough in her hands. "My brother said there had been graffiti sprayed on school buses parked at the middle school."

"I'd say from the words sprayed on my garage these kids are not fond of school." I took a sip of my coffee. "I sincerely hope middle school kids don't know some of these words. But I suppose I'm naïve to think that."

"I wouldn't call you naïve exactly." Dixie grinned. "But you may have been named Rosetta because of those permanent rose-colored glasses you wear."

Ignoring her comment, I gathered up our cups and carried them to the sink. "I'm going to run out to the Farmers' offices and pick up that sponsor list from Minnie. Is there anything you need while I'm out?"

"Not that I know of." She placed the dough in a big bowl and covered it. "I'll call you if I think of anything."

"Sounds good." I retrieved my purse and my keys.

I was halfway to the Farmers' offices before I remembered I'd forgotten to fill Dixie in on the Looking Pretty makeup party invitation.

Maybe a Freudian slip.

* * * *

I found the Farmer family's offices without any trouble at all. (Okay, I used my GPS but don't tell Dixie.) The parking lot was a bit busier than when Dixie and I had come for our early morning meeting with Kenny's sister. Two of the reserved spots for the family's cars were filled. Neither car was Kenny's Cadillac.

I parked in the visitor area and then went inside. It was the same receptionist and I let her know I was there to see Minnie.

"She's out on an errand but should be right back," she explained. "If you'd like to have a seat, I'm sure she won't be long."

"No problem." I settled into one of the chairs in a corner of the waiting room. I pulled out my phone and tapped on my notes app. Looking through where we were and what we still had to get done, I saw we were in pretty good shape, given all that had transpired. I saw at the bottom of my list a note to follow up with a couple of other groups that had expressed an interest in a cookbook project. I needed to do that in the next couple of days. If they were sincerely interested, they might move on to someone else if they didn't hear. And we needed to move directly to the next project once we were done with this one.

"What am I supposed to do with this?" A young man tossed a piece of paper on his co-worker's desk.

"What did she tell you to do?" The girl looked up.

"She said, and I quote, 'No more. We are done paying for my brother's lavish lifestyle. He can pay his own bills.'"

"Then I guess you have your answer. Don't pay it." The girl went back to her computer screen.

I shrunk a little further into my chair. I didn't think Karla Farmer would be happy one of her employees was quoting her where anyone who walked in could hear.

I few minutes late, Minnie came through the outside door and spotted me. "Oh, hello. I have that list of sponsors for you. Follow me."

I followed her. As she walked past, the agitated young man from earlier handed her a file and said, "Karla said no more expenses for Kenny. He's cut off."

She frowned at him but took the folder. Once back at her desk, which was just outside Kenny's office, she retrieved an envelope from a drawer and handed it to me.

"Here, you go, all the sponsors." She dropped into her chair. "Sorry for the confusion yesterday. Harriet was not clear about what you needed."

"No problem at all." I hesitated.

Her desk phone rang and she quickly picked it up. "Hello, Tina. No, he is not in and I don't know when to expect him." She listened for a few more minutes. "He's been through a lot lately, so I don't know when he'll be ready to start looking at houses again." She paused. "Or if he will. Good-bye."

Minnie hung up the phone and looked at me expectantly.

Flustered to be caught to blatantly eavesdropping, I said I'd see her at the next committee meeting and hurried out.

* * * *

Back at the office, I shared what I'd overheard with Dixie.

"I think we'd better tell the sheriff what we know." We should have probably come clean before now, but there was nothing to be gained by waiting.

Dixie was silent. I was sure she was weighing the options. I waited.

"Okay, let's get it over with then." She tossed the apron she'd been about to put on toward one of the stools.

"You could go and I could stay here," I suggested. "We don't both need to go."

"No way," She picked up her purse, "This is your idea, you heard the conversation, you're coming."

The Jameson County Sheriff's Office was at the edge of town. I think the northern edge, but don't hold me to that. Dixie drove since she knew where it was and we were there in an all too short five minutes.

When we walked in the door we were greeted by a young uniformed deputy who stood behind a long faux marble counter.

"Can I help you, ma'am?"

Man, I hate that. It makes me feel so old. I know it's very polite and all, and I should be happy about that, but I don't think of myself as being a ma'am.

"Hi, Butch." Dixie leaned on the counter. "We're here to see the sheriff. Is he in?"

"I can check." Which I was almost certain meant he needed to find out if the sheriff wanted to see us or not. "What are your names?"

"Dixie Spicer and Sugar Calloway."

He disappeared and I turned to Dixie. "You really do know everyone in town, don't you?"

"Not everyone." She grinned. "He's the younger brother of someone I went to high school with. Quite a lot younger if I remember right. Always wanted to be a cop since he was little."

"Ms. Spicer, Ms. Calloway." Butch was back. "The sheriff will see you now."

He opened a door that led down a hallway to a big corner office. Sheriff Griffin sat behind a large oak desk, a serious expression on his face.

"Good morning." He didn't smile. "Can I offer you a coffee?"

I started to accept but Dixie said, "Never mind the pleasantries, Terry."

"Okay, Dixie, have it your way."

Why did I think there was a double meaning to that statement?

"We need to tell you a couple of things." Dixie took a deep breath. "I assume now that my aunt is back in town and has explained her absence that she's not longer your prime suspect?"

"Bertie is back, but I can't say she has explained where she went and why." His mouth was a thin grim line. "Your aunt has been very uncooperative. Which makes me think she has something to hide."

"Think what you want."

"Bertie doesn't really have a motive though, does she?" I asked. "I mean being upset over a scone recipe isn't a murder motive, right?"

The sheriff nodded. "You said you needed to tell me a couple of things." He looked at Dixie, his jaw tight.

She looked at me.

"The night we talked to you, when we were parking on Kenny Farmer's street," I began, "we started to leave but just then Kenny got in his car."

"And we kind of followed him," Dixie finished my sentence.

"You kind of followed him where?" He gave her a hard look.

"To a motel in Churchville." Dixie didn't look away.

"The Weary Wanderer Motel," I added.

"Sugar had seen him with someone at Elsie's funeral and we thought he was probably meeting her at the motel."

"But he left, uhm, really quickly. Really quickly," I repeated.

The sheriff crossed his arms. "And..."

"And after he left we knocked on the door of the motel room and a guy answered and claimed Kenny had never been there." Dixie crossed her own arms as well.

"Good grief!" the sheriff exploded. "What in the Sam Hill did you think you were doing? He could have been armed. He could have had a knife."

One of the deputies stopped by the door. The sheriff walked over and slammed it shut.

"He didn't have a knife but he did have a knife tattoo," I explained as the sheriff paced back and forth from one side of the office to the other. "Right here." I pointed at my forearm but the sheriff wasn't looking.

We waited for him to calm down and stop pacing. He showed great restraint. I think he really would've liked to punch the wall.

Finally, he dropped into his swivel chair and looked at us. "Please tell me there's not more."

"There a lot more," Dixie said evenly. "Tell him about seeing the guy at Disco's store."

I recounted seeing the guy from the motel at Flashback and explained that Disco didn't get a name or phone number. "I saw the van pull away, but I didn't get a license number. I'm sorry about that."

"Disco said the guy was mostly interested in what Kenny had been selling of Elsie's," Dixie added.

"Also, I think it's worth mentioning that we've heard Kenny had asked Elsie for a divorce and the discussion had not gone well."

"Who shared that little tidbit?" The sheriff leaned back.

"Do I have to tell him?" I asked Dixie.

"Up to you." She shrugged.

"I don't really want you questioning her," I explained. "She'll know I was the one who told you."

"Minnie Silberhorn?" he asked.

"How did you do that?" I'd been sure there were a lot of possibilities on who could have shared the gossip but he'd zeroed in on Minnie right away.

"Stands to reason." He tipped back in his chair. "She's got access to all that goes on, given her job."

"She does," I agreed. "And though she's convinced Kenny would never do anything so awful, I think she's a bit naïve."

"I won't tell her I heard it from you." He rocked forward and placed his arms on the desk. "Unless I have to. I'm surprised she'd say anything bad about Kenny, though. She's been a devoted employee for years. Sticks up for him whether he deserves it or not."

"I don't think she thought she was saying anything bad about him. I think she was trying to get me to understand that Elsie was not...well liked. And that there were any number of people who are happy they don't have to deal with her anymore."

"That part's true. But it's a long way from murder."

"That's exactly what I said to Minnie. You don't think she's in danger, do you?"

He didn't answer right away. "No, I don't."

"Then today when I was at the Farmer family's offices—" I began.

"Did you follow someone there, or just decide to go question someone?" The sheriff's dark eyes snapped.

"I went there to pick up a paper from Minnie related to the cookbook project, but while I was there I overheard talk between some of the employees that Karla, Kenny's sister, had cut him off financially."

"So, there you have it." Dixie spread out her hands. "Everything we know."

"I sincerely hope that's everything." He leaned forward. "You are not to do anything else. You are not to ask any questions. If you see that van," he looked at me, "you jot down the license number, you call me, you do not approach it. You do not talk to this guy that you've seen. You walk the other way."

"And..." He took a breath. "If you can get your aunt to give up the information and where she was and why, that'd be helpful. I'd like to eliminate her. I really would. But bottom line, she's not helping much."

"There was one more thing." I'd forgotten to mention the employee that'd been fired. "I was told that Elsie had been responsible for the firing of an employee, Joey Waters, who backed into her Cadillac. I've been told he sort of went downhill after that and that his mother had threatened Elsie."

"We've already talked to Teresa Waters." He stood. "Anything else?"

"No, I think that about covers it." I met his gaze.

Dixie was staring at a spot across the room.

He crossed the room and stood silently for a few minutes, his hand on the doorknob. "I am dead serious about this, so listen carefully." He paused. "This is not murder mystery dinner theater. This is real and you have put yourselves in real danger. No more. Got it?"

Neither Dixie nor I answered.

You'll be happy to hear that we exited with our dignity intact. Though from the looks of the faces of the deputies in the front when we walked out, I think they were impressed we'd survived the dressing down.

Once back at the shop, I sank into my desk chair in relief. I felt so much better knowing the sheriff knew everything we knew.

Well, except that part about the rat poison.

I offered to get lunch for us so Dixie could get back to the test recipes.

There was a new waitress working at the Red Hen. She must have had some experience because she moved easily from table to table. I didn't recognize her, but I knew so few people. Dixie might know her. The girl wore her collar up, which nearly concealed a tattoo on the side of her neck. It was good to see that Toy had finally found someone interested in the job.

I had called in our order earlier, so I checked in at the register. I have to admit I was a little disappointed that it was ready. I'd been looking forward to sitting down at one of the tables to wait and seeing what other tidbits I could find in the newspapers under the glass.

As I walked back to the office, I looked around the square in admiration. So many small towns were struggling, and yet St. Ignatius managed to stay vibrant. I guess it was because it had changed with the times. The era where everyone in town shopped at places around the square was long gone. Probably many in town bought a lot of things online. But the storefronts had changed and now carried things you couldn't necessarily buy online.

"I'm back," I called as I opened the front door.

"Good because I'm so hungry I could eat a horse." Dixie came out from the back wiping her hands on a towel. "I never thought I could get tired of cooking, but this project may get me there."

"Usually you have breaks in the cooking, don't you?" I asked. "When you do your State Fair entries, I suppose you don't. But otherwise you do, right?"

"That's true." She reached for one of the bags I carried. "I may take a break once this book is done and not cook for a couple of weeks."

"I bet not."

"You're probably right." She reached in pulled out a handful of French fries. "They were really fast. I didn't expect you back so quickly."

"Toy has a new waitress so Marge was back working in the kitchen. I'm sure that helped," I answered.

"The new girl anyone we know?"

"Not that I know." I laughed. "You probably do,"

"What's she look like?"

"You know I'm not good at ages, but she's younger." I chomped on a fry. "Thin, long hair, pulled back. I'm not helping you any am I?"

"Not at all."

"Oh, I know." I suddenly remembered the one distinctive trait I'd notice. "She has a tattoo on her neck here." I pointed at the side of my neck. "I'm not sure what it is, maybe a dragon."

"Doesn't ring a bell." Dixie shrugged.

We finished up our lunches and then went our separate ways and got to work.

Chapter Sixteen

Dixie had cooked up a batch of red velvet cupcakes, one of the cookbook entries, and I decided to take some of them to The Good Life for Greer. She would get a kick out of having something she could share with her friends. And I needed to explain that I'd somehow misplaced the strawberry cruet.

The day was overcast and so I wasn't surprised not to find Greer outside. I rang her doorbell and heard a yell from inside, "Come in."

She was settled into her recliner, feet up, a book in hand. She picked up a crimson ribbon and marked her place before laying the book aside.

"A good book?" I asked.

"*Murder Is Easy.*" She held up the book.

"An Agatha Christie book?" I asked. "That's kind of tame for you, isn't it?

"Maybe." Greer smiled. "But I watched this on television last night and it didn't seem like the book at all. At least not how I remembered it. So, I had to dig it out and see if that was really the case or if I was losing it."

"I'm sure you're not losing it." I sat down on the couch. "But I might be."

"You?"

"I have to confess something crazy."

I described the scenario. I'd gone to the attic and couldn't find the cruets, the lights had gone out. When they came on I was startled by the clown face and dropped it. It hadn't broken but when I set it back on the shelf I found the box with the cruets. I remembered taking them downstairs and washing them, but now they were missing.

"And, Greer, I would swear that after I washed them I put them right by the door. You know that little table that fits perfectly in the alcove."

"Honey, don't you worry about it at all." Greer clasped my hands. "It's not a big deal. Those things are just trinkets."

"Here's the thing though. I can't find them. I looked around to see if I'd simply thought I'd put them there. They are nowhere to be found."

"Well, that is odd." Greer closed her book.

"I even went back up to the attic and looked around. Nothing."

"A mystery." She smiled.

"I'm going to look again, but I wanted you to know and I wanted to drop off the cupcakes." I felt like I'd let her down.

"They look tasty." She touched a finger to the frosting of one.

"When is your book club? Maybe you can share them with the group."

"It's tomorrow and they'd be the right amount."

"Good. They're delicious, as is everything Dixie bakes, so I was hoping someone would be able to enjoy them."

"We will definitely do that."

"Okay, I won't keep you. I'm going to go home and try to figure out what I did with your cruets."

"Please don't worry about it, my dear." She waved a hand. "Before you go, I wanted to mention to you. You'd asked if there'd been any rumors about Kenny Farmer having an affair and Bunny says the rumor is that he'd been seen with Tina Martin, the real estate woman."

"I'm sure he was seen with her." I nodded. "When I was at the offices earlier today, Minnie, his assistant, said Tina had been showing him houses."

"Sugar, honey." Greer looked over her glasses at me. "I think Tina was showing him more than houses."

"Oh." I gave Greer a kiss on the cheek and promised to let her know if I found the missing cruets. In the meantime, she thought maybe I should bring the clown mask so she could take a look at it. She wasn't sure she remembered having a clown mask.

Who was I to judge? I couldn't remember what I'd done with those strawberry cruets.

I thought about the possibility of Tina as Kenny's affair as I walked to my car. But it couldn't have been her at the church. I'd seen her earlier when she sang, and I'd have remembered that dress with the cherries on it.

Wait. When she sang, she'd had on a choir robe. It could have been her.

I needed to call Dixie as soon as I got home.

Chapter Seventeen

"I cannot believe you talked me into this." Dixie picked up her purse and followed me out to the Jeep. "I had avoided getting caught in Tina Martin's pretty web all this time and now you lead me right into it."

"I am not going alone to face that group," I said. "Besides who knows what gossip we'll pick up with this crowd."

"Can't you think up a different way to torture me?" Dixie frowned.

"Just an hour," I promised. "That's all we have to stay and then I swear we'll go."

We arrived at Tina's modern two-story in the newer part of town in no time. I think Dixie was wishing for a longer trip. There was a festive wreath on the door with a mirror in the middle. A bright red ribbon proclaimed, "You're Looking Pretty today!"

We could hear a cackle of voices from inside. It sounded like the party was in full swing.

"Just an hour," I reminded Dixie as I pushed the doorbell. "And it's for a good cause."

Tina answered the door and shrieked her hello. "I am so excited you're here!"

Maybe she'd had a few too many of her special energy drink. She grabbed our hands and pulled us into the fray.

I spotted most of the Founders' Day Cookbook committee members. Harriet, Dot, Toy, who had her new waitress with her. Even Minnie, who I could swear I'd never seen with a stitch of makeup. They'd all probably been guilted into accepting Tina's invitation just like we had.

"Why don't you girls help yourself to some food and drink, and then you can take a look at the display table?" She pointed toward a table stacked with cosmetic products. "The eye shadow I'm wearing this evening is Aegean Isle, one of our new colors."

Up close it appeared that she'd applied everything on the display table to her face.

I swear I have never seen that much makeup on a woman. (Okay, once. But that was a drag queen, so not technically a woman.)

"I've got to run upstairs for more order forms." Her face was flushed with the excitement of, I could only assume, fresh victims and big orders. "You help yourself to some snacks."

The snacks were the kind you pour out of a bag and dipped out of a plastic container.

"Seriously?" Dixie rolled her eyes. "She couldn't stir a few ingredients together?"

I glanced around, hoping no one was close enough to hear.

"Shh." I held a finger to my lips. "We don't want to get thrown out before we have a chance to look around." I picked up a few chips and a ladled half a spoonful of dip onto a pink cocktail plate. Okay, so tasting all those great homemade recipes Dixie'd made had turned me into a bit of food snob too.

"Fine, I'll be good." She picked up a celery stick. "What's the strategy?"

"You see if you can locate Tina and once I know you have her busy, I'll see if I can find any evidence of an affair," I suggested. "Maybe even *The Dress.*"

"Good idea," she whispered. "I don't see her right now but—"

"There you are!" Tina had come up behind us. "I see you have snacks. I'm sure you could have done better. You two with your fancy recipes and all."

So maybe she had heard Dixie's earlier comments. I frowned at my business partner. If I hadn't felt so bad about being caught disparaging our hostess's food, I might have been more on guard. As it was, I wasn't on my toes and found myself being led to the cosmetics table along with Dixie.

"Everyone." Tina clapped her hands. "I want to show you some techniques that anyone can use." She made sure her smile hit each person in the room.

"Let's start with Dixie Spicer and her awesomely gorgeous red hair and pale complexion." Tina brandished a large makeup brush. "Dixie here has volunteered to be my model for the evening."

I was certain Dixie had not volunteered. Maybe it was payback for her comments about the lame snacks.

"Just take a seat here." Tina had pulled up a stool.

"But—" Dixie looked at me.

I shooed her toward the stool. It would be the perfect way to make sure Tina was busy while I looked around.

"First off, you want a porcelain but not pale look, and to get that you need the complexion primer." She opened a jar and slathered Dixie's face with a substance. "If you want to hide freckles or other imperfections, you can use the Looking Pretty Super Gone concealer."

I didn't think Dixie saw her freckles as imperfections. I sure didn't, but I gave her a hard look. Hoping I'd telegraphed that she should stay in place.

Tina moved quickly from product to product. In a matter of minutes Dixie wore some of everything from the table on her face.

"Now doesn't she look wonderful?" Tina asked the group who continued to munch crackers and celery, their attention on Dixie's transformation. "Doesn't she look ready for a date?"

I glanced around at the assembly. Dixie looked ready to choke Tina.

"Let me get a picture of this." The hostess held up her phone. Dixie clapped a hand on Tina's arm and lowered it.

"First, can you show me how you did this?" Dixie pointed to her face. Her sarcasm was lost on Tina and truly on the rest of the room as well.

"Of course," Tina answered. "I went a little fast and it can be a bit confusing. Let me show you the step by step."

Once Dixie had Tina busy answering questions, she motioned to me and I immediately headed upstairs to the second level. I peeked in the first open door. Bathroom. I slipped in and back out. Nothing there. Then I hurried to the next closed door. Linen closet. I tip-toed farther down the hall and stuck my head inside a bedroom. This had possibilities. Gauzy curtains, a bright flowery wallpaper, and pillows everywhere. I didn't want to flip on a light because my excuse, if discovered, was going to be that I was looking for the bathroom.

I crossed the room and quietly slid open the door to the closet. I listened. Still snippets of conversation from downstairs drifted in, but no one coming. I pushed aside a few items, sliding the hangers across the rod and noting the groupings by length and then by colors. Though Tina was a clothes horse, I had to give it to her she was an organized one.

Then I spotted it. The white dress with bright red cherries on it.

It *had* been Tina that day at the church. The picture of Kenny with a woman in his arms flashed back into my brain. What nerve. And at his wife's funeral no less. I thought of him shoveling food in his mouth and talking about her the day we'd taken food to his house. I could almost smell his cologne.

Wait a minute. I could actually smell his cologne. I lifted the dress to my nose and sniffed. That embrace had been so tight, it was likely the scent had transferred. Heck it was so tight, they'd probably transferred DNA.

My mind raced. Now that we'd confirmed that there was something going on between them, how did we convince Sheriff Griffin that he needed to concentrate his investigation on Kenny? I could hear the sheriff in my head. Just because they were having an affair didn't mean Kenny had killed Elsie. But if you put it with the denied divorce, the life insurance, the disposal of her prized possessions…Well, it was just fishy. Probably not enough for the sheriff or the DCI, but hopefully enough to get him investigating.

I closed the closet and turned to leave. The bed was unmade and there were pillows scattered around that were the same pattern as the wallpaper. The light from the open doorway landed on the white nightstand. There was a half-empty drink container of Tina's special energy drink and a bowl of apples. She was devoted to her healthy lifestyle.

Tina should not have been messing around with a married man. At some level I felt bad she was involved with a guy who was such a creep and most likely a murderer. Maybe when Kenny went to prison she'd find someone else.

I peeked out and still didn't see anyone. I could hear the chatter of voices from downstairs so hopefully I was home free. Stepping into the hallway, I had started to pull the door closed when I spotted something on the floor. Good grief, had I dropped something from the closet?

Leaning into the room, I quickly flipped the light on.

I clapped a hand over my mouth. Kenny Farmer was not going to be going to prison. He was on the floor tangled in Tina's bright flowered bedspread, face up, his sightless eyes wide open.

I flipped the light off and raced down the hallway. Peeking over the bannister, it didn't appear anyone was looking my way. I raced down the stairs, spotted Dixie who was talking with Dot Carson.

I grabbed Dixie's hand and tugged her into a corner. I couldn't speak.

"Did you find the dress?"

I nodded.

"Good. Can we go now?"

I shook my head and finally found my voice. "I also found Kenny Farmer."

"His stuff?"

"No, him. The real him." I gulped. "And I think he's dead."

"What?" Dixie's raised voice attracted the attention of a few ladies clustered around the makeup table.

"Shhh." I pulled her a bit farther away. "I'm not sure what to do."

"Did you check to make sure he wasn't just asleep?"

"He wasn't asleep." I tugged her toward the front door. "Listen, we need to call a doctor or 9-1-1 or the sheriff or somebody." I knew I was babbling but couldn't seem to pull my thoughts together. I also knew a doctor was not going to help Kenny.

"Maybe we should go upstairs and check and make sure before we—" She was interrupted by an earsplitting scream.

I looked around. Tina had disappeared. My money was on that she'd gone back upstairs. Maybe for more order forms again and discovered Kenny.

I started toward the stairs with Dixie on my heels. Tina appeared at the top.

"Call 9-1-1," she gasped. "Oh, Lord. Call an ambulance." Her cell phone was clasped in her hand so she must have thought to make a call herself, but at that moment seemed incapable of doing so.

Dixie pulled her own cell from her pants pocket and dialed. I could hear her explaining that we had an emergency, and she didn't know what kind. I'd already reached the top of the stairs, and I put my hand on Tina's arm. She collapsed in my arms and wailed.

Dixie was now beside us and I tried to keep from dropping Tina on the floor. Dixie gave me a questioning look. I pointed down the hallway to the door that now stood open.

Dixie shook her head.

I pointed again.

"Tina, let's have you sit down somewhere." I maneuvered her into the bathroom, sat her on the edge of the tub, and opened a cupboard. Taking a wash cloth and dampening it with cold water, I offered it to her. Her mascara and Aegean Isle eye shadow had melted into a river of tears that slid down her cheeks.

I looked away long enough to poke my head out to check on Dixie. When I looked back, Tina had slid to the floor in a heap.

"I have to go check and see if the ambulance is here," I said to her.

She nodded.

I popped back out into the hallway and Dixie handed me the phone. "You take over with staying on the line. I'm going to go downstairs and see if I can rein in the chaos down there."

I took the phone. "Hello?"

"Yes, stay on the line. We have paramedics on the way."

"I don't know that's the right choice at this point," I said.

"What do you mean?" the dispatcher asked. And then without waiting for an answer. "They should have arrived now."

I could hear Dixie at the front door letting the rescue crew in. "I'm hanging up," I told the lady on the phone.

In St. Ignatius, Fire and EMS are all volunteers, so they were probably known to most of the ladies in attendance. If Kenny Farmer had in fact had a heart attack in Tina Martin's bedroom, and that was my best guess, that fact was not going to be a secret for long.

The two medics climbed the stairs. I pointed them to the bedroom. I couldn't hear their conversation, but I could tell there was no scramble to try to revive Kenny. I checked back in the bathroom. Tina still sat on the floor. She'd stopped crying but sat staring sightlessly, her polka-dot dress crumpled around her legs.

"Can I get you anything?" I asked.

She shook her head. I started back out to the hall and almost ran directly into Sheriff Terry. See now Dixie had me doing it too.

"Whoa," he said. "What are you doing here?"

"I—uh, found Kenny," I mumbled.

"I thought Tina found Kenny."

"She did, but I'd already found him." I waved him on. "Long story."

He stood for a couple of minutes like he wanted to say something but then moved down the hall to where the medics were waiting for him. Then he came back.

Looking into the bathroom at Tina, he said, "I'm going to need to talk to her." He started to leave again and then stopped. "And you."

I looked back at Tina. She'd begun to shiver. I found the linen closet again and pulled out a blanket and tucked it around her. I wasn't sure what else to do for her, maybe the paramedics needed to check her over.

"I'll be right back." I touched her arm. I was sure I could find some tea or water for her.

When I got downstairs, it was clear that Dixie had not given any details. Other than to assure the guests that Tina was okay and that the ambulance was not for her.

"What's going on, Sugar?" Dot stood at the foot of the stairs.

"I need to get Tina some water." I avoided Dot's question.

The other ladies were seated around the room. Their eyes were wide and bright. And I didn't think it was Tina's Looking Pretty eye brightener.

"I'll make coffee." Dixie headed to the kitchen. I started to follow her.

"I really need to be going." It was the dark-haired girl with the neck tattoo from the diner. Being new in town and not knowing anyone probably made it even more awkward for her.

I didn't think there was any reason any of us had to stick around. Except maybe me, now that I'd confessed to the sheriff that I was again the dead-body-finder.

Speaking of, I could hear him clumping down the stairs. He was followed by the two medics who headed outside. They weren't going to leave Kenny there were they? My question was answered when they returned with a stretcher.

"If everyone would stay put for a few more minutes, I'd appreciate it." The sheriff looked around the room.

"I need to go," JoJo (that was her name) said again.

"Not yet." He was firm.

Dixie came in from the kitchen with a tray of cups and a full coffee pot. She placed them on the dining room table.

Sheriff Terry stopped when he saw her.

"I'll be right back." He turned on his heel.

The ladies gathered around as Dixie offered coffee. I headed to the kitchen and opened the refrigerator. I moved three more bottles of Tina's special energy drink that were lined up on the top shelf like Buckingham Palace guards.

Probably not the best option for her right now. Locating a bottle of plain water, I took it, slipped past the group in the living room, and climbed the stairs to Tina. She thanked me.

When I returned the sheriff was back in the living room, his face grim. He held a sheet of paper and a pen.

"I'm going to need for everyone to provide their name and contact information." He handed the pen and paper to Minnie who was standing closest to him.

"What's going on Sheriff?" she asked.

"Kenny Farmer has died," he explained.

"No!" If Tina's scream had been ear-splitting, Minnie's was otherworldly. "That can't be." She collapsed on him.

I felt so sorry for her. I'm sure Sheriff Terry had forgotten that Minnie worked closely with Kenny, and I could see on his face that he'd misjudged the impact of delivering the news.

My eyes were on Minnie and the sheriff, but I could hear the ripple of a gasp that went around the room. I looked over at Dixie who was still handing out coffee.

"So, if you'll just write down your information when the paper reaches you." The sheriff took the pen and paper from Minnie and handed it to the next person. "In the meantime, can someone tell me what you all were doing here?"

"Tina was having a Looking Pretty party," someone answered. It might have been Toy.

"A what?"

"Makeup, cosmetics. Tina is a Looking Pretty consultant." I pointed to the folding table that held all the bottles and jars.

He still looked confused.

"She sells makeup."

"Okay. And did anyone go upstairs during the party?"

"Tina did." Toy George spoke up. "She had to get more order forms."

"And I did," I said quietly to the sheriff.

"Why?" He pinned me with his gaze.

"I—it's…" I stopped. "I'd prefer to tell you privately."

He gave me a hard look, but didn't press the issue. "So, Tina went upstairs but only just before you all heard her scream?"

"No," Dot Carson said. "She went upstairs earlier and then again right before she screamed. To get more order forms," she clarified.

The others nodded. "So, none of you were upstairs at all?"

"I was." Dixie spoke up. "But just so I could call. Sugar was dealing with Tina."

Sheriff Terry turned away, his back to us all, and said something under his breath.

I wasn't sure what it was that he said, but it didn't really matter: I got the point he was completely out of patience.

Chapter Eighteen

I think I'd used the expression herding cats to describe the Founders' Day Cookbook Committee from time to time. The committee meeting the day after Kenny's death was a lot more like herding feral cats.

Harriet tried to get everyone to quiet down a couple of times but the group would quiet down for a bit and then pretty soon whispered conversation would turn into this yowling sound. There was no pie served today to keep them busy and everyone helped themselves to coffee or tea. Toy was short-handed because JoJo, her new waitress, had not shown up for work. After she'd been so nice to the girl, too. According to Dot, Toy had even given JoJo an advance to help her out.

Needless to say, Tina was not in attendance but she was the topic of every conversation. Once again, I found myself seated by Minnie. She sat head down, moving pens, flipping pages, not looking up and seemingly not listening to the chatter. We sat for a while in silence. She looked like she was still in shock. And I felt like I was.

I wanted to ask how she was doing. The woman had been absolutely devastated last night. She didn't make eye contact though so I didn't want to intrude. I know from experience that it can be more difficult sometimes when people are kind to you. Sometimes you need to just continue dealing with the day-to-day to get you through. I imagined for her it added another layer that she probably didn't know if she was going to have a job. With Kenny gone, her position with the company might be in jeopardy. When Dixie and I had been at the Farmer offices that day, it was clear that wrangling Kenny and his schedule was her one and only responsibility.

"Committee members." Harriet finally raised her voice to the point that she got everyone to stop talking. "We simply must get through this agenda." She turned to point at me. "Sugar, can you begin with a status update."

I stood and spoke loudly so that I could be heard over the few who continued despite Harriet's attempt to bring some order to the meeting. "I can. The recipes have all been finalized and the layout work is done. Later this week, we'll complete the photos, and then those will also be added." I took a deep breath. "As you know, we've allotted some space for town history. With Mr. LeBlanc's help and cooperation, we've stayed with the original number of pages."

"Thank you." Harriet dismissed me. "Minnie, can you give us an update on sponsors."

Minnie didn't look up from her notepad. I touched her arm and she jumped.

"What?" She pushed her hair out of her eyes and looked around.

"The sponsor list," I prompted.

"Oh, sorry." She flipped to a page in her notebook and read off the businesses who were underwriting the cookbook project. The Farmer family was the biggest sponsor and so far, I'd heard nothing to the contrary, but again something we probably needed to confirm.

"Thank you." Harriet moved on. "Bertie, you're in charge of pre-orders, right?"

Dixie's aunt stood. "Yes, and I've got order forms here for everyone to take. You should try to get as many pre-orders in advance as you can. I need them turned in in two weeks, so I have time to put them in a spreadsheet. Big orders we'll get to you. Otherwise, people can pick them up at our table at the celebration."

"Will you be needing to mail any?" Dot Carson asked.

"Well, I don't know yet, Dot." Bertie looked over her glasses at the postmistress. "They haven't ordered them, thus the need for filling out the pre-orders."

"Now, let's see. Who was supposed to be in charge of signing up people to man the table?" Harriet consulted her notes. "Good grief." She stopped and suddenly the room got quiet.

"It's Tina." She swallowed hard. "Who is not here today. I don't know if, I don't suppose we'll be able to get her notes…" her voice trailed off.

"How about we start a new sign-up sheet?" I tore a page from my notebook. "What are the times?"

"From nine o'clock in the morning to nine at night," Jimmie LeBlanc spoke up. "That's on Saturday. And then noon 'til six on Sunday. Because the Founders' Day planners didn't want to interfere with church services."

"Okay," I said. "Let's send this sign-up sheet around." I quickly wrote out the available shifts and handed the sheet to Minnie. "Maybe you could take the handwritten one and put it in a spreadsheet for us." I leaned down to speak to her. I didn't want to commit her to something if she wasn't up to it. Clearly, she was grieving over Kenny Farmer, and I thought it might be better for her to be busy right now.

Minnie looked up and nodded.

"If you'll pass the sheet to Minnie once you've signed up for your time, she has volunteered to put our info into a spreadsheet. How should we handle the people who aren't here today?" I asked, looking in Harriet's direction.

She still looked a little dumbstruck but quickly recovered. "I'll get in touch with the others and can have them sign up, if you'll let me know when we have gaps."

She regained control and got through the rest of the details in short order.

Everyone filed out, still talking about Kenny's death and I wasn't too surprised to catch snippets of conjecture over whether this might be a murder rather than a heart attack. I guess it's a reasonable jump to think so, after all, two deaths in the same family so close together. But I also caught bits of conversation that pointed to Tina as the possible killer.

As my Aunt Cricket would say, jumping to conclusions is an Olympic sport in some circles.

Once back at the shop, I was exhausted from the frenzy. The smell of fresh coffee and hot pastry hit me as soon as I came through the door. I found Dixie in the kitchen and filled her in on the meeting and the rumor-mill.

"I'm so glad you agreed to handle that part of the business." Dixie opened the oven and slid in another sheet.

"And I'm glad you agreed to handle this part." I plucked a puff pastry from the cooling rack and headed back to my office.

I pulled out Max's card and dialed the number. The call went straight to voicemail and I left a message letting him know that I was simply confirming the photo shoot for the next day. It was comforting, a bit, to be back to doing something so familiar. We thought we could do the shoot in one day because there weren't a lot of photos. Though I thought that might be too much for Dixie. She assured me that she'd grouped things together so that the more complicated dishes were at different times.

Dixie stopped in before she left. One of her nephews had a baseball game and she'd promised to attend.

I looked up from my papers. "I'm leaving soon, too."

My cell rang just as I was walking out the door and I glanced at the display. It was Greer. She had another request. This time for a piece of green Frankoma pottery. She wasn't positive which box it might be in, but she was almost certain it was in a box of its own. I told her I'd see what I could do.

When I dropped it off I hoped for a chance to talk to her about what I'd seen at Disco's store. If Disco was helping her sell items she no longer wanted or needed that was entirely her choice. But the requests had become more and more frequent and I worried there was a financial angle to the whole deal too. Was Disco taking advantage of her? I didn't think he'd cheat her, but I also didn't think business was booming. I had no idea what any of those items were worth and could only hope she was getting good information from her friend. And my real worry was whether Greer was selling the things because she needed the money?

If she needed money, maybe the reasonable rent I was paying was not enough. I would be willing to pay more. I didn't want to offend her by sticking my nose in her business so I would need to tread lightly, but I was concerned.

Chapter Nineteen

I arrived at the shop early the next morning in order to make sure everything was set for Dixie and Max and the photo shoot. I opened up the front curtains. Max had explained that daylight was really best for photographing food. I thought I'd heard that before, but when I was with the magazine the departments were so big that I often didn't even meet the photographers who were assigned to a particular story.

The square was quiet and there were very few cars parked. It looked like the lights were on at the Red Hen Diner. Toy was probably there getting ready for the day. When I talked to her yesterday, she had confirmed that her new waitress had run out on her. It wasn't that the diner was a bad place to work, it was simply that young people had so many other options for employment. The "Help Wanted" sign was back in the window.

St. Ignatius's story was one of grit and stamina and a very strong sense of community and I'd worked hard to make sure the cookbook content reflected the town's personality. I thought we'd put together a mixture of recipes that the community would enjoy and moreover I thought it told the story.

We'd planned a full day for photographing the recipes that would be in the book. First the sections would have photos, and then there were a few more we'd chosen to give some variety to the content.

I'd also decided to include four historical photographs that Max had been able to retouch. The thing to remember when you're putting together a cookbook is that it's just like any other book: people are drawn to a great story.

Max arrived in a short time to set up. He unpacked a tripod, some special lighting and a couple of reflectors.

We'd met before and selected the dishes we would use for the photos as well as any table settings or accessories so I already had those laid out. He'd been all about color and making sure that we made best use of it. I understood that. If you were paying the price to print something in color, you wanted to be sure that it was worth it.

"Dixie's already in the kitchen and has the first recipe baking." I stood back to keep out of Max's way as he situated the tripod and other equipment.

"Cookies, I think." He looked up from setting up his camera and smiled. "Unless my nose deceives me."

"You are correct." I was already wishing they were done. "Can I get you a cup of coffee?"

"I'd love one." He placed his camera on the counter and shifted his bags underneath and out of the way.

I headed to the backroom to grab a cup for Max and refill my own. I stopped by to see how Dixie was doing.

"I'm just going to stay out of your way," I told her. "If you need something give a yell."

"Sounds good." She looked up from the mixer.

This was old hat to her. When she entered the Iowa State Fair, sometimes she entered thirty or more recipes. The food was judged on taste but also on presentation, so she understood the need to have the food look good.

I took Max his coffee and he already had everything set up for the first shot. This first recipe was Greer's Garbage Cookies and he was going with an overhead position so he'd used the side arm.

Dixie brought out the plate of cookies and placed them on the counter.

Max positioned the plate on a piece of wood that looked like it came from an old barn. The red paint was bright in some areas and faded in others and the white plate stood out in relief.

"Could you bring a glass of milk?" He turned toward me. "A plain clear glass if you have one."

"Sure." I knew just the glass. I hurried to the back and pulled a tall glass from our storage cupboard. I picked up a towel and shined it up a bit as I took it out to Max.

"Perfect." He poured the creamy white milk in with a funnel so it didn't splash the sides and strategically placed it near the plate of cookies. I could see what he was going for. The plate of cookies, the barn wood, the glass of milk. Not the fancy polish of the food I'd watched photographed at the magazine. This photo would look like a short break between chores or an after-school snack.

Several clicks and he was satisfied.

He handed me the plate of cookies and I inhaled the warm sweet smell. I wondered if it was too soon to eat the props.

Next up was Betty Bailey's Broccoli Gratin. As I walked the cookies back to the kitchen area, Dixie pointed to a table in the corner that she'd set up.

I dropped off the cookies and she handed me her silicone oven mitts.

"That's the next one." She nodded at the casserole dish on the counter.

I picked it up carefully and carried it out to Max. I would hate to drop something after Dixie had spent her considerable time on it.

Placing the casserole dish on the counter, I could see that Max had removed the barn board and replaced it with a marble slab. I wondered if he'd had this stuff lying around or how he'd decided what was needed for each dish.

This food he was shooting up close with the broccoli directly on the marble. He took a couple of photos. Misted the broccoli with his water bottle, tried a couple more, and then stepped back frowning.

"I'm sorry to keep sending you to get things." He turned to look at me. "But I need a bit of oil. Vegetable oil. Olive oil. Doesn't matter."

"No worries. That's what I'm here for."

I quickly found some vegetable oil and took it out to him. I'd picked up a pastry brush on the way, thinking that might be helpful. "Will this work?"

"Yes, it will." He took the items from me. "We can brush the oil on and get that shine that will make the green look fresher."

By the time Max was satisfied with the Broccoli Gratin, Dixie was ready with Mona Patten's Meatloaf. I couldn't wait to see what Max had planned for this one. Here I'd been worried that he was a nature photographer and out of his element. So far, his picks on props and angles had been right on the money.

The meatloaf was center stage on a simple cutting board, sliced to show the texture, and with the knife left in the picture as if the loaf had just been cut for serving.

Unfortunately, the knife reminded me of the tattoo on the arm of the big guy we'd seen with Kenny. I kept that thought to myself.

Dixie was a dream to work with. Unflappable. Calm. But kept those dishes coming.

I cleared the meatloaf and carried it back to the table in the kitchen. Next up was an apple pie that Dixie brought out herself. I knew she'd spent a lot of time on it and I was glad it was in her hands and not mine.

"I didn't know if you would want to photograph it whole, just a slice, or what." She slid it on the counter.

He looked at it and spun the dish around. Then looked up at the front window and shook his head. "I wondered why I was getting shadows."

I followed his gaze. There were several faces pressed up against the window, undoubtedly attempting to figure out what was going on. I hadn't unlocked the front door, on purpose, and when we'd started none of the shops were open. Now, as stores opened and people were out and about, they'd come to peer in at the photo session.

"I can pull the curtains if you like." I offered.

"No, I need the natural light. It's much better for the photos. I could drag out my lights but I don't think you're going to like the effect."

"Okay, then I'll go chase them away." I pushed up my sleeves.

I took some time to make a sign that said, "Closed for Photo Session." Then, tape in hand, I unlocked the front door and prepared to step outside to chat with the usual suspects. They were a curious lot but I was sure they'd understand when I explained what the problem was with them peering in.

Just as I stepped outside, the crowd suddenly turned and like a bevy of bees moving to a new flower, they shifted down the street.

I looked back inside at Max and Dixie, and Max gave me a thumbs-up. "Much better,"

I shut the door and went ahead and taped up my sign. The crowd had stopped in front of Tina's real estate office.

Oh, no.

Not wanting to join the busy bees, uhm, crowd, I walked across the street to see if I could tell what was happening.

There was an Iowa Department of Criminal Investigation car parked in front of Tina's office. As I watched, a man in a jacket that said "DCI Police" in bold letters on the back escorted Tina to the car and helped her into the backseat.

I stood, trying to sort it out in my head, until the car pulled away. And then I headed back to the shop.

While I was gone, Max and Dixie had decided to photograph the apple pie with one slice out so you could see the sliced apples inside. Brilliant choice, I thought.

"Good job on moving the crowd along." Dixie handed me the pie to take back to the kitchen.

"I can't take credit." I grabbed the server they'd used as well. "They simply moved on to a bigger happening."

"What was that?" Max looked up from his camera.

"Tina just left her office in the backseat of a state DCI car."

"What?" Dixie stopped brushing up crumbs.

"I don't think she was arrested." I continued toward the kitchen. "She wasn't handcuffed or anything anyway."

After the excitement, no one came back to look in our window and we continued through the day with my list of photos. By two o'clock we were done.

We offered to feed Max but he had other commitments and declined. Dixie started her clean-up process and I walked Max to his car, carrying one of his bags.

"Sorry to have you work with all that food and then not feed you." I felt bad. And a little guilty because I knew I was about to devour a slice of that apple pie. They'd sprinkled it with extra sugar to get the look Max had wanted, but I didn't mind. I'd take one for the team and eat it anyway.

"I promise to make it up to you at some point before this project is done."

"Say, I just had a thought." He paused in loading his equipment into the Land Rover. "Are you busy this evening?"

"Not really," I answered. "I had a hot date with Ernest but he'll be fine as long as I pay up with some food." I paused. "Ernest is my cat."

"Oh," he chuckled, "you had me going for a minute."

"I have a gig and it involves dinner," he explained. "If you don't mind a short drive, I'd enjoy the company."

I loved the informality of his invitation. He made it easy to say yes.

"That sounds like fun. What type of place is it?" I wondered if I was dressed appropriately or needed to run home and change.

"Outdoor venue, very casual." He stopped his hand on the car door. "That's partly why I agreed to do it. Why don't I pick you up at your house about six?"

I gave him my address and then went back inside to help Dixie clean up. We made short work of the dishes, and I had my piece of apple pie.

As I pulled into my driveway, I noticed a white Lexus parked on the street a couple of houses down. It was similar to the one that had been parked on Kenny Farmer's street. I wondered how long it had been there. I'd love to ask the neighbors but I knew most weren't home during the day. Mrs. Pickett was, but if I asked her it would somehow be my fault it was there.

I traded my jeans for a multi-colored maxi skirt and paired it with a dark blue knit tank. Still casual I thought. I grabbed a lightweight jean jacket to throw on if the evening cooled off.

"Ernest, I am going out," I explained. "I've refilled your food and water."

The doorbell chimed and I jumped.

Not good to be found talking to the cat.

I opened the door and stepped outside.

"Nice neighborhood." He looked around.

"I like it." *Most days*, I added in my head. I could only imagine what Mrs. Pickett would think about a strange car picking me up. I glanced at the Lexus down the street but didn't see anyone inside. I didn't know what drug dealers drove but wished I'd paid more attention to the cars that had been in the parking lot at the Weary Wanderer Motel. Maybe Tattoo Guy or his supplier drove a Lexus.

Max held the door and I settled myself in the passenger seat. We made small talk about the weather, always a good topic in a state where crops were dependent on the elements.

"Dixie's from a farm family," I commented. "I think you know her brother, Hirsh."

"I do." He turned onto the highway and I thought it was the same direction Dixie and I had taken when we followed Kenny. "Hirsh and I hit it off when I first moved here because we're both Cubs fans."

"Dixie and her brother are close. I always wished I had a brother or sister," I confided. "Do you have siblings?" I turned to look at Max.

"No, I'm an only child, too." He glanced my way. "My mother died when I was young and my father remarried. He and my stepmom, a very nice lady, live in Puerto Rico."

"My mother is still very much alive and running the world, but my father died several years ago." I felt my throat tighten. "We weren't close."

"Losing a parent is tough no matter how close you are," Max said quietly.

A silence settled between us, but was comfortable rather than awkward.

I noticed Churchville and the Weary Wanderer Motel as we passed them. Someone else driving, watching fields of corn and soybean whisk by, I felt the stress wing away. I hadn't known I'd longed for blue sky and open fields when I was growing up in the bustle of city life, but I guess I had.

A few more stretches of corn and crops, and there was a small sign that said "The Farmstead." We turned onto a winding gravel road and followed it a little way to a driveway where Max turned in.

We rounded the curve and...wow. Picture postcard, wow. Movie set, wow. Just wow.

I don't think I'd said the wow aloud, but my quick intake of breath and my mouth hanging open must have conveyed the same thing.

Max smiled at my reaction.

The restaurant was a converted barn and the waning light touched it and the tall grass just right so it seemed to glow. A patio of sorts had been added to one side and it was lit with festive lanterns. Their glimmer was reflected in the small pond nestled against a bank of river rock.

Max parked and opened the back to retrieve his camera equipment. At the entrance we were met by a couple who I assumed to be the owners. Max made introductions and they escorted us to a table on the patio.

"Excuse me for a bit." Max didn't sit down. "I need to walk the perimeter."

"No problem." I sat down and looked around. The atmosphere in the restaurant was basic and simple. Tables were covered with off-white cloths, and silverware was tied up in cloth napkins with a piece of twine and a sprig of lavender. I looked over the menu while Max walked around with the couple.

The conversation we'd had on the way to The Farmstead had me thinking about family. I watched the lights dance on the pond and let the quiet of the evening wash over me.

Family. What a complicated topic. My mom and her sisters and their own special brand of crazy. Dixie's brother and her big traditional but rowdy family. Max's lack of family. I still had my mother and as crazy as we made each other, I hoped to have her for a very long time. But I knew what it felt like to have that hole caused by a missing parent.

My own dad had been gone out of my life for a long time before he passed away. He and my mom had been estranged for years before his liver disease killed him. A direct result of his drinking, according to my mother. But I'd hoped someday to get to know him, now that would never be possible. Never.

He was from Iowa. From a place like this, but I'd not found any trace of the Calloway family. Yet. My mother had never met them. Had no desire to find them.

Maybe it was for the best. Maybe. Who knew? Maybe there was a sordid past. Maybe he was the black sheep of the family. Maybes were all I had. That and a very dim memory of a smiling dark-haired man who laughed a lot, and was willing to playact with a little girl with a big imagination.

As I let the thoughts of family swirl around in my head, it suddenly occurred to me that as focused as we'd been on Kenny and his affair, we'd never followed up on Elsie's past. Maybe we needed to go back to the very beginning. When we looked into Elsie when trying to find Bertie, it had seemed like every bit of information related to her once she and Kenny married. But Greer had said she was from some other town.

What was the name of the town? I closed my eyes and tried to think. It had made me think of outer space.

"Mars," I said aloud.

"As in the planet?" Max had approached while I was lost in reverie and now slid into the chair across from me. "This would be a great location if you're into planet-spotting or star-gazing."

"Sounds like fun, but not the planet." I thought I might be onto something. "Elsie Farmer was originally from a town called Mars."

"I take you to this fantastic setting and your mind is still on murder." He picked up his camera and snapped a quick photo of the twine-tied napkin.

"Sorry, I was thinking about our earlier conversation and got to musing about families, and it occurred to me we know nothing about hers."

"If she had relatives in the area, I would think they would have attended her funeral."

"You would think so, wouldn't you?" I pictured the packed church in my head. "Maybe they did. There was such a crowd it would be hard to say."

"Are you hungry?"

"I am." I confessed. "I'm afraid being around the food as we get ready to publish this cookbook has caused me to think about food all the time."

"They don't have their full menu going." Max nodded toward the barn. "I think they were waiting on some photos before putting it together, but they put together some samples for us. If you're ready I'll let them know."

"I'm ready." I smiled.

Max left his camera on the table and went to talk to the couple. When he returned it was with a platter of food.

"I hope we're not going to be in trouble if we don't eat all of that." I eyed the plate. "I know I said I was hungry but this is enough for a family of four."

There was a small plate with different types of cheeses, some slices of apple, a handful of grapes, and couple of pieces of brioche. And then on the larger platter were roasted potatoes, chicken wings with blue cheese dip, and battered morel mushrooms.

Max snapped a couple of photos before we dug in. The food was amazing but I couldn't decide if it was the food alone or the ambiance of the place that made it seem especially tasty. The owners stopped by with a glass of wine from a nearby winery. Iowa had recently become known for well-crafted wines and I guess it made sense. The rich soil that had made the state perfect for farming was also prime for grapes. The wine was light and crisp and the perfect complement to the variety of fare.

As the sun began to set, I felt myself relax into the moment. Maybe getting away from the cookbook project and the murder was just what I'd needed. Not thinking about the murder, I'd had a breakthrough on it. Maybe not thinking about the cookbook would work in the same way.

"I'm going to walk to the other side of the pond to get a couple of shots of the sunset." Max laid his napkin aside and picked up his camera. "You're welcome to come along or stay. It's up to you."

"I think I could use a walk after everything I've consumed." I patted my tummy. "If you don't mind, I'll tag along."

"I don't mind at all." Max stood and held out his hand.

We walked arm in arm across the deck and then down into the field behind the barn. He let go and stopped to take a few photos and then moved toward the pond to get a few more. The opportunity was fleeting, as very quickly the sun was behind the trees and the shadows overtook the light.

Max offered his hand, and we headed back to the restaurant. My prediction was The Farmstead would be a great success. Enough off the beaten path, but not too hard to find. A solid menu, high-quality food, and a unique experience. If I were still employed at the magazine, I would have gladly covered its opening. As it was, I hoped someone did.

We said our good-byes and walked back to Max's Land Rover. I climbed in.

I'd enjoyed the evening and the drive back to St. Ignatius was filled with get-to-know-you conversation that no longer seemed awkward. We discovered a shared love of good coffee and great jazz, and disagreed totally on the perfect vacation. Mine beach. His mountains. By the time we were back in town, it no longer felt like a first date. It felt like the beginning of a friendship. Friendship was a perfect way to start.

We pulled up in my driveway. The house was dark. I probably should have left the porch light on what with all the vandalism going on. And having not left an inside light on for Ernest, I was sure to be soundly scolded.

"Thank you." I turned to Max. "That was a wonderful evening."

"I'm happy you enjoyed it." He got out and came around to open the door for me.

There were no lights on next door at Mrs. Pickett's. I hoped that meant she was already in bed or somewhere in the house watching television, and too busy to notice the kiss on the cheek I gave Max as I got out of the car.

When I got inside, of course, Ernest had been close to expiring from starvation while I was gone and insisted on a snack before he herded me to the couch for a neck scratching session. I kicked off my shoes and sunk into the cushions of the couch. I couldn't think of the last time I'd had such a great evening.

Had that been a date? I wasn't sure. If it was, I loved the concept. No dress-to-impress what to wear, no awkward small talk, no pressure.

"Manage your expectations, Sugar," I told myself. "If it was a date. It was just one date. No need to figure out what it means tonight."

Great. Now not only was I talking to the cat, I was talking to myself. I wasn't sure which was worse.

Chapter Twenty

Dixie had coffee started when I arrived at the shop the next morning, I could smell the rich aroma as I opened the door. I sniffed again, hoping for a muffin, a breakfast roll, cookies. Nothing. There wasn't any reason to bake today, but a girl can hope. Right?

I'd given Dixie a spreadsheet of all the recipes and she'd selected which ones to test, and then together we'd decided which ones to photograph. Dixie and Max had finished up everything yesterday. Max would work at his place on the photos today.

Everything was digital so we should have proofs in a couple of days, depending on what else he had in the hopper. The first order of business would be to make sure he had what he needed. If we needed to re-take anything, we'd want to know that right away.

I pulled out my project folder and Dixie groaned.

"I know my lists and charts make you nuts, but this is how I work." I poured coffee into a mug and found a granola bar in my bag. It would have to do. Moto trotted over and gave me the puppy-dog-eyes look. I reached back in for my stash of dog treats and slipped him a couple.

Dixie and I sat down at the counter to go over everything that remained to be done before we were ready to go to print. I'd talked with Liz, our graphics person, and sent her all the recipes and text. I was excited about the history bits and the historical photos and Liz was too. She had embraced the concept immediately and understood my vision for the history being interwoven with the recipes and the community. On the technical side of how to accomplish that, I'd connected her with Max and they'd been able to sort all that out. She would do the layout and add finishing touches once she had his photos from yesterday's shoot.

We were almost there. I had reviewed the sponsors' logos and sent them off to Liz as well.

"The only thing that's left is the tribute to Elsie." Dixie looked at me. "What do we want to do about that?"

I slapped my forehead. "That's what I wanted to talk to you about and I completely forgot."

"What?"

"When I was at the farm-to-table restaurant with Max yesterday evening, which was wonderful by the way. We've got to go there when they're fully open. Anyway, while we were there I was thinking about family," I began and then stopped at Dixie's expression.

"Stop it," I laughed. "How old are you?"

She shrugged, unfazed. "Go on."

"I was thinking about families in general and mine specifically. The fact I know little to nothing about my dad. My aunts and their strong sister bonds. Your family and how close you are. And suddenly I remembered Greer talking about Elsie and that she wasn't from St. Ignatius and didn't have any family in town."

Dixie nodded. "All true, but I'm not sure where you're going with this."

"I remembered Greer said she was from a town not far away called, Mars, but that she didn't remember ever meeting any of Elsie's family. Or them coming for a visit. Don't you find that strange?"

"A little, I guess." She reached down to absently pat Moto who had followed us, undoubtedly hoping for more treats.

"I got to wondering about it and thinking maybe we should do a little research into Elsie's past. I checked for what I could do online, and the answer was not much. So, what do you think of a little road trip?"

"I think it's a wild goose chase." Dixie crossed her arms. "But I am not going to let you try to get to Mars and get lost."

"Great. You fell into my trap." I smiled. "How soon can you be ready?"

Dixie sighed. "I always forget that you started out in sales. You seem nice, but under that innocent girl-next-door look, you're a closer. And you're good. Give me thirty minutes to finish cleaning up from yesterday, drop Moto at home, and I'm game."

I went back to my desk and took care of a few items I needed to finish up. I'd worked with a printing company in a suburb of Des Moines. They were able to give us the best price, and in projects like this one, the more you can keep costs down the better value you can offer to your clients. In this case, that meant the Founders' Day committee would be able to sell the books for a reasonable price and would also make some decent money from their project.

A call to my contact confirmed that we were still good as far as lining up with their schedule. I printed the little information I'd been able to find out about Elsie and tucked it in my bag.

"Ready?" I called as I heard Dixie come in the back.

* * * *

Dixie gave directions and I drove. The town Elsie had been from was a little more than an hour away and in the opposite direction from where Max and I had gone the night before. She'd packed a bag of snacks for the trip. A large bag of snacks. From what I could see, the provisions would come in handy if we were somehow stranded in the wilds of rural Iowa and needed to live on junk food for a week.

"Turn at your next left." Dixie used a red licorice stick to point at a country road sign.

I pulled off the highway and onto a much narrower road where she'd pointed. The sign said Deersville.

"But—" I didn't think we wanted to go to Deersville.

"Just keep going straight until I tell you to turn," Dixie directed.

"Okay." I slowed my speed and kept going.

"Pressfield, population, two-hundred and fifty-seven." I said the names of the towns aloud as we drove through them. Some were no more than a handful of houses. Others a little bigger. Most had their population on a sign at the edge of town.

"Moose City, three-hundred and thirty-one." I continued driving.

Dixie laughed at me and handed me a cookie.

"What?" I took a bite and glanced her way. "I like that they tell how many people live there. How often do you think they update the sign?"

"I have no idea."

"I mean if a baby is born, is the sign updated?"

"Signs are expensive. I'm sure not." Dixie rummaged in the treat bag and this time came up with cheese puffs.

"I wonder."

I was tremendously entertained by the names of towns in my adopted neck of the woods. Sure, we had unusual names for towns in Georgia, but the names, like the people were sort of lyrical and, well, southern. Like they were named while folks were sipping mint juleps. Dewy Rose, Sugar Hill, Talking Rock, Burning Bush, and my favorite, Flippen, Georgia.

But Iowa small towns had straight-forward monikers. Plain and hard-working but with a bit of wit and attitude stirred in. Names that made you curious about what the story was behind the name. There was What Cheer, Defiance, and Gravity. And then, Correctionville.

Doesn't that one just make you wonder if they were registering something exotic like Whisperville and someone said, "Wait there's a correction"?

Then there was Diagonal, Lost Nation, and Last Chance. I especially loved the ones named for other places in the world like Jamaica, Peru, East Peru, and Nevada. Now, Jamaica was pronounced in the usual way, but not Peru, which was pronounced Pee-Roo, unlike the South American country. And Nevada was Ne-VAY-da, not at all like the state.

I pulled into Mars, disappointed there was not a UFO in sight. There was a simple sign at the edge of town that said, Mars, Population, 1,397. Smaller than St. Ignatius, but still way more people than East Peru. And no red planet graphics to be seen.

I wanted spaceships and planets. Maybe a Mars rover replica on the playground. I could hear "Fly Me to the Moon" in my head. (Or "Life On Mars," if you prefer. Your pick.)

"Where do you think we should start?" I drove slowly. Unlike St. Ignatius and many other Iowa towns, Mars had no courthouse or town square. The main street had a diner, which appeared to be closed, a laundromat, a hardware store, and a storefront that said Mars Public Library.

"Let's try the library." Dixie suggested. "Maybe they'll have old yearbooks or newspapers."

"Seems like a great place to start." I parked the Jeep and we went in.

There was a petite lady behind the desk; her short dark hair gave her a pixie-like appearance. She greeted us with a smile. Her nametag said, Mrs. Schwebach.

"Welcome to the library," she said. "Is there something I can help you find?"

"We're working on an article about a former resident and thought we might be able to find a little background information about her time here in Mars," I explained.

"I see."

"Do you keep newspaper articles?" Dixie asked. "Or yearbooks?"

"The town hasn't had a newspaper in years," Mrs. Schwebach explained. "However, we do keep yearbooks. Up until we stopped being an independent school district, that is. Our children now go to Consolidated County schools. What year were you looking for?"

"We're not exactly sure." I gave her a range of dates.

"Let me show you where we keep those." She moved from behind the counter and walked us to a back room with shelves of yearbooks. "They're arranged by date."

"Thanks, we'll look through these." Dixie was already running her fingers over the spines.

The years we were interested in were on the bottom shelf. It didn't take long to find Elsie Banks in the yearbook, but there was nothing at all about her. No extra-curricular activities, no sports, no awards. Nothing. There was a blurry picture of a young woman, but I felt like we'd found nothing of who she'd been.

We located some telephone books from the time she would have lived in town and found a Eula Banks listed. We wrote down the address, 318 Maple. Shouldn't be hard to find.

Thanking the friendly librarian, I dropped a few dollars in their Bucks for Kids' Books jar, and then we went back to the car.

"What now?" Dixie asked.

"Let's try the post office." I pointed across the street to a small house that had a U.S. Post Office sign out front.

"Okay, let's go." She opened her door. "Then maybe the diner will be open."

"Are you hungry?" I asked. I couldn't believe she could possibly be after the junk food we'd eaten in the car.

"A little." She grinned at me.

"Okay, after this we'll check." I walked across the street to the post office.

A young woman with big hair looked up as we entered. "Hello."

"Hi, we're in town doing a little research on someone who used to live here." I explained.

"Elsie Banks."

"Sorry, never heard of her." She smiled politely.

"Any Banks live in town?" Dixie asked.

"None that I know of," the woman answered. "Sorry I can't be of more help, but I just started this job a month ago."

"Okay, thank you for your time." I held the door for Dixie and we headed back across the street.

"Now can we check the diner?"

"Sure." The diner was not at all like our own Red Hen Diner. There was no "cluck" as we walked in the door. In fact, there was no sound at all when we entered, and yet every one of the six people inside turned to look at us.

We settled ourselves at a booth in the corner that had seen better days. Tan plastic was held together in some places with duct tape. A young woman in overalls stopped by the table with glasses of water.

"The special today is our club sandwich." She handed us each a menu.

I've always found that if you're not too sure about the fare in an eating establishment that the special is usually a good choice.

We ordered and she headed back to the kitchen.

"Okay, so maybe my idea of researching Elsie here in her hometown was a little ambitious."

"A little." Dixie shrugged. "It's okay. It's been intense, so I think we both needed to get out a bit."

"I can do the bio on her with what I've got." I leaned back in the booth and took a sip of my water. "I had a thought that if we couldn't find any more than what was in her obituary that I might pitch the idea of doing something on the Farmer family instead, and include Elsie and Kenny in that. What do you think?

"I think it's the perfect way for the one who got us into the promise of having an Elsie tribute to get us out of it." Dixie raised her brows.

"You got me there."

In short order, the club sandwiches arrived. Though I wouldn't put it up there with The Farmstead fare, it was good. The bread lightly toasted, the bacon crispy, and the tomatoes garden fresh. What the Mars Café lacked in ambiance, it made up for in good food.

We finished our sandwiches and then stopped at the cash register to pay. A guy, perhaps the owner and I suspected the cook, came out from the back. He wore a burgundy sweat suit and a baseball cap. Pushing the cap back on his forehead, he said, "I hear you been asking about the Banks family."

"That's right," I said. "Any of the family left in town?"

"You could stop by and see Fred and Edith and I suppose Eula, too."

"Where would we find them?" I handed him our check and some cash.

"You just go to the end of main and hang a right." He gestured with the hand holding the cash. "And you'll find 'em right there in the town cemetery." His smirk said he thought that was clever.

"So I guess no living family left in town." Dixie gave him a look that said she didn't think so.

"Nope." He placed the money in the ancient cash register and handed me back my change. "Not for years. Eula stayed after her folks died. Had a daughter Jocelyn Jane. The girl got in all kinds of trouble after her mom died. Don't know what ever happened to her."

"We're working on a write up about Elsie Banks. Anyone still in town that might have known her?" I asked.

"Nah, I don't think so." He raised his voice. "Darrell, you remember an Elsie Banks?"

A man across the room, apparently Darrell, shook his head.

"The family was dirt poor," Darrell hollered back. The man that was with him nodded in agreement. "Used to live over on Maple. Nobody lives there now, it's just a shack. I think the city uses it for storage. That right, Pat?"

A woman on the other side of the restaurant answered, "Yes, that's right."

"I think Eula's sister's name was Elsie," the man across from her called out.

"Could be," Darrell agreed.

Everyone seemed comfortable with a conversation that spanned the length of the diner. It felt a little strange, like we'd wandered into their living room, but the group was friendly enough.

"Thanks for your help." Dixie moved to the door.

"Thanks," I said to the guy at the register.

"Wanna buy a ticket to the pancake breakfast?" He pushed forward a couple of tickets. "They're only five bucks a piece. We're raising money for playground equipment for the park."

"Sure." I handed him a twenty and picked up four tickets. "Good luck with your fundraiser."

"Sugar?" Dixie stood holding the door open.

"Coming." I stepped outside and joined her.

"Thought I'd better get you out of there before you gave them all the money you had."

"It was for a good cause," I said as I climbed back in the Jeep.

"I'm sure." Dixie got in and buckled her seatbelt. "Let's take a swing by the cemetery and then call it a wrap."

"Sounds good."

The cemetery was fascinating and I made a mental note to come back for a longer visit once the St. Ignatius cookbook was complete. There were old tombstones from the mid-eighteen hundreds. It was a good-sized cemetery and well-maintained, the bushes trimmed, the grass mowed.

"I wonder if there aren't more people in here than live in town," Dixie mused.

"I was thinking the same thing." I turned back toward Main Street and took a small detour to go down Maple.

The lady in the diner had been right. The house was nothing more than a shack. The windows were boarded up, the paint peeling, the cement on the front steps crumbling.

We sat in the car and looked at it.

"I feel sad for her." I turned to Dixie. "It explains a lot doesn't it?"

"That it does." She shook her head.

"When you come from this I guess it makes you want to be more. Maybe her putting on airs had less to do being important and everything to do with Elsie's own insecurities."

We were both quiet as we drove out of town.

I stopped at Deersville to get gas before we got to the main highway, at the little convenience store I'd noticed when we'd turned off before. I probably could have waited but I was afraid to take a chance. When you have my sense of direction, or lack thereof, you learn to keep plenty of gas in your car.

I filled up and went inside to get drinks for the drive back to St. Ignatius. No need for snacks: we still had that covered with Dixie's magician's bag of bottomless junk food. The convenience store had a coffee machine that made cappuccinos. The pictures of coffee drinks looked good, but the concept seemed a little iffy to me. I opened the cooler, picked out a couple of bottled waters, and took them up front to pay.

The counter around the cash register was jammed with plastic buckets of impulse buys. I am a merchandiser's dream customer. I picked out a postcard with a pig in red galoshes, a fudge cow patty (If you don't know what a cow patty is, you should look that up.), and a black and white pen that mooed when you clicked it. Quite a haul.

As I walked out to get in the Jeep, I noticed a gray van parked across the street at a place called the The Dive. What were the odds? There couldn't be two vans in that kind of shape, could there?

The Dive appeared to be a bar. One whose owner called it like it was. The van was one of only a few cars parked on the street and there didn't seem to be anyone around. I waved to Dixie trying to get her attention but she was on her phone.

I decided that approaching the vehicle didn't fit the description for "dangerous." As long as all I did was get close enough to read the license plate number, I was perfectly safe. I would write it down and walk away. I would be in no danger at all.

I tried one last time to get Dixie's attention and then walked slowly across the street. Stepping over the grass that grew up between the cracks of the sidewalk, I approached the van until I was close enough to read the license plate.

Just as I did the bar's door opened and out walked JoJo the AWOL waitress.

Yes, that JoJo. The one who had bailed on Toy after she advanced her a week's wages. No notice at all and then poof the girl had just disappeared.

Outraged on Toy's behalf, I was ready to give the girl a piece of my mind. Toy had been sure the money went to a family in need but here was evidence it had simply gone for booze. She didn't see me, but I continued across the street toward her.

When she was even with the van she stopped. Then she opened the passenger door of the van and got in.

What the what?

No sooner had I processed that, or tried to anyway, than the bar's door swung open again and out walked the big guy with the knife tattoo.

Oops. Now I was in the danger zone.

Quickly turning away, I held my handbag in front of my face like a bright red Kate Spade mask, and I scurried back to the Jeep.

I could hear the engine rev and peeked from behind my car to see. As the van sped away I got a good look at the license plate. I pulled out the cow pen I'd just purchased, and wrote it down on the pig postcard.

"Moooo," it said as I yanked open the door and hopped into the Jeep.

"What was that?" Dixie asked.

"My cow pen," I answered. "Did you see the van?"

"What van?" Dixie looked around.

"It's gone now." I handed her one of the bottled waters. "I tried to get your attention but you were looking at your phone."

Twisting open the other water and taking a drink, I tossed the rest of my purchases in the back seat. We headed out of town. I couldn't wait to get back to St. Ignatius and give the sheriff the license number.

Who knew what the connection was between JoJo and the guy with the knife tattoo was, but whatever it was, it involved Kenny Farmer. And, come to think of it, JoJo had been at the Looking Pretty party and had disappeared after the police showed up. We'd all just thought she was a flake, but maybe there was a reason she'd suddenly shown up in town.

Chapter Twenty-One

As soon as we arrived back at the shop, we called Sheriff Terry. He listened carefully and took down the information I'd given him.

Dixie was still skeptical about this being a big breakthrough, but I was convinced there was more to JoJo being at the Looking Pretty party and then disappearing from town than just coincidence.

She and Moto waved good-bye while I was still on the phone. Earlier she'd mentioned a big family birthday party for her niece. Her niece was majorly into dogs and so this was a canine-friendly event. There were pupcakes as well as cupcakes planned for the guests. Dixie, of course, had baked and needed to stop at home and pick them up.

I had waited for an opening to ask her about her Aunt Bertie's comment about her and Sheriff Terry being an item and had failed to find one. I was going to have to get bolder if I was going to solve that mystery.

* * * *

When I pulled into the parking lot behind the building the next morning, it looked like Dixie had just arrived as well. She got out of her pickup and stood. A Jameson County Sheriff's Department vehicle blocked the entrance to our building.

I felt my heart sink. Now what?

Had there been another murder? Had Bertie gone missing again? The possibilities zipped through my head as I put the Jeep in park and got out.

Dixie and I approached the back door which stood open. A deputy stood just inside.

"Can you wait here a minute, ma'am?" He was polite but firm.

The sheriff soon joined him. "You've had a break-in."

He motioned for us to follow him.

As I turned the corner into the office, my heart sank. All of the papers I'd painstakingly sorted into piles of recipes for the various sections had been tossed on the floor. It looked like some of them had been wadded up and walked on. Every drawer in the desk had been pulled out and the contents dumped on the floor. The file cabinet where I'd put the historic pictures was tipped on its side.

"How bad is the kitchen?" Dixie asked quietly.

"Pretty bad, I'm afraid," Sheriff Terry answered.

I linked arms with Dixie and took a deep breath. "Let's get it over with." The sheriff was right, it was bad.

Glass dishes had been smashed on the floor. Flour and sugar had been thrown everywhere. Butter smeared on the counter and on the front window.

Unbelievable.

I was at once angry and broken-hearted.

"How you know?" Dixie asked. "Who called you?"

"A jogger noticed the door open and went to close it and saw the mess," Terry answered.

The one saving grace was that Max's photos from the shoot weren't there. They were with him.

He showed up just as the Jameson County Sheriff's Office people were leaving.

"What happened here?" he asked.

"We had a break-in." I could feel my throat tightening and I fought to keep the tears at bay.

His laser blue gaze searched my face. "Anything taken?"

"Not that we can tell." I shrugged. "But it's a real mess." I pointed to the doorway. "Take a look inside."

Max walked through the backdoor and I could hear him exclaim as he got a good look at the destruction.

I used my cell phone and called our insurance company. The agent was just across the square and he said he'd stop by in a few minutes.

Dixie came outside shaking her head. She walked to where I stood and I told her I'd called about what we needed to do to file an insurance claim.

"He said to be sure and get pictures." The sheriff's deputy had taken a bunch of pictures already, but if we needed them for insurance, maybe we also needed to take some.

She leaned against the side of my car. "We are a week away from going into full production. I don't see how we can make it."

"We'll make it." I tucked my phone away and straightened my shoulders. "I don't know who did this or why they would target us, but we are not going to let them win. We'll make it."

"All right then." She linked her arm through mine. "Let's get started."

Heading back inside, I realized I wasn't sure where to start.

Max stepped over a jar of pineapple that had been smashed in the doorway between the kitchen and my office. "If you can give me a few minutes before you start cleaning, I'll take photos." His expression was grim. "I'm sure you'll need them for insurance purposes."

"I've already called, and you're right. We will."

"Okay, it won't take me long." He went back to the Land Rover for his camera and re-entered the building.

Our insurance agent had arrived and after a brief conversation with him, he did a walk-through. When he came out he looked a little shell-shocked.

"Worse than I thought." He wiped his shoes in the grass. "I talked to Max Windsor while I was in there and gave him my card. He'll send the photos directly to me and we'll get a claim filed."

I thanked him and once he'd gone, started making a list of supplies we were going to need for the clean-up. Top of the list was garbage bags. A lot of garbage bags. Hardly any of the perishables would be salvageable.

Max stepped outside and walked to where I stood in the shade. "I'm done. I'll send these to your insurance agent right away."

"Thank you, Max." I touched his arm. "We appreciate your help."

He walked toward his vehicle and I headed to the store with my list.

When I got back Max had commandeered a couple of large rolling trash cans from one of the neighboring shops and he and Dixie were already carrying out one large bag of trash. I waded into the fray.

Dixie had propped open the front door to get some circulation going as it was hot work. As usual the activity collected a crowd and I finally had to put up a sign so that people didn't walk in on the slippery floor and get hurt.

By noon we had the floors cleared and had begun the process of trying to save paperwork that had been trashed. I set up some boxes and labeled them to make it easier to sort. The intruder had poured cleaning solution on my computer and I couldn't get it to turn on. I wiped it down and carried it outside to my car. I'd have to take it to someone who knew more than I did to see if it could be saved. And if it couldn't, if any of the files on my hard drive could be.

I tried to fish my keys out of my pocket in order to open the cargo area of the Jeep to set the computer inside and fumbled to balance it.

A voice spoke from behind me. "Here, let me get that."

It was Sheriff Terry. I almost didn't recognize him out of uniform. Without the trappings of the office, he looked younger and somehow less serious. In jeans and a T-shirt, I could picture the high school heartthrob he might have been back in the day when he and Dixie were an item. In spite of the warmth of the day, he wore a light jacket so I assumed he was still armed even though he was off duty.

He took the computer from me and I opened the back. Setting it carefully on the blanket, I said a little prayer that the liquid cleaner hadn't totally destroyed the last several months' work.

"I brought you guys something to eat and some water." He picked up a bag he'd put down in order to help me. "Looks like it's been a long day already."

"It has." I agreed.

"Come on in, Sheriff." I headed back into the shop. "Dixie needs to take a break and maybe I can convince her if there's food involved."

"Let's make it Terry since I'm off duty." He grinned. "I'd like to help with the cleanup."

"I think I can get you inside the door with the food, but I'm not sure Dixie will tolerate any more than that. She won't bite, but I can't say that she won't bark."

"And I can't say that I'm not scared."

Dixie had piled her auburn curls on top of her head and was pushing a pile of broken glass into a dust bin.

Tears ran down her face.

"Jerks." She wiped her cheek with the arm of her shirt. A shirt which had started out the day white but was now covered in so many stains it looked like one of Disco's tie-dyes. "It wasn't enough to make an unholy mess of things, they had to break my grandma's mixing bowls."

"I'm so sorry, hon." I put my arm around her shoulder. "Let's take a little break. We've been going at this since we got here. Terry here brought us some water and, uhm…"

"Sandwiches," he finished for me. "Nothing fancy, just some sandwiches."

I could feel her tense, but to her credit she didn't lash out at him. It could be the woman was so darn exhausted she couldn't, but I was going with that she was taking the high road.

"Come on, let's wash up." I steered her to the lavatory at the back.

We looked at each other in the mirror over the sink.

"We look scary," she said.

"No," I countered. "We look fierce."

When we got back out front, Terry had finished sweeping up the broken crockery from Dixie's grandmother's mixing bowls and the debris was out of sight.

Sliding onto one of the stools, Dixie pulled the bag Terry had brought toward her and pulled out a bottle of water. She handed one to me and then looked around.

"Where's Max?" she asked.

"I think he's still working in the storage room." I headed in that direction. "Let me look."

I found him moving supplies that were still useable to the top shelf and tossing others into a box he'd fashioned as a trash can.

"I can't believe you're still here." I was so thankful for the help he'd provided. "You sure didn't need to give up your day."

He shrugged. "I had it blocked out anyway, because we were going to go over the photos today."

"Now that we can't, what will that do to your schedule?"

"We'll work it out."

I sure hoped so. I'd been worried about losing support for the project. I'd been concerned that the details wouldn't come together. I sure as shooting did not see this coming.

"You're a peach." I smiled at him. "Take a break. The sheriff has stopped by with some food and I've talked Dixie into taking a break."

"You didn't leave them alone in there did you?" Max raised a brow.

"You've noticed the tension too, huh?"

"Hard to miss it."

When we walked into the outer area, there seemed to be a cease fire. They weren't exactly chummy with each other but they were talking.

"The deputy who responded this morning said it was a high school kid out for a run who noticed the door standing open. When he stopped to close it, he noticed the mess. He didn't go in but called 911 on his cell. The deputy checked things out carefully before entering but the vandals were long gone."

"I hope you catch them." Dixie tore into the submarine. "They'd better hope you find them before I do. Why make such a mess?"

Max grabbed a sandwich and sat down. I brushed off my jeans and did the same.

"We don't keep any money on the premises." I peeled back the wrapper.

"They were probably looking for money and when they didn't find any decided to trash the place." Dixie took a swig from her water.

"Have you noticed anything at all missing?" Max asked.

"Not a thing so far." I looked around at the shop that had been so cheery yesterday.

I finished my food and stood, ready to get back to work. The others soon followed. Max headed back to the storage room, and Dixie went back to sweeping up flour, sugar, and broken glass. And Terry took the other broom and headed to the opposite side of the room from Dixie.

The next hour, I picked up papers. Sorted and organized. Saved what I could. It wasn't as hopeless as it had at first seemed. My mind worked as I sorted. Who had done this and why?

I knew the sheriff's office had talked to surrounding business owners, but they'd been busy with the teen who'd called in the break-in. And then crowd control as word got out. They seemed certain it was part of the wave of vandalism, but I wondered. Maybe.

But why us? Everyone knew we didn't keep money in the shop. Maybe someone from one of the stores close by had seen something.

It wouldn't hurt to take a short break and ask around. I decided to start with Disco.

* * * *

The neon Flashback sign in the window of Disco's shop was only half lit so it looked like the name of the store was Flash.

I approached the counter where Disco leaned forward on both elbows. Today his attire was authentic 1970s polyester. I didn't know where he found the stuff he wore, or if it was his own well-preserved personal collection, but this was the most awful powder blue leisure suit. (Make a note, we should pass laws that prohibit this trend from ever coming back into vogue.)

"Hey, Disco," I said. "Your 'back' is out."

"Whoa, how did you know?" He straightened carefully rubbing his lower back. "You must be psychic. I've been unpacking a new shipment of Trolls and I think I hurt myself."

"No," I laughed. "Your sign." I pointed at the window. "The 'back' part is out."

"Wow." He rubbed his head with a hand that sported multiple mood rings. "That too."

"I wondered if the guy who'd come in asking about Kenny ever came back." I leaned against the counter trying to see if he had been doing any packing for shipping.

"No, that dude didn't come back, but a girl came in asking the same thing."

"Shorter than me, dark hair, tattoo here?" I pointed at my neck.

"Wow man, you really are psychic." He blinked and wiped a hand over his face. "How did you know?"

"I saw her with the guy today."

"So you're not psychic." His shoulders dropped in disappointment.

"No," I sighed. "If I were I'd figure out who really killed Elsie and Kenny Farmer."

"So, you don't think it was Tina?" His eyebrows shot up. "Everybody thinks it was Tina."

"No, I don't think so." I could partially see into the back, but didn't see anything I'd delivered to Greer. Maybe I'd imagined seeing the frog statue.

"Say have you seen anyone hanging around the store?"

"I haven't been out much." He rubbed his back again. "Because Trolls." He jerked a thumb toward the backroom. "I did stop by yesterday around noon, but you guys were gone and the door was locked."

Probably looking for food was my guess.

"Did the county sheriff's office people ask you about seeing anything early this morning?"

"Yeah, or if I heard anything." He folded his arms across the pockets of the awful leisure suit. "I wasn't here real early or anything and when I got here I had the music sorta loud."

"Thanks, Disco." I turned to leave. "Hope your back feels better soon."

"I hope so too."

Next on my list was Lark Travers, the owner of the jewelry store right next door to us. The possibility he'd been there early was much more likely than Disco. I asked the same question, and Lark had arrived about just before the Jameson County Sheriff's car had. He also was surprised we were targeted. It was clear he was worried about his own shop. The routine was to lock everything, cash and jewelry, in the safe at night, but the property damage and the lost sales would be devastating.

I glanced at my watch to see if I had time for one more. Probably time to check back in on Dixie and Terry to make sure they hadn't come to blows.

Dixie and Terry were no longer at opposite ends of the room, but had partnered to clean around the island. Max had filled two boxes with unsalvageable supplies and was dragging them toward the back door.

I stopped to clear the way. Once outside, I grabbed the other end of the box and we lifted it into the dumpster.

"Great teamwork." He grinned. "I'm going to take off in a few minutes. I'd stay but I've got a photo session with the track team."

"I can't thank you enough." We lifted the second box and tossed it in.

"If tomorrow works to go over the photos, I'll come by in the morning."

"Thanks to you and Terry, we should be able to do that."

"Terry is it now?" He raised a brow.

"He said to call him Terry when he's out of uniform." I brushed my hands together to remove the flour. "I'm trying it out."

"I'll come by around ten o'clock. If that doesn't work, just call me." He gave a little salute and headed toward his vehicle.

Back in the shop, I resumed my paper sort. I'd cleared most of the files and my back had begun to ache. I felt Disco's pain in a real way. It seemed like minutes but when I looked at my watch, I could tell it had been more than an hour. I took a batch to the trash and met Terry on his way out.

"I'm going back to the office for a bit," he said. "I told Dixie to call if you two need anything."

"Thanks, Sheriff." I'd slipped back to the title. It was a hard habit to break.

"We'll get these kids." His jaw hardened. "They're not just TPing trees or soaping windows like we did when Dixie and I were in school. Spray painting and this kind of damage, this is serious."

I walked back inside and went to check on Dixie. She'd finished sweeping up most of the broken glass. She looked exhausted, both mentally and physically, and I had to assume I looked the same.

"Hello," a male voice echoed from the back.

"Hello," we both answered.

"We're in here," I added.

It was Hirsh. Dixie's brother, and he'd brought a posse.

"Hi, Sugar." He bobbed his head in my direction. "Hey, kid." He rubbed his sister's shoulders. "How you doing?"

"Okay," she answered, biting her lip.

"Good. It's time for you two to get out of here." He gave Dixie a little push. "Time to go home and clean up." He looked at her and held his nose as if he smelled something bad.

"You don't tell me what to do." She gave him a shove back.

"This time I do, sis." He gave her a squeeze and headed her toward the exit.

I could tell how tired she was by the fact that she went without further protest.

"You, too." Hirsh pointed at me.

I smiled and followed, but stopped as I got even with Hirsh. "Who called you, Max or Terry?"

"Both." He grinned and suddenly I could see the Spicer family resemblance.

"Thank you." I gave him a hug and followed Dixie out the door.

There were bad people in the world, but there were also a ton of good people.

Chapter Twenty-Two

The next morning, I woke up with a start realizing in all the excitement, I had not yet painted over the graffiti on my garage. I was surprised I didn't have a nastygram tacked to my door reminding me.

I showered and threw on some clothes. Ernest looked at me like I'd lost my mind. Getting dressed before there's coffee and kibble. The nerve.

I didn't find any white paint in the garage. Greer had been sure there was some, but maybe whoever she'd hired to paint hadn't actually left any behind. In any case, it would require a trip to the hardware store before I could get started.

I walked around the side of the garage and stopped. It had already been painted. The awful words in red were completely covered. I was relieved and a little uneasy. Nice that it was taken care of, but baffling that whoever had done it had not said anything.

Walking back inside, I called Dixie's number.

"My garage is painted," I said without preamble. "Do you think Hirsh and his crew did it?"

"I don't know. Maybe." She yawned. "I think he would have told you. Do you know what time it is?"

"Sorry, I didn't look at my watch."

"It's okay." She yawned again. "I needed to get going. Someone needs attention."

"I hear that." I could hear Moto barking in the background. "Want to meet at the Red Hen for breakfast before we get started?"

"Sure."

"How about we meet at nine? Max is coming at ten to go over photos with us so that will give us time."

"Works for me. See you there." She disconnected.

I finished getting ready for the day, and Ernest kept me company while I did.

"I wish you could actually talk," I told him. "Then you could tell me who it was that painted over the graffiti."

He switched his tail and meowed.

I'm guessing I was being scolded for not understanding that he could actually talk.

No sign of Mrs. Pickett this morning and I made it to the Red Hen in record time. I secured a booth and Toy brought coffee. I couldn't help but compare the bright cheerful atmosphere to the tired décor of the diner in Mars. Toy had done a wonderful job and I hoped she could find a replacement for JoJo.

Dixie walked in as I was on my first list and my second coffee. Again, Toy was on the spot.

"Heard what you girls have been through." Toy put a cup in front of Dixie and refilled my cup. "Don't give up."

"We won't."

We ordered food and had just finished. I fished in my bag for my wallet.

I could sense Dixie tense before I saw the reason for it. The sheriff had just walked in the front door of the Red Hen.

"Ladies." He nodded at us and slid into the booth next to Dixie.

"Terry," she answered.

"Sugar, we ran the license plate number that you wrote down and the van was stolen."

Man, I thought I'd done such great detective work. All within the confines of not stepping on police toes or putting myself in danger. And I'd hoped it would become obvious they were on the wrong track.

"However," the sheriff continued, "when I talked to the man who had reported it stolen, he was almost certain it had been stolen by a 'friend' of his who he owed money to. The friend matches the description of the guy you described to me and that Dick Fusco also described."

"Who?" I asked.

"Disco," Dixie answered for the sheriff.

"Right." Since no one called him by his real name, I'd forgotten what it was. "So, will you be able to find him?"

"We have ways." He drummed his fingers on the table. "Law enforcement ways."

I guess in spite of the "Call me, Terry," and his help with the cleanup, he hadn't quite gotten over us waiting so long to share the information we had.

* * * *

Back at the office, it was almost like the break-in had never happened. Almost. Dixie's brother and his friends had done such a complete cleaning job that you couldn't tell there'd been food and flour everywhere and butter on the windows. I was grateful for what they'd done. However, all the utensils Dixie'd had hanging up were gone, and the pantry was nearly empty of supplies.

Max arrived promptly at ten and proceeded to set up his laptop, a mini-projector and a portable screen. Photo proofs have come a long way since I started in the magazine business. Once everything was set up, Dixie and I sat back and watched the show.

The pictures were perfect. I was glad we'd dimmed the room lights in order to see them better, because I have to tell you, I got a little teary they were so perfect.

Crazy, I know, to be teary over pictures of meatloaf and apple pie, but there you have it.

Once I'd gotten over the hump of how much I loved the photos, I took a deep breath and switched gears.

"Max, these are wonderful and just what we hoped for." Dixie brushed her finger on the corner of her eyes, and I knew she had been just as entranced as I'd been.

"Could you go back to the side dish series?" I asked.

He hit the back key on the laptop several times and we looked at that group again. "Your pick," he said. "But I like this one the best." He moved forward a couple of photos.

The three of us spent the next hour, reviewing, debating, and reviewing again until we were in agreement on which ones to use.

"I'm heading back home, and I'll send these to your Liz," Max said, as he packed up the screen.

I disconnected the projector and helped him get all the electronics in their proper bag. As we walked to his car, I thanked him again for helping with the cleanup, and for being so flexible on the project.

"And, Max, those photos...I'm in awe of your talent."

"It's what I love." He smiled as he slid the bags into the passenger seat. "The food angle is new to me, but I enjoyed learning about it and doing something different. Now I can apply that to other work."

"We'll be lucky if you can fit us in on the next project."

"I'll get the photo files to Liz and let you know when they're sent." He gave me a quick hug before he got in. "You're almost there."

Back inside, I found Dixie in the kitchen and on the phone with Tina Martin, who insisted she needed us to stop by her house.

Chapter Twenty-Three

When Tina answered the door at her house, she looked like death warmed over. There were bags and dark circles under her eyes and I didn't think the Looking Pretty Super Gone concealer would help.

Instead of her usual sharp appearance, she sported gray sweat pants and a washed-out pink sweater than had seen better days. The ever-present energy drink was, well, not present, today. I'd be willing to bet it would be a long time, if ever, before she'd be swigging down one of those.

"Hi, ladies." When she held open the door her hand shook. "Thanks for coming."

The products that had been so nicely displayed the night of the Looking Pretty party were piled in a heap on one end of her dining room table, and her unopened mail was stacked on the other end. Aunt Cricket would've said she looked like something the cat dragged in.

I don't care what the DCI or the County Sheriff's Office results were; I didn't think this looked like the home of a killer. It looked like the home of a woman who was falling apart.

"Have a seat." Tina pushed a wadded-up blanket off the couch and onto the floor.

"How are you doing?" I asked and then immediately regretted the question.

How was she doing?

Oh, about as well as anyone who was about to be arrested for murder.

"I've been better." She smiled weakly. "I have to take it a day at a time. It's been hard to keep busy. My real estate business is non-existent. I'm not even going in to the office anymore. No one wants to buy a house from a murder suspect."

"I'm sorry." I couldn't imagine what her days were like. "What can we do to help?"

"The reason I asked you to drop by was I wanted to give you all my things for the Founders' Day cookbook." She handed me a file with some forms and notes. "I know you've got more meetings and can't bring myself to come."

Tina teared up.

"I'm sure this will be straightened out soon," Dixie spoke up.

"I don't know how." She wiped her eyes with a tissue. "To tell you the truth, the committee stuff was kind of a ploy to get you here. I know you did some checking around when Bertie was a suspect and was missing, and I don't know who else to turn to. You've got to help me clear myself."

We should have said "no" right then. But, of course, we didn't.

"Have the police been back to talk to you?" I asked.

"They did that first night." She twisted the hem of her sweater. "Then the investigator from the DCI questioned me. I told them everything I know."

"Do you know of any reason why someone might have wanted to kill Kenny?" Dixie asked.

"I honestly can't think of any reason." She tucked limp blond hair behind one ear.

"Were you having an affair with Kenny?" I asked bluntly.

Might as well ask the question and get it over with.

"We had been seeing each other for a while." Tina looked down at the floor. "Call it whatever you want. I'm not proud of the fact I was dating a married man."

"Did he tell you he planned to divorce Elsie?" Dixie straightened the stack of mail absently.

"We hadn't really talked about it, but I hoped." Tina reached for a tissue. "We were very discreet."

"What was Kenny doing at your house when you had a whole house full of guests?" I'd thought about this ever since I'd found Kenny. Why would he be there? "That doesn't seem very discreet."

"You know, Sugar." She looked up rubbing the bridge between her eyebrows. "I haven't the faintest idea."

"You didn't know he was up there at all then?" Dixie stopped lining up envelopes.

"You probably think I'm lying, but it's the honest truth. I don't know when he came. I don't know why he would chance it. And my energy drink. Why in heaven's name would he drink it? He was always giving me a hard time about having it with me at all times."

"Were you aware of any illegal drugs he may have been taking or buying from someone?" I wasn't sure the sheriff or the DCI investigator had even considered that possibility. I hoped Sheriff Griffin had shared our information about Tattoo Guy, but it seemed the investigation into Kenny's death had centered about Tina and only her.

"No. I can't imagine Kenny taking drugs." A tear ran down her cheek. "He wasn't a druggie. He was a lot of fun, a big spender. Bought me all kinds of jewelry and clothes, but he could afford it. But it wasn't about the things."

I couldn't believe she was defending the louse and I wasn't sure he really could afford it. At least not based on what I'd heard while waiting for Minnie at the Farmers' office. But no one seemed to buy the idea of Kenny being into drugs. If not drugs, what was his business with the guy with the knife tattoo and the runaway waitress?

"I'm not sure there's much we can do, but we'll definitely do anything we can." Dixie leaned forward. "Do you have anyone who can stay with you? Family close by?"

"No one." Tina shook her head. "At least no one who would come. I've worked hard for what I have, and the only family I have left are people who think I owe them something. But me needing something? No, I don't expect to see them."

"Do you have an attorney?" I asked.

"No." The tears started again. "Do you think I need one?"

"I'm sorry, hon, but yes I do." I patted her arm. "Did the DCI people tell you what's next?"

"They took a bunch of stuff from my house and my garage." She dropped her face into her hands. "A container of anti-freeze I had in there. Do you suppose they think I put anti-freeze in my own drink and then gave it to Kenny?"

"That's possible." It would explain why the sheriff was not forthcoming with what the poison was. This was different than the rat poison they thought had killed Elsie.

"We'll get the names of some attorneys for you." I stood. "And you try to get some rest."

"Thank you." Tina reached out and grabbed our hands. "I can't thank you enough."

We left Tina with what I was sure were empty promises. Other than the promise to get her some names of some good attorneys.

Back at the shop, the sheriff waited by his car. We pulled in and parked. He followed us inside and took a seat at the counter.

"I want to be clear, I am telling you this not because I want or need your help." He paced back and forth. "But because I don't want you to attempt to help."

"Got it." Dixie handed him a cup of coffee. "Now spill the beans."

"We brought Robbie Clark in for questioning this morning."

"Who?" I wasn't following.

"The guy with the knife tattoo." He tapped his arm.

"That's great." Dixie had apparently decided it deserved a cookie because she brought a tub out from under the counter and opened it.

Sheriff Terry took one and continued, "He says JoJo, his girlfriend, has been getting monthly checks from Elsie Farmer for years to stay away from her."

"To stay away?" I took a cookie for myself. "Why?"

"She is apparently a relative. A great-niece it sounds like." He paused and took a gulp of coffee. "And Elsie was paying her to stay away and keep her mouth shut about any connection between them."

"JoJo." I looked at Dixie. "Jocelyn Jane."

"That's right." She dragged a stool closer and sat down. That was Eula Banks's daughter's name."

"Her meal ticket ran out when Elsie died and JoJo moved on to Kenny." Terry bit into his cookie and smiled. "We've got a BOLO out on JoJo Banks. She's bad news and I'm sure is tied up in the murders of Elsie and Kenny in some way."

I was sorry to say I now knew what a BOLO was. "I don't get it though. Why kill off someone who'd been writing you a check?"

"We don't know. And we don't need your help." He was quick to add, "Maybe she thinks she'll inherit money. Hard to say. We'll know more once we pick her up."

"I hope that's soon," Dixie looked at her hands. "We just came from Tina's house and that woman is in bad shape."

"I know there was some sort of poison found in her garage." I paused. "But you can't really think she had any reason to kill Kenny."

"I can't say much about the poisons, but I can tell you this." Sheriff Terry paused. "According to the DCI, that's part of why this case is so baffling. The amounts of these substances it takes to kill are very exacting. Not something an amateur would know."

"But you're still not willing to clear my aunt?" Dixie ran a hand through her hair.

"Or Tina Martin?" I added.

"No." His face was unreadable. "Not yet."

The sheriff left with more reminders that he'd shared what he'd shared to keep us from attempting to help. Dixie sent the rest of the cookies with him.

Chapter Twenty-Four

I looked up from putting the final touches on the proof I planned to present at the final meeting of the Founders' Day Cookbook Committee. Dixie stood in the doorway of my office.

"The sheriff is here to see you." She pointed toward the front.

"What now?"

"He wouldn't say." She shrugged. "He needs to talk to you he said."

I smoothed the papers and clipped them together. Carefully placing them in my bag, I headed out front to see what the sheriff wanted.

"Yes?" I stopped in front of him.

He shifted his weight and looked at me.

"Sugar, I'm sorry but I have to ask you about a number of items that you may have taken from Greer Gooder's house."

"Yes?" I waited.

"So, you admit to taking the items?"

"Of course," I couldn't see where he was headed with this. "A frog statue, a cup, strawberry cruets, and a piece of pottery."

"Why would you take those things?" He frowned.

"I took them and gave them to Greer. She asked me to get them from her storage in the attic. I don't know what exactly she's doing with them but I suspect that she may be giving them to Disco to sell for her."

"Ah, now that makes more sense."

"Have you talked to Disco?"

"I have not." He wiped his hand over his face. "I wanted to talk to you first."

"So, you did know he's been doing something with Greer's stuff." I shook my head. "I'm worried about what she's getting rid of and why she's doing it, but it's none of my business really. And I can't see how it's any of yours."

"We had someone come in and want to file a complaint about you."

"What?" Dixie popped out from the kitchen. She had obviously been listening. "A complaint about Sugar?"

"Because I've been taking things to Greer?"

"I told you that you were being way too nice." Dixie pointed a finger at me.

"This person thought you were taking the things for yourself."

"I'll bet it's my neighbor, Mrs. Pickett." I shook my head. "She hates me. I don't know why she hates me but she does."

The sheriff stuck the paper in his pocket. "It wasn't Mrs. Pickett, though she might be sort of involved."

"Well, if not her who was it?"

"Greer's son had some concerns about his mother after he got a call from Mrs. Pickett about you living next door. And then these items started showing up online for sale, so he asked us to check into it. Because he'd been told you were observed with the items, Spiff assumed it was you selling them."

"You have got to be kidding me." I looked at Dixie. "His name is Spiff?"

"It's Spencer but everyone in town called him Spiff," she explained.

Greer had talked about her son. I thought back to when she mentioned the insurance policy. She seemed proud of him. She hadn't come right out and said so, but I'd gotten the impression she was disappointed he didn't call or visit more often. Minneapolis was not that far away. She hadn't said he was nuts.

"You said I was seen with the items." I tried to understand how he'd gotten the idea I'd taken things. "Who saw me?"

"Spiff wouldn't say who saw you, but when he questioned Disco, the guy refused to give him any information about how he'd obtained the items. Spiff felt like Disco was hiding something, possibly protecting you."

"How did he know things were missing? And were showing up for sale?" This was not adding up.

"He says he'd seen items he knew his mother had online for sale and the account he traced to Disco. And then when Disco wouldn't admit to selling his mother's things, he says it left him no choice but to file a complaint."

"Well Disco probably was hiding something but he was protecting Greer. Not me."

"Okay, then." The sheriff leaned against the counter. "I wish the rest was as easy to sort out as this."

"We heard you picked up JoJo," I said.

"We did, but she's not talking." He ran a hand through his hair.

"On the items from Greer's house?" I wanted to make sure I understood clearly. "You'll follow-up with her and with Disco, right?"

"Yes, we will." He headed for the door. "We'll sort it out."

Chapter Twenty-Five

It was the final *St. Ignatius Community Cookbook* committee meeting and so we were almost to the finish line. As the meeting wrapped up, I pulled Minnie to one side.

"Do you have a minute?" I asked, keeping my voice low.

"Sure." She was packing up her colored pens, putting them in their slots in the pencil case. She zipped it shut and put it away before she looked up.

"You know the sheriff has taken Elsie's niece JoJo into custody, right?"

She nodded, continuing to stack and straighten copies of the minutes she'd passed out at the meeting.

"He's waiting for the state investigator to come, but he needs some proof of these payments you said were made to her. Do you have check numbers or anything like that they can use to get Kenny and Elsie's bank records?"

"The sheriff asked me about that and I told him I don't. I can show them on my computer, the debit each month, to another account. I suppose they can figure out where the money went from that."

"I'm sure they can." Thank goodness Minnie was so meticulous. "Is your computer at the office?

"No, it's at home." She looked at blankly. "I work on a laptop. It's a lot easier."

"Great, can you let the sheriff know you have that?"

"Sure," she agreed. "I've got to get home now though. There's a documentary I've been wanting to see, and this is the first night."

"I won't keep you then." I smiled at her. "You hang in there, hon."

"Thanks." She finished collecting her things and left without saying good-bye. I shook my head. Such a serious woman. So intent on getting to her television program.

I took my time gathering up my own papers.

This was it.

We were at the end of our first community cookbook project. In spite of pretty drastic obstacles, we'd made it. Everything was ready to go. I'd go back to the office and call the printer with a few minor corrections and it was a go.

Sheriff Terry had JoJo and Robbie in custody and as soon as the DCI investigator saw the money trail, it would be clear JoJo was the killer of both Elsie and Kenny.

Not Bertie. Not Tina.

Though I was still miffed about Mrs. Pickett calling Greer's son and convincing him I was stealing from his mother. It had all been sorted out. I wasn't sure what the woman had against me, but I was going to break her. I would convince her to like me, even if it meant picking up every leaf the wind blew into her yard.

I laughed at myself as I tucked the last sheet of paper into my bag. I went out, waving good-bye to Toy, who was at the cash register with a customer.

"Cluck" the door said as I went out.

It was that trip to Mars. I'd felt like it had been a wasted road trip, but if we hadn't gone I would not have seen JoJo and her boyfriend. The sheriff would not have had the license number. I don't really believe in fate, but it sure felt like our trip to Mars, and my gas stop, had been a lucky break.

Humming "Fly Me to the Moon," I walked back to the office lugging my bag and feeling that all was soon to be right with the world.

The good feeling didn't last very long, once I entered the shop.

Sheriff Terry sat on a stool at the counter with Dixie, a bite of tiramisu halfway to his mouth. They both wore sober expressions.

Dixie's tiramisu was out of this world and could not be the reason for their dejected faces.

"What's wrong?" I looked from one to the other.

"I wasn't able to hold them," he said. "The man whose van they stole refused to press charges. The DCI says we don't have enough evidence to hold JoJo on suspicion of murder."

"But her boyfriend is the one who said she was extorting money from Elsie and then they moved on to Kenny." I dropped my bag on the floor and joined them at the counter.

"He's recanted his story." Dixie poured a coffee and pushed it across the counter to me.

"The state says they may be able to get them on extortion once they see the transactions and can confirm those. But that doesn't make a case for murder."

"So they're on the street?" I couldn't believe it.

"Yep." Dixie handed me a plate with a slice of tiramisu. I knew it was her personal entry in the Founders' Day cookbook. I also knew it was Sheriff Terry's favorite dessert. For once, I knew when to keep my lips zipped.

"Until we have proof of the blackmail and even if there was money that changed hands, JoJo can claim her aunt gave her money. There's no one to refute it."

"Except Minnie." I jumped up. "She said she balanced Kenny's account for him all the time and has all those spreadsheets on her computer."

"That will help." Terry slid off his stool and began to pace.

"She also told me she overheard a phone call where Kenny said to someone, 'You may have gotten a payoff from my wife, but you're not getting anything from me.'"

"Why didn't I know this?" He swiveled to look at me.

I held up my hands. "I asked her to call you."

"I'm going to call Agent Bell and share this with him. Hopefully it will change his mind." He went out the door.

Dixie and I sat there for a while in silence. Something was nagging me.

"I'm worried about Minnie." I finally broke the silence. "I'm going to call her."

I dialed Minnie's number on my cell phone, but she didn't pick up. "Now, I'm even more worried."

Dixie started picking up the cups and plates. "She told you she was going home to watch some program, right?"

"Yeah, something on the science channel." I couldn't remember what she'd said, but she had seemed focused on getting home in time.

"You know Minnie." Dixie wiped down the counter. "Laser focus. She probably won't answer you until it's over."

"I'm sure you're right, but I'm going to check on her just to be sure." If she was in danger, I felt responsible. Like I had put her in there by insisting she talk to the sheriff initially when she hadn't wanted to.

What if JoJo and Robbie had figured out it was Minnie who'd had the information? They'd go after the laptop for sure. If they didn't find it at the office, they might try her house. And, according to Greer, she lived alone.

"Okay, I'll close up here." Dixie started to the kitchen with the dishes. "Don't get lost."

"Come on. I've been there before."

"Like I said. Don't get lost." She grinned.

Chapter Twenty-Six

I found Minnie's house without any problem. (Okay, I used the GPS again.) It was in an older part of town and was a quaint little bungalow. Compact and unassuming, much like Minnie. I knocked on her door and then knocked again. She didn't answer.

I tried again and waited.

Now I was beyond worried. I looked up and down the street. No gray van parked anywhere in sight, but what if JoJo and her boyfriend were driving something different now? What was I thinking? Of course, they were.

I turned the doorknob and the door opened easily. I took my cell phone out of my purse and placed it in my jacket pocket. Easy access, just in case.

"Minnie?" I leaned in and called out. "Hello?"

Taking a deep breath, I reminded myself she could simply be somewhere in the house where she couldn't hear my knock. Maybe in a room at the back of the house engrossed in her television show.

I stepped inside.

Lights were on in the living room. The furniture was from a different era. According to Greer, the house had been Minnie's parents' home. I guessed she'd not updated.

I glanced around, there were pictures on the mantel of her parents. No siblings. No extended family.

"Minnie?" I called out again. "Are you home? It's Sugar."

Listening to see if I could hear a television, I moved toward a hallway where the wall was home to several framed certificates.

Minerva Silberhorn, Academic Honor Roll, St. Ignatius High School.

Probably achievements her parents had been very proud of and had displayed. Yet, there was something sad about them still hanging on the wall, decades later.

I kept listening for any sort of sounds, my eyes moving to the next frame, a certificate and a newspaper article. A very young Minnie, at college, along with one other student.

Minnie Silberhorn, OCA, Outstanding Chemist Award, for her work as an undergraduate researcher.

I crept down the hallway, ears attuned to anything unusual. What if she couldn't answer because she was injured? What if they had her gagged?

There was a light at the end of the hall. Just a little crack of light. Another room with the door closed.

I ran my hand along the wall, moving carefully so I didn't give away my presence. The wallpaper whispering beneath my hand. My fingers bumped another frame. The photo was a building I recognized. One of the historic photos Max had helped restore. The home of Otto Styles, the chemist who discovered a weed killer that made him oodles of money. The inscription on the photo simply said, "Great Grandpa Otto's House."

Wow. A whole lot of chemistry going on in that family.

The words echoed in my head. The thing that had been nagging me gelled.

I stopped where I was.

Sheriff Terry had said the DCI didn't think the poisonings could be suicide or accidental because of the understanding of chemistry that would be needed. How much it took to kill someone was not something an amateur would know.

JoJo and her boyfriend were amateurs. Their approach had been to get Elsie to pay them money to keep quiet. When Elsie was gone they'd moved on to Kenny, thinking he'd continue the arrangement. Not much skill in that plan.

I now stepped backward. My mind raced trying to put it all together. My eyes never left that sliver of light at the end of the hallway.

I turned to head for the door and caught a glimpse of what they used to call the sitting room.

There was a large lighted curio.

Many families have them. My family did.

It was where my mother kept her awards, my Aunt Cricket kept pictures of her critters, and my Aunt Celia kept pictures of her grandchildren.

The last piece of the puzzle snapped into place.

It was where Minnie Silberhorn kept pictures of Kenny Farmer.

Not just a few pictures. Hundreds of pictures.

I couldn't breathe. Couldn't move.

Get out. I had to get out of the house and call the sheriff.

My feet felt like lead but I forced myself to move. I turned.

Minnie stood in the doorway. Her stillness chilling.

"Hello," I choked out. I started to try to bluff my way out, but I'm afraid all the terrible realizations showed on my face.

The right amount of poison to kill.

The access to Elsie's kitchen.

The energy drink bottles lined up so exactly in Tina's refrigerator.

I brushed past her and headed to the living room, but before I could get to the front door, she grabbed my wrist.

"I need to go, Minnie." I twisted my arm hoping to free it. "I just stopped by to check on you. Dixie's expecting me back at the office."

"No, she's not. You know..." she tipped her head and looked at me like I was a specimen under a microscope. Her voice was hard and cold. "Sometimes I think you're brilliant and other times I can't believe how incredibly stupid you are."

"Stupid," she repeated for emphasis as she twisted my wrist, her eyes gleaming.

I furtively slipped my free hand into my jacket pocket, grasping for my phone. I tried to hit a button without looking hoping against hope that I dialed someone. Someone who could help.

I heard Dixie's voice.

"What was that?" Minnie'd heard it too.

"Just the auto-assistant on my phone." I tried to cover the phone hoping to muffle the sound. "I must have bumped it."

"Nice try. Hand me the phone." She reached out her hand. The hand that didn't have a death grip on my wrist.

"Minnie, let me go," I said loudly, hoping the phone would pick it up as I pulled it from my pocket and handed it to her.

She tossed it across the room where it fell with a clatter.

"What are you going to do?" I asked. "Another poisoning death? One where your presence might actually tip the scales and make you a suspect?"

"I'd hoped this wouldn't be necessary. Hoped when they zeroed in on Tina you'd give up." Her voice was hard. "But you were so persistent, and I realized you were never going to give up."

Do you know what that feels like when your own words come back to haunt you in the worst possible way? Yeah.

"The authorities will think it's either Elsie's relative JoJo or Tina and personally I'm hoping for Tina. What an immoral bitch."

I was shocked at her language and wanted to point out that Kenny was as much, if not more, at fault than Tina. After all, he'd been the married one. I decided this was not the time to point out Kenny's fault in the whole mess. Not with her still gripping my wrist.

"Why kill Kenny?" I asked. If I could keep her talking there was at least a small chance Dixie had heard and would send help. "I thought you cared for Kenny. It seemed like you did."

"I loved him." Her eyes filled with tears.

Good grief, the cold-hearted killer was going to cry.

Maybe if I could get her thinking about Kenny I could rip my wrist loose.

"Then why? Why kill the man you loved?"

"He wasn't supposed to drink stupid Tina's energy drink. She never shared it with anyone. Her secret recipe." Minnie wiped at her eyes.

A new realization hit me. "It was Tina you intended to kill."

"Yes, never my Kenny. She'd led him astray. He would have come to his senses."

"So, Elsie and then Tina, clearing the way for you?"

"We were meant to be together." She heaved a big sigh.

"And now me? Three murders on your conscience." I hoped to appeal to whatever moral sense she had.

"I have no choice." Her face suddenly went chillingly blank.

"But if they find me here." My hand had started to go numb from her grip.

"I'll say that you told me you were just at Tina's and that you came by and then started feeling sick. They'll think you ingested something like Elsie and Kenny did. It will seal her fate."

What did she think? That I would drink something? That she was strong enough to force me?

I made up my mind at that moment to fight.

The others hadn't seen it coming, but I had the advantage of knowing I was about to die. The police would find scratches on Minnie and bruises on me that wouldn't support Minnie's story of me stopping by Tina's house. Dixie would know differently. She would force Sheriff Terry to investigate. He would force the DCI to find the truth.

I yanked on my arm and at the same time kicked out toward Minnie. Minnie dropped to her knees, letting go of my arm. I was loose.

Get out. Get out. Get out. My mind screamed.

I made a dash for the door but Minnie grabbed my ankle and pulled.

I went down hard. My cheek slammed against hardwood floor. Pain exploded in my head and the room began to spin.

I blinked a couple of time trying to focus. Then I noticed the syringe in her hand.

No, no, not this time. It wasn't going to be that easy. I bucked and kicked ignoring the pain.

There was a loud pounding on the front door as Minnie brought the syringe down, aiming for me. I rolled away and it just barely missed.

"Help!" I tasted blood as I screamed.

Sheriff Terry burst through the door followed by Dixie. Dixie stomped on Minnie's wrist and she let go of the syringe with a cry.

Minnie scrambled to her feet and lunged for the syringe.

I raised my leg and with force that came from somewhere deep, I planted my foot right in Minnie's backside and pushed. She sprawled forward on her face. Stunned, she hesitated for a moment and then staggered to her feet and ran toward the kitchen.

Sheriff Terry ran after her and I heard a scuffle. Then silence. Suddenly we could hear the sheriff booming voice ordering Minnie to the floor.

"Dixie," I sat up.

"What?" She looked at me.

"It was Minnie all along."

"I know, sweetie." She sat down beside me on the floor and put her arm around me.

In a matter of minutes, the house was swarmed with lights and sirens. The medics insisted on checking me over, though I was certain nothing was broken.

"I'm fine." I was sure when the adrenaline stopped pumping that I would be sore, but all in all I was fine.

The paramedics had moved me to the couch. From there I could see through the open doorway that a crowd of neighbors had already collected outside and their numbers were growing.

Dixie and I waited to see if it was okay for us to go. The sheriff was still in the kitchen and had Minnie secured. The DCI Special Agent pushed through the crowd and headed that way.

In a few moments, Sheriff Terry joined us.

"Are you okay?" He crouched down so he could see my face. "Did they check you over?

"They did and I'm fine."

"I think someone should take Sugar home," he said to Dixie. "Special Agent Bell says we can get her statement later."

"I'm right here." I waved a weak hand.

"Sorry about that, Sugar." He and Dixie shared a look. "Do you want to go home?"

"I do." I didn't want to be there when they took Minnie away.

You might think it would be good to see the perpetrator of so much awfulness taken away in handcuffs. She'd killed two people. She needed to be held accountable for what she'd done. I had no problem with that.

But at the moment, my heart hurt and my mind felt numb.

Chapter Twenty-Seven

The day of the Founders' Day celebration dawned bright and steamy as only a July day in Iowa can.

Dixie's Aunt Bertie was on shift at the Founders' Day Cookbook table when Max and I arrived. She'd wanted an early shift because the Jefferson Street B & B was at full capacity and she needed to take care of her guests. Folks who had pre-ordered the book stopped by to pick up their copies, and those who had not were subject to Bertie Sparks's high-pressure sales tactics.

The committee had the idea to provide some samples from recipes in the book to entice people to approach the table. Then they pounced. A brilliant tactic I thought, and if my former employer had been as creative and engaged on their marketing, perhaps they'd still be in business.

The cookbook was absolutely stunning, if I do say so myself. It was a team effort and I was proud of how it had turned out. The pictures and the recipes told a story. Dixie's brilliance on the recipe choices, Max's amazing photos, and even Jimmie LeBlanc's pieces of history had been stirred together in just the right amounts.

The whopper of a bruise on my cheek had begun to fade. It would be a long while before the memory of Minnie's death grip on me and the gleam in her eyes would do the same.

JoJo and her boyfriend Robbie had been arrested for extortion based on information recovered from Minnie's computer. Minnie had proudly confessed to the murder of Elsie Farmer, but continued to insist that Kenny's death had been accidental. Her court-appointed attorney had a tough road ahead of him.

Greer had insisted that Spiff apologize to me. He'd not only filed a complaint with the police after getting a call from Mrs. Pickett and finding the items online, he'd also been in the house. He had a key and had gone in and taken the strawberry cruets. He'd probably also been the reason Ernest was outside, but I didn't tell her that. He was in enough trouble with his mother. I accepted his apology.

The Founders' Day Festival was in full swing. The sights and sounds swirled around us. Max snapped photos as we stood watching. People were beginning to jockey for places to view the parade.

The marching band, in their St. Ignatius Saints uniforms, lined up, waiting for the go. They had to be cooking in those long-sleeved uniforms.

Sheriff Terry looked exasperated as the crowd refused to part for the red convertible that carried the newly crowned Miss Iggy. He and his deputy would move people and clear a path and then others would move in.

I saw Dixie and Moto across the way and waved frantically. She spotted me and headed over.

A sea of silver heads and pink T-shirts waved from the next float in line. Greer and the group of ladies from the retirement center rode on a flat-bed decorated with miles of foil that had The Good Life plastered in big cut-out letters on the side.

Dixie made it across the street and we hugged.

We'd made it. No words were needed. I reached in my pocket for a treat and slipped it to Moto.

I looked around at the familiar faces.

People who, though we didn't share any bloodlines, felt like family to me. My family of the heart.

I leaned my head on Max's shoulder.

It *was* a good life.

Recipes

Bertie Sparks's Proper English Scones

Ingredients
2 cups and 13 tablespoons of self-rising flour
1/4 teaspoon salt
1 teaspoon of baking powder
3 tablespoons of caster or regular sugar
3 ounces of cubed butter
3/4 cup of milk
1 teaspoon vanilla extract
Squeeze of lemon juice
One beaten egg, to glaze
1 cup of raisins or craisins or dried fruit of your choice

Instructions
1. Preheat your oven to 425° F. (Bertie recommends also preheating your baking tray.)

2. In a mixing bowl, add the sifted flour, salt, baking powder, and combine.

3. Add the butter and rub in with your fingers until the mixture looks like fine crumbs.

4. Using a knife, stir in the sugar.

5. Put the milk into a cup and heat in the microwave for about 30 seconds. Add the vanilla and lemon juice, then set aside for 2 minutes.

6. Make a well in the dry mix, then add the liquid and combine it quickly with a knife. Dust some flour onto the work surface and place the dough on the surface. Shake some more flour on the dough and your hands, then fold the dough over 2-3 times until it's slightly smoother. Gently pat it into a round about 1 1/2 inches deep.

7. Take a 2-inch cutter and dip it into some flour. Cut into the dough, then repeat until you have four scones. Then press what's left of the dough back into a round to cut out another four. Try not to over work the dough, be light with your hands when reshaping.

8. Brush the tops with beaten egg, then carefully place onto the hot baking tray.

9. Bake for 10 minutes until risen and golden on the top.

Elsie Farmer's Irish Scones

Ingredients
3 1/2 cups all-purpose flour
5 teaspoons baking powder
Pinch of salt
1/4 of a cup of white sugar
1 stick butter
1 egg
2 ounces of cream
7 ounces of whole milk
Milk to glaze

Instructions
1. In a large bowl mix the dry ingredients together.
2. Rub in the cold butter with your fingers until it resembles breadcrumbs.
3. If you want to add dried fruit such as raisins or berries, add them now before you add liquid.
4. Mix your egg with the milk and cream and pour into your flour mixture.
5. With an open hand mix your scone mix until a dough forms.
6. Turn your dough onto a floured work surface.
7. Knead lightly to give your dough a smooth surface.
8. Pat your dough down with your hand until it's about an inch thick.
9. With a round scone cutter, cut out your scones. You should have about twelve.
10. Put on a baking tray, glaze the tops of your scones with some milk to give them a golden top when baked.
11. Bake at 350°F for 35 minutes.

Enjoy with Irish butter, jam and freshly whipped cream.
Scones are best the day they are baked.

Betty Bailey's Broccoli Gratin

Ingredients
Kosher salt, to taste
2 lb. broccoli
2 tablespoons of unsalted butter
1/4 cup all-purpose flour
2 cups milk
1/2 small yellow onion, thinly sliced
1 bay leaf
1 cup grated Gruyère cheese
Freshly ground pepper
1 cup panko
1/4 cup grated Parmigiano-Reggiano cheese
2 tablespoons of olive oil

Instructions
1. Bring a large saucepan of well salted water to a boil over high heat. Cut the heads from the broccoli stalks and cut the heads into small florets. Add the broccoli to the boiling water and cook for 2 minutes. Transfer the broccoli to a bowl filled with ice water, then drain well.
2. In a 10-inch fry pan over medium heat, melt the butter. Add the flour and stir well.
3. Slowly whisk in the milk and bring to a boil.
4. Reduce the heat to low, add the onion and bay leaf and simmer, stirring frequently, until the mixture thickens.
5. Remove and discard the bay leaf and add the Gruyère, stirring until the cheese is melted.
6. Carefully fold in the broccoli and spread in an even layer.
7. In a small bowl, stir together the panko, Parmigiano-Reggiano and olive oil, and season with salt and pepper.
8. Sprinkle the panko mixture over the broccoli mixture.
9. Transfer the pan to the oven and bake at 350° F for 40 to 45 minutes.

You can make this in a stove-top to oven pan as Dixie does.
Or if you don't have that type of pan this recipe works just as well in a casserole dish.

About the Author

Mary Lee Ashford is the "Sparkle" half of the mystery writer Sparkle Abbey, author of the Pampered Pet mysteries from Belle Bridge Books. She is the founding president of Sisters in Crime – Iowa and a member of Mystery Writers of America, Romance Writers of America, Kiss of Death, the RWA Mystery Suspense chapter, Sisters in Crime, and the SinC internet group Guppies. Prior to publishing the Pampered Pet Mystery series with Bell Bridge Books, Mary Lee won first place in the Daphne du Maurier contest, sponsored by the Kiss of Death chapter of RWA, and was a finalist in Murder in the Grove's mystery contest, as well as Killer Nashville's Claymore Dagger contest. Mary Lee is an avid reader and supporter of public libraries. She lives in Central Iowa with her husband, Tim, and Sparkle the rescue cat namesake of Sparkle Abbey. In her day job she is an Information Technology manager. Any spare time she spends reading and enjoying her sons and daughter-in-laws, and six grandchildren.

Made in the USA
Columbia, SC
12 December 2018